The Waterwi

Perilous Peripl

By

Michael Fitzalan

Periplus – A Narrative of a Coastal Voyage

Perilous Peregrinations

Dedicated to my brother with love and thanks. He taught me how to have fun.

PART ONE

Chapter One - The Storm

The sixteen-ton boat surfed over the gigantic waves. Its metal hull was all that prevented the boat from breaking up, yet it was this steel that within minutes of flooding would sink to the ocean floor like a stone slung into a pond. This smallness in the immense ocean, the vulnerability of our situation, these were the major worries.

The Atlantic is a cold and lonely place in a gale. Safety, the Portuguese coast, was twelve miles off, but it was becoming further away with each wave; we were being driven in the direction of America, over three thousand miles to the west, with only enough water for two days at the most.

The Azores to the southwest might as well have been the same distance. Both wind and wave drove our vessel westwards; the waves were in command, and we had no control.

Clouds hung in stratus layers, rain fell at the wind's whimsy, drops angled to the back of the head or darted diagonally on to the deck as another wave of water crashed over the bow. Helplessly we bobbed into the shipping lanes. Waves ten metres high raised us above the blue boiling water below; we rested on the foaming crest, afforded a glimpse of a ship or a tanker or just the grey cloud horizon, before plunging down, sliding along the wave into a deep trough where another wave would splash over the bow as our boat dipped its nose into the bubbling brine.

In a heartbeat we were lifted up again on a swell. As it grew higher, we floated up like a chair on a Ferris wheel. This undulating motion took us along twenty metres in twice as many seconds. There was no better description for it; we were storm surfing. The sensation was slightly unsettling, like being in an express lift going up and down repeatedly.

Our boat was a heavy fifty-two-foot sailing cruiser, a yacht designed for day sailing in safe seas with the occasional overnight anchorage. This boat was not built to be buffeted by waves its own size. The sea rose and fell all around us, and we were dwarfed by the swirling swell.

I had heard of storms in the Bay of Biscay that broke boats in half, but I had never heard of storms so bad in the Atlantic; I had always associated the Cabo de San Vincent, Faro and the Golfo de Cadiz with sunshine and sand. This was a storm straight from the Bay of Biscay: all rain, high seas, and spray.

There I stood, soaked to the skin, my polo shirt clogged with water sticking to my wet flesh. My denim shorts felt twice as heavy with the water that they had absorbed. This was not what I had expected, but I was too scared to be concerned about that. Sanctuary, Vilamoura, lay shrouded in a mist.

Where our vessel had once been had become obscured by this same sheet of stratus. We were in a frosted bowl of fierce activity; a canopy of grey surrounded us above. Below the sea bubbled, swirled, and foamed, spitting cold flecks of salt water over our prow.

Our ship was shaken by the constant battering. The crew were concerned, helpless and frightened. As the boat perched again on the peak of the wave, the Captain spoke.

'That jib needs to come down, you'll find a harness below,' he shouted above the wind, keeping the tiller as straight as he could. I sat on the starboard cockpit bench catching my breath.

'If you want that jib down, you can take it down yourself; I was almost swept over the side taking down the mainsail,' I complained.

I was nineteen, I knew real danger and recognised it now. Water dripped from my brow and sodden shorts and shirt. My legs were soaked, I felt water run down my neck; my hair was so wet that I had to flick my head to shake off the excess rainwater.

Every five minutes my hair was washed forward, and I had to run my fingers through the sodden strands to push it back over my head and out of my eyes. I was already breathless and shaking, having earlier crawled over the cockpit roof that bucked, like a wild beast, beneath my body.

Once I had almost been claimed by the sea but had been saved by a firm grip on the gunwales which ran along the roof It had been arduous work, clinging with one arm to the mast as I slowly released the winch that held the rope and tried clumsily to furl the sail, a dripping slippery nylon mass.

Every few minutes I would have to change arms as I slowly lowered the halyard. It had to be a slow process, if I let the sail down in one go then it would spread all over the deck, a slippery mess that would leave me stranded and exposed for the rest of the trip. Slipping over wet sails in a storm was like skating on ice, particularly as the boom would be your only form of purchase and that would be covered in the sail.

One slip, a sudden unsettling wave, and that would be it, over the side. There was, of course, the alternative of slipping down through the bow hatch, but that meant struggling past the flapping jib, going further forward than was safe, over slippery fore deck with no mast or shrouds or gunwales to hang on to, and then struggling with the two heavy metal clips that secured the hatch.

It was the least favoured of my options. I just had to take my time and slowly and steadily release and stow the sail as best I could. I had enough loops of rope to lash the sail to the boom and even though my stowing was not perfect, it would have to do.

Furling a sail of that size would perhaps take two men to do it properly- one man with one arm can make a real hash of it. I had, but at least the mainsail would not capsize us.

All that was needed was the boat to topple due to wind against canvas, a wave of water to slop into the cockpit, and four people and a sailboat would be on the ocean floor.

There was no way that I would go forward again.

The jib was not full of wind; it tugged at the jib sheets that we had released earlier, but apart from the fact that it twirled itself around the forestays or danced in the wind like a kite, the only bothersome problem was the racket it made, from manic flapping to a muted clapping as it wrapped itself around the wire, before spinning off the wire and flapping like mad again. It was not a danger to anything but our nerves.

As the sail got damper, the sound got worse, almost like a continuous cracking. I was adamant that it could stay up, annoying as it was.

'Hold the tiller while I go below and check the lifejackets,' the Skipper ordered.

Geoffrey was upset by my mutinous retort, but he knew that taking down the jib was too perilous a task. He was frightened; he wanted to make the ship as safe as he could, but in this case that was impossible.

Needing me to help him steer, he decided against sacrificing me. Instead, trying to hide the fear in his eyes, he looked ahead. I was ready to take the tiller; I stood up and moved next to him.

'We'll leave the sail,' he hissed through clenched teeth. Perhaps by refusing to follow his order, I had exposed his cowardice; after all he had not volunteered to take the jib down in my place. I had not intended to do so. I was merely relieved I did not have to go forward. 'Will you keep her steady while I'm gone?'

'No problem.' I assured him.

He was an experienced sailor, a decade in dinghies and a decade on the seas.

If he was fearful then the situation had to be bad.

'It's hard work- the waves are all coming from behind, but at different angles and from different directions all the time. I've never seen a sea like this. Steer her so that the stern faces the incoming wave. That way we ride up on the top of the wave. Don't whatever you do allow the wave to break over the sides or we've had it. As we ride down the wave, keep the boat following the same direction as the wave. When you reach the depression of the wave, look around for the direction of the next one to carry us up. You want to have it directly behind you, or near as, damn it.'

He handed me the tiller. I appreciated the trust. I, a novice, held all our lives in my two hands.

Two hands were needed; the turbulent seas were like a bog. The metal rudder dragged in the ocean and the wooden handle was barely responsive.

'Okay, you check on the jackets and see how the girls are,' I called after him.

He looked down into the cabin as he slid the hatch cover back, then he turned his rain-lashed face towards me, his features contorted in both horror and disgust.

'They're still spewing on their bunks,' he complained.

With that sympathetic phrase he opened the double doors and disappeared below. He came up as we rode the incline of another wave, an escalator ride to the top and a steel slide down to the bottom; the ascent took two-thirds of the time, the descent one-third. The sea underneath us swelled up like a balloon and then deflated. We never knew on which side of the wave we would come down, which part would fall away beneath us, sending us sliding into another cavity in the sea.

'There are only two life-preservers; they're both for children.'

He stood close to me as he relayed this piece of choice news.

That was it, divine intervention; we were being punished for taking those two German hitchhikers for a day's sailing. It was not my idea, but I was an accomplice; it was important that such a transgression should deserve a fitting sentence and that was death. I accepted it quite casually. Fishermen died in storms, sailors died at sea, the Captain was a dirty old leech and I wanted to be a clean, young one. We deserved to drown. It was the hitchhikers that I felt sorry for. I had never heard tell of a hitchhiker lost at sea.

'There's Vilamoura,' the Captain announced, without a hint of relief.

That, after all, was our destination. I could see him pointing to one o'clock, off the starboard bow. A wave took us down as my gaze followed his finger and for a few seconds all I could see was a mountain of water, its shiny slopes; they were blue, black, and marbled with white foam. Then we rose to meet the sky and through the haze of cloud I could make out what looked like a shoreline sitting on the horizon and a white mass, which I took to be the marina.

'Thank God, we've almost made it,' I gasped feeling relieved.

I was ignorant and relieved.

'There's no way we can turn the boat in this storm. If we start heading nor'-west, we'll be rolled over, and besides Vilamoura is due north; we'd be capsized straight away if we went across these waves.'

Vilamoura had been at one o'clock a few minutes ago, but I looked at the compass for a second and saw that what he had said was true. We were surfing in record time. I looked over my shoulder to deal with a few more waves, one from the left and the next from the right. I concentrated on prising the stern into the swell so that we could ride over, and not be swept under the wave.

Looking out north, on a crest, I glanced again at Vilamoura, the harbour, refuge, our haven, had so suddenly moved to three o'clock. It was difficult to control my anger and disappointment.

This 'so-called' experienced sailor had overshot the port. My thoughts were less than charitable towards my fellow crewman.

'Brilliant, my brother sends me to get sailing experience and we end up heading for Sagres.'

My sarcastic words fell on deaf ears.

Maybe he thought I was trying to make light of the situation, or perhaps he was incredibly thick-skinned because he just looked ahead and smiled.

'There is another port we could head for, by which time the storm should have dissipated.'

'Great, where is it?'

'It's near Albufeira, about three hours away. We've been travelling for one hour.'

He looked at his professional-style mariner's watch, all stainless steel, three dials, five hands, luminous characters, and digits.

'Great, that sounds wonderful,' I enthused.

'The fastest time from Olhao to Vilamoura was two hours, we've done it in less than half that. The fastest time from Vilamoura to Portimao was eight hours, so we should make Albufeira in four.'

Hearing about racing records failed to reassure me.

Yes, we were going almost as fast as a small speedboat, but the spray and the lurch of the boat constantly reminded me that we had to survive for those hours.

It was exhausting; wrenching the tiller with both arms, turning my head to line up the boat, twisting my body as we came down the wave to see which direction the next wave would be coming from. I wanted to be warm and dry, on a beach, just like anyone else in the Algarve in April. I distrusted the Captain after he had overshot our destination.

Was he really that good?

We had planned for a three-hour cruise. There was nothing on board. Olhao had limited provisions and limited fresh water. We were the least well-equipped boat out to sea that day. We had one flare, the harness had in fact gone missing, only two tiny lifejackets, no food and little water.

The black silhouettes of tankers could be seen clearly as we neared the shipping lanes. The force of the storm was pushing us into one of the busiest shipping lanes in the world. I was not overly worried at this prospect.

'When your number is up your number is up, it's as simple as that,' I told myself constantly.

There were lots of things I still wanted to do; perhaps we would be lucky and survive this ordeal by water. Everyone who has sailed in these parts had heard of some boat or other run over by a tanker, or worse and less quick the wake from those large propellers capsizing a yacht, once even a catamaran. We had only one hull, so we were twice as vulnerable.

I could imagine the scene, four adults tearing at two children's lifejackets as the gallons of water poured on board, pushing the boat under. All we needed was a little extra weight of water. Already, the gunwales were being lapped by the choppy water that moved around our hull.

These small waves, which escorted us through the peaks and troughs, were a real danger. Too much water over the side and into the cockpit would lead to us sitting lower in the water.

We had no real control; more water on board would make the rudder even stiffer, perhaps impossible to move. A rogue wave would finish the job.

Danger is a funny thing, you either remain calm and accept whatever hand you are dealt, deal with the situations as they arise in a cool manner, or you panic.

The only really experienced sailor on board, our esteemed skipper, was close to the latter of these options. I was veering towards the former idea, but ignorance is bliss.

We had been on the same course for a long time and nothing adverse had happened. The jib was still up, but so were we. The situation seemed fairly stable.

Once the vessel was submerged, that was the time to panic. We wouldn't last long in the water, hypothermia is such an efficient killer, but it had not come to that. I comforted myself with the thought that we could all abandon ship, jump into the yacht's tender and we'd be safe for a few days, starvation our only worry.

However, the fact that such a small boat would be overturned immediately in such high seas suddenly occurred to me, and then I remembered that the tender, the rowing boat that could have provided us buoyancy, had been leant to someone in Olhao.

Therefore, it was a case of sink or swim. Would I be able to overcome the rest of the crew and use the two jackets as water wings, the buoyancy aid of toddlers, or would I be a gentleman and offer my lifejacket to the landlubbers who had not envisaged this situation and did not deserve to be here? That was the question.

There's the rub - what do you do when the instinct of survival cuts in, a real situation where death stares you in the face and you want to survive?

Were these girls responsible for being stupid enough to agree to come with us?

Did that make them culpable?

Should that be punishable?

Was the Captain culpable, and therefore, did he deserve to go down with his ill-equipped ship?

Could I live with myself, knowing I had survived, if I did survive, by taking the lives of others? I felt sure that I would be noble. The girls were safe, unless the Captain decided to bludgeon all of us to death with a windlass handle.

It was with great relief that I realised Captain Instability was as capable of doing something like that, as I was of getting us confidently into any harbour.

His view was to see if the storm eased and bolt for port. This assumed a lot, particularly as the storm was getting worse and we were only a few hours into it.

Storms can last for days and nearly always get worse before they get better. I had the time to think, although I was wrenching the rudder from port to starboard as each wave came from another direction.

I challenged myself to appear completely calm. I wondered how long I could keep up this subterfuge as we surfed successfully down another slope of sea.

This was bravado, but it was necessary for morale; if I seemed unconcerned and got on with the job in hand, it might reassure and calm our Captain, give him a respite, a chance to think of solutions rather than imagine appalling scenarios.

My equipment was astonishingly inappropriate. I needed a lifejacket, a sou'wester and full oilskins, a harness with lifebelt to feel secure. Instead, all I had was my belief that we would survive, with or without the help of our skittish skipper.

My mind ran from concern for the poor girls, to the next big wave and then to whether the Captain was up to the task. The poor young teenagers hitch-hiking through Europe had been asked if they wanted to have a day's sailing.

They had refused at first but had relented after Geoffrey's persistent pestering. It was difficult to refuse him. Perhaps they thought it would be an experience they would not forget.

How right they were.

If we lived, then we could all report one of the most life-threatening experiences anyone could endure. If we sank and subsequently died, we were assured of being immortalised.

Someone would be presented a paper from the day he was born, a facsimile perhaps, and our tale of woe would most probably put the two of the two both off sailing forever.

I wondered, having read Moby Dick and being well aware of the deprivations suffered by Cook and Nelson, how I had ever contemplated a life at sea, with its brine dampness and lack of predictability. Even in fair weather it was uncomfortable, cold, damp, and windy most of the time.

The sun barely warm, a cold ocean below, chilling everything. This storm was something else. Mental concentration along with physical strength would save us. Our minds had to focus on the direction of the next wave, and we needed brawn to steer the boat into the right path. It was an exhilarating and eerie feeling sliding down those waves.

Would we take on water at the bottom? Could we correctly predict the next roll of the waves? As we came up would we be tossed by a freak wave on to our side? I was cold and thirsty. In this rough sea, making a cup of coffee could be fatal. If the storm drove us out to sea, we would either starve, die of hypothermia, or be run over by an obliging tanker, unable to see us in this foul weather. I had always sailed in warm climes to avoid such a situation.

In Greece I had only ever once been in a rainstorm, although I had heard tell of terrible storms and knew enough Greek mythology to be aware of the rough time that the Argonauts had experienced. I had assumed, though, that these storms were most probably in wintertime.

I had travelled so little at this time of year that I had expected sunshine all the way from May until June, with perhaps the odd shower. The previous year I had been in Canada for the eight weeks of the summer holiday, and it only rained twice and that was at night, it had been hotter, too.

The year before that, England and the rest of Europe had a summer-long heat wave, which had started at the end of May. There was realism in my expectations, showers could be encountered, the odd chill wind, but a full-blown storm, from force eight to ten, was not on the agenda, and the shock was almost numbing.

If I was sailing in February or September, if we were off the Bay of Biscay or anywhere in the North Atlantic, then fine, but we were forty miles away from the Mediterranean, due south. Turn left (or to port, I should say) at the Rock of Gibraltar and the next stop was Morocco with its deserts and its tropical weather.

From a previous trip I knew that parts of southern Spain were deserts. This was not an area of the world that you associated with storms, and yet we were in one and it was bad. The rain never stopped, its persistence jarred my nerves, but surprisingly it felt warm. The cold spray from the sea made up for that though.

The low temperature surprised me most, only three or four degrees, not far from freezing point. The wind cut through everything. My hands and face were raw from the spray of icy water and the lash of cold air. My skin tingled. My teeth may even have chattered, but for the fact that they were set tight together to enhance the grimace I wore.

I was at the tiller for over an hour, and it was with relief that the Captain popped up from below to bellow a report that he had bedded down the girls and I should go below and get dry and warm up a little. It was a comic sight, the two of us changing positions, both with our legs apart to balance more fully.

For the first time I realised that the metal deck was in two inches of water and the Captain came towards me slipping and sliding on the white-painted metal sheet that formed the floor, totally impractical for wet sailing. I handed him the tiller, gingerly, as we rode up a wave, I had waited until our stern was aligned with the wave before beckoning him forward from the cabin hatch. Geoffrey took the tiller and looked nervously over the cabin roof, down the wave, as we slid along the water. The waves had got larger. I was used to them by now; he was not.

I sat next to him and watched him look over his shoulder and line the boat up to a wave coming from a completely different direction yet again. We rode up it and down into the dip and I watched him take the next wave. The rain poured off his oilskins and I noticed with envy he was wearing gloves. I rubbed my sore hands together between my knees and felt the dampness of the rain weigh heavily on my clothes.

I asked him if he was all right. He nodded with little confidence. I needed to be warm so I danced across the slippery deck, sliding on the wet floor, hanging on to anything I could get purchase from: the seat, the mast ropes and boom, both now redundant as wave not wind pushed us on. I went through the cabin, past two moaning heaps on the two bunks.

Going straight through into the master cabin, I saw two towels and with one I started to dry my hair. I walked unsteadily back, past the two groaning bodies, feeling the roll of the boat at every step and sure that I would fall on one or other of them and compound their problems by crushing them. They were most probably wondering what had possessed them to go off with two strangers on a voyage, which increasingly looked like it would end in disaster.

I, too, wondered what I was doing here. I had left my home comforts to sail with my brother on his wooden yacht and after a series of mishaps he had persuaded me to get some sailing experience with another skipper. Here I was, wet and tired, being jostled about the Atlantic by the worst storm imaginable, while my brother lounged in a safe harbour which may not have even had rain, let alone force eight gales.

Added to the obvious discomfiture of being in a storm, I was cold, hungry, and wet, and that did not take account of my hopelessness at being driven by an unrelenting sea, the bucking and swaying of the boat, the sight of two casualties on the bunks and my utter lack of faith in the skipper.

Being naive, I had assumed that the weather on the Algarve would be mild, not tempestuous, and I had packed accordingly. I did not mind being just cold, I did not mind just being soaked, but being both together was miserable.

I reasoned that I should have stayed at home in England; too late for that. I should never have left my brother's boat; too late for that. It slowly dawned on me that it was too late for anything. There were four scenarios: we either capsized, or sank, starved, or survived. I favoured the latter option, but the elements seemed to favour one of the former scenarios. Despite my unsteady gait, I managed to locate my overnight bag amongst all the debris and ignore the moans and groans of the hapless girls.

The skin was wet, but the lining was dry, I had bought a good quality sailing bag, thankfully, and was rewarded by dry clothes.

The walk back to the cabin with the added weight of the bag meant my progress was even slower than before and my legs were buckled like a horse rider's to give stability. I was impressed that I had managed to avoid the contents of the now-upturned bowls, which the girls had used to vomit into.

Drying myself was a problem. I did not want to get the bed wet, as it was the only dry part of the boat; fortunately, the forward hatch had been closed before we set sail so that the girls could sunbathe there. Most boats leave harbour with the hatches open to air out the dampness of the previous night.

The problem was not so much staying upright as I peeled off the layers of damp cloth, but that the motion in the depths was increased and I was beginning to feel seasick. The smell of sick from the heads and from up- ended bowls by the girls did not help matters. I cursed myself forever believing sailing would be fun. I cursed my brother for allowing me to go off with a relative stranger, whose sailing capabilities were more hearsay than concrete.

After all, it was his suggestion.

His words rang in my ears: 'Go and get some experience, we have a day or two before Patrick joins us. We haven't done much sailing; it is a marvellous opportunity.'

It was a marvellous opportunity to drown. I cursed my eldest brother, Patrick for his inopportune arrival date, for good measure. Geoffrey had never seen seas this bad and nor had I, nor did I want to see them.

Up until that moment I had thought it was a smart move to spend the summer sailing around the Mediterranean, but even at that time it seemed naive to believe that it would be plain sailing. Along with the sunshine there had to be a little rain sometime. I just wished that it had not come all at once. Trapped in a fifty-foot boat when Portugal is experiencing one of the worst storms in its history is not my ideal holiday. Perhaps I should start at the beginning.

Chapter Two - Sail Away, Sail Away

Pristine white walls, twinkling white hulls, mirrored masts in blue calm water, a sun that shone with Mediterranean intensity. That was the marina at Vilamoura on the Portuguese Algarve. Modern cleanliness pervaded the harbour; even the air was clean, fresh, and new, a breeze being blown from off the Atlantic Ocean. Rows of yachts, stainless-steel rigging straining, clicking in the wind, furled white sails, sun bleached as if they had just been fitted, clean decked to reflect the sun.

We stood, my brother and I, at a white counter in the cool cafe, our figures reflected in the clear glass of the mirror. Behind us stood an unhappy looking Portuguese girl in a pressed white shirt and a black skirt to her knees, a starched apron around her waist. Whether her sad expression was due to her genetic make-up or her disposition, it was hard to tell.

It made me feel that perhaps the Portuguese were not as friendly or as relaxed as the Spanish people I had come across. Certainly, the customs men who insisted on our unpacking all our cases when we had arrived at Faro airport the previous evening seemed officious and cold. That and the miserable attitude of the girl who served us coffee coloured my judgement.

The whole place seemed soulless and unwelcoming. The cafe we had come to was in the middle of a row of whitewashed buildings, which lined the east side of the harbour. Big plate glass windows formed black mirrors against the white, and above the apartments of absent owners had their white, wooden shutters closed. The tiled floor on which we stood still gave off a scent of bleach; the counter and serving area was showroom standard, cutlery, and coffee machine, china plates and saucers, white, again, of course, and glasses polished to perfection.

There were no stools or chairs. You were not expected to stay. Even on the veranda outside the shop, there were no plastic chairs and tables, but I was sure if they had been, they would have been white.

I sipped my cafe galao from the tall, thick glass. An elongated spoon stood in it to prevent the glass from cracking with the heat; I dared not remove it and put it on the spotless saucer, particularly as the coffee had been poured so efficiently without spilling a drop. Galao is delicious, one part espresso coffee, strong and dark, to which is added three parts of hot milk; it was a fantastic breakfast tonic.

In contrast to the order of the place, Norman and I wore cut off jeans-shorts and bright T-shirts; his was yellow, mine was turquoise. Neither of us was in a talkative mood that morning. It was about half past eight and we had not really woken up.

Norman outlined the plan for the next few days, which was basically getting the boat ship-shape and ready to sail I'd bought some cigarettes at a bar the night before, but I didn't feel that I should smoke on an empty stomach and there was no ashtray to be seen. The coffee had certainly got my gastric juices flowing.

After a small pastry custard tart, a *pastel de nata*, we walked in the bright, early May morning sunshine, the warm sea breeze at our backs. There was a sandy dirt track tat led out of the complex, on either side of this roadway lay building site debris: empty cement bags, a collection of bricks, a small hill of coarse builders' sand, plastic buckets which once held whitewash and a few paint pots.

Walking along the beach to the old village, we passed through the shantytown and for the first time that day I felt that I was back in the real world.

The town consisted of shacks made of wood chipboard or sheets of corrugated iron draped with the Mozambique flag.

The inhabitants were refugees from the African continent; the authorities tolerated them because they had no policy to find them somewhere to live. I wondered how long they would last on this beach once the development of the coastline was complete. Everyone was busy washing for the day or cooking breakfast on open fires or gas stoves. They returned our smiles.

We walked on to the town. Everyone stared, a continental habit, perhaps at our clothes or wondering if we were French, German, or English. They would never have guessed we were Irish, a factor, which was to prove indispensable later in our voyage.

Norman bought a baguette, a quarter kilo of local cheese that smelt suspect (a fine recommendation), a jar of apricot jam and a tin of Danish butter.

Returning to the boat, we breakfasted on the provisions and brewed a pot of tea using the tea bags we had brought out with us. There was no kettle, so we boiled a saucepan of water on the gas flame. That was our kitchen: a small, blue *Calor* gas bottle, four inches high, with a valve controlled by a black knob, and three steel bars flattened at the top for balancing the one and only saucepan on. I mused as I munched the soft, doughy bread, spread with butter and jam -what was I doing there?

I'm not sure which is the longer story, why I was there or what happened on our three-month adventure. Briefly, I had left school two years previously with plans to travel to either South America or Africa. I had not considered that the recession in 1980 would prevent me from gaining useful and lucrative employment.

As a holiday job I had worked for Jean Machine, in their fashion warehouse, stacking and unpacking jeans from Hong Kong, but there was no permanent work to be had. Things were different now that I was no longer cheap student labour.

In 1981, I went to Spain, ending up looking after a villa for ten weeks. It was idyllic and the only job I had to do was Hoover the pool once a week to keep it clean.

My girlfriend and I had a wonderful time, sunbathing, reading books and exploring the Andalusian villages of: Alhaurín el Grande, Coin and Mijas. We even went to Malaga a few times and to Puerto Banus to have a drink at Sinatra's bar and watch the holidaying rich pose in the luxury marina. It was modern, but it had soul, a cheerful buzz of activity. When I got back, I started work for a small company doing their bookkeeping for them, nominal and purchase ledgers and the rest. It was very dull stuff.

I was happy to leave it all behind.

My brother had been in a terrible motorcycle accident a few years prior and with his compensation money he took up sailing in the Canary Islands and around the Mediterranean.

Whilst staying in Vilamoura, he came across one of the most beautiful boats he had ever seen, *Waterwitch,* built in 1937 by Uffa Fox, a famous boat builder who had been based in Cowes. The yacht had been sunk in Gibraltar harbour and salvaged by a hippie called John, who spent his time playing his guitar in bars along the southwest coast of Portugal.

My brother wanted the boat and John, bored with ten years in one place, wanted to go to the Seychelles and strum there. The deal was done; in return for a single ticket to the Seychelles via London, Norman took possession of a handmade, mahogany, Sitka spruce and teak racing yacht, forty-two feet long.

There was very little persuasion needed to convince me to help him crew the boat. I handed in my notice; they kindly let me leave within a week and I booked a return through Mon- arch Airways to Faro airport, not realising that I would be visiting Faro many more times than I planned.

The fact that I had little experience in the sailing field, if that is not an incorrect expression, seemed to matter very little. Norman had his in-shore and offshore certificates as a yacht master, and I had sailed twice before. I could hardly wait to get going. How naive I was.

My sailing days had been spent around the Greek islands, first year off the west coast, Paxos to Levkas, and the second year the east coast, Skiathos and Ithaca to name a few islands. The school had arranged the trip, part of a flotilla sailing holiday, a great two weeks at Easter.

There was nothing to it, no tides to speak of, or to worry about.

The boat was twenty-four feet long, which was small, but comfortable, a cruiser with a cooker, shower and comfortable bunks and cushions in the cockpit.

I imagined our boat being bigger would be even more luxurious.

The relationship with my girlfriend had finished and I was sharing a flat with a friend from school. There was nothing to keep me in

England. In fact, the flat had become a Mecca for all our friends from school and the number of people wanting to room there, who slept on the floors of the two bedrooms and the front room, guaranteed that my absence would not cause problems, I would worry about finding accommodation on my return.

Norman had a girlfriend called Joanna and she drove us to the airport. The evenings were getting lighter, and the days were getting warmer as spring had arrived.

The plan was to work on the boat through the rest of May, leave the marina on 1st June and meet up with Joanna and some friends of hers on the island of Ibiza at the beginning of July. We would stay in the Balearic Islands for the month of July, sail to Sete in the South of France and up through the Rhone into the canals of France ending up on the French side of the channel. From there, we would sail to moorings in Kent or the Southampton area. That was the plan, but 'the best laid schemes o' mice a' men Gang aft a-glee' and believe me they went 'a-glee'.

Chapter Three - A Series of Shocks

The first shock was the cost of cocktails at the revamped departure lounge; the second was the amount of alcohol that they put in the drink and the third was the boat when I arrived. It was nothing like I had expected. It was embarrassing watching my brother kiss his girlfriend goodbye with a quite unnecessary display of intense passion, almost as embarrassing as walking in on them that morning while they were saying goodbye, but that's another story.

I passed out on the flight due to the cocktails and drinks on the plane, not a wise idea since I had not eaten since breakfast. I woke for the descent on to the tarmac, looking out of the window; I hadn't been lucky enough to get an aisle seat, but my brother had. Satisfying myself with the view of the lights of Faro and the glinting blue black sea as we banked to line up with our landing path, my mind was full of feelings of a great adventure about to begin.

The bubble burst when we picked up our holdalls from the baggage carousel. Each of us had an extra bag with equipment and stores needed for the boat. We were eyed, most suspiciously, by the customs officials who could not pigeon-hole us.

Even to this day I cannot work out what it was that made them search us so thoroughly. Was it our bulging bags, our Irish passports, or the fact that we were both tall with light coloured hair, almost Scandinavian looking, in contrast to these Latins? Weren't the Irish generally of a similar Latin colouring, with dark hair and similar stature?

We were not fair skinned either.

My brother had been in the Algarve and the Canaries for a month; I had spent the summer in Spain, mostly outside, plus I had been back to Spain in February for a top-up. We had tans. Despite our casual dress of check shirts and jeans, we were quite obviously smugglers as far as they were concerned.

Maybe they just didn't like the look of us or maybe they didn't like their jobs.

We declared everything, but the bored customs men were not satisfied that we had done so. I had decided to refrain from saying that I had nothing else to declare but my genius. I was far too sensible, and the officials looked far too mean.

They were also armed, which always makes one uncomfortable and terribly polite. They had nothing else to do; it was the end of a long and tedious day for them. It was about nine thirty and they would not be home before eleven. I didn't blame them, but unpacking and re-packing our bags was a trying experience.

The bags had been packed with such care and precision that trying to fit everything back into the bags, once it had been inspected, proved very trying, particularly as the effect of the two cocktails, followed by drinks on the flight, had not quite worn off We had brought over an awful lot: filler powder, special paints, special finishes and varnishes, parts for the engine, a new sail, canned goods.

All of it had been brought out for inspection, and then thrown in a heap by our bags. It was up to us to put everything back if we could. They scattered our belongings and all we could do was look on and try to replace everything as best we could - a right regal welcome to the Algarve.

We found a cab outside and Norman warned me that their driving was dangerous. The driver must have been in a hurry to get home, making this his last job of the evening.

Sitting in the back of the car I was worried that it might be his final job and our last ride ever. Despite the driver, who dropped us off at the corner of the yacht pool, we arrived safely.

Carrying the heavy bags along the pontoons was no joy. I was hoping that the boat would be close by, but alas it was one of the furthest away. Norman pointed it out to me, and my heart sank. It needed an awful lot of work done on it, I could tell, even under the artificial glow of the marina floodlights.

When we reached the boat, he unlocked the hatch, and I passed the four bags down to him in the cockpit. Finally, after some swearing, the bags were stowed. It was disconcerting to notice that the gunwales were only two foot above the water line and that most of the forty-two foot was out of the water forming tapered ends, great for streamlining and racing, but not leaving much room for living space.

Inside the cabin neither of us could stand, the roof being only five feet high. This was grandly called the lounge but should have been called the crawl.

We had left England on 8th May.

Rising early, our first task on Sunday was to unload the boat and sort through the equipment, making sure there was a place for everything, and everything was in place.

It was not a day of rest, but we had barbecued pork at a restaurant called the Cabana. It was cheap and cheerful, with bench seats, a long refectory table and plenty of cheap red wine, exactly what we needed after a day in the sun.

Rehydration was not a priority.

On Monday we took the cockpit apart, sanded it down and sorted through the equipment there. If this sounds repetitive, it was.

Supper was at the Ritz; it was the name yachts-people gave for a local transport cafe. Swordfish was on the menu, the fish steaks fat and succulent, with a cheap white wine to complement them.

On Tuesday we painted the cockpit and sorted through more equipment. Supper was at the Mayflower, squid this time. I lived for eating. It was the highlight of a hard day.

The name Mayflower rang a bell. I was sure the Puritans set sail promptly, though we would not. The next day we tidied up the cabin which involved sorting through more equipment, or the same equipment yet again.

We spent a week sanding down the hull and deck, filling gaps in the timber and generally patching the boat for a smooth coat of wood primer. It was unpleasant work without shelter.

The daily ritual consisted of having a shower and then breakfast, followed by smothering our skins in suntan lotion, which made our hands greasy, holding the sandpaper awkwardly and we were sweating almost immediately.

Working in the heat with dripping oil running off your body is no joy, but finally we were ready to apply the paint. This was even less enjoyable, but progress had been made. We could abandon the suntan oil at this stage because we had such a solid base tan. Besides, it was so annoying to be so greasy all day.

Despite the fact that this boat looked as if she would never leave harbour, I remained hopeful that one day I would sail again. Supper became a hunt for variations.

We had swordfish at the *Ritz*; octopus at the *Cabana*, you get the idea.

Three restaurants, a limited menu, still our sails remained firmly furled. Sailing involves moving to new places, variety of location, that sort of thing. I could have made it to any of the restaurants blindfolded. Also, I was working hard, not as a crewmember, but as a restorer. For this reason, I started to become more than a tad resentful of my own flesh and blood.

It was only eleven o'clock and yet the heat from the sun was oppressive, certainly not conducive to working out of the shade. The bright light of the sun was painful to look at and the heat generated by it had warmed everything: paint tin, skin, stone pavement and even the white deck. A sweat had already formed on my brow, and I was aware of a clammy feeling under my armpit.

It was one of those skies that look pale and glow blue, which everyone associates with summer in the 'Med'.

For some strange reason my brother was already writing the logbook, which I thought was only written when one went to sea, but apparently it is necessary to keep a good watch on things in harbour and note down any incidences of drunkenness amongst the crew or mutinous rumblings.

This was all very well, but with all things considered, treachery from one crewmember, and your brother at that, seemed highly unlikely. However, a note could be made of what provisions had been bought and what equipment was needed or had gone missing, not that this was in any way a regular occurrence.

More likely it would be a case of some boathook or paddle going over the side, or a can of beans being dropped overboard by mistake.

Accidents did happen and we had our fair share both out to sea and in port. As I slapped another coat of paint on yesterday's work, it struck me that this religious half an hour of writing allowed my brother time off from manual work.

I stood in the dinghy with the hot sun on my back, trying to keep balance while my brother, pen in hand, wrote spasmodically, smoking one of his filthy roll-up cigarettes which took an age to make and even longer to burn down or sipping a chilled glass of shandy. I could see the bottles hauled up occasionally from the cool water and then hear the plop as they were returned to their saline fridge.

My filter tips were in the cabin, and I ached for one. Concentrating on the brush strokes of primer, I had pretended not to have seen or heard the making of the first drink of the day. All I had since eight o'clock was a cup of Galao and a pathetic pastry.

Due to time constraints, we had abandoned our early morning perambulations into town and saved our appetite for our evening meal of roast quails at the trucker's cafe or chicken barbecued over a charcoal grill at the Cabana.

We would pick up bread and cheese for the next day from the shops along the way. If we didn't make it to town by seven in the evening, we negotiated for bread from the restaurant and eked out our supply of cheese. We had jam on board in case we were not cautious enough with our other rations. It was important that we tried to keep to our schedule.

The possibility of spending the whole summer working on the boat was a real one. We therefore elected to get her seaworthy. This, inevitably, involved working long hours in the hot sunshine. The skin on my shoulders and back was peeling and I felt that if I didn't have a drink of any kind soon, then my throat would begin to peel also.

Just as I was about to curse my own flesh and blood, my brother arrived with a shandy and a pack of my *Sagres* cigarettes. I never bought duty-free, but always smoked the tobacco of the country. Besides being cheaper in Europe, it gives one more of a feeling of being on holiday.

Some holiday.

Chapter Four - The Riddle of the Sand Banks

Dealing with bureaucracy is the most frustrating of clerical tasks and leaving Vilamoura was the most frustrating of bureaucratic nightmares.

Norman remained calm, but I could not. I was bored of being painter and powder monkey. The sharing of menial tasks was not equal and if I had wanted to paint, then I could have got four pounds an hour painting any house in London, accruing capital rather than spending it. I was there to sail and meet the girls on time in Ibiza.

I didn't want to let them down in any way.

Norman could not have cared less. The more time spent in harbour, the more work I could do on making his yacht ship-shape and Bristol-fashion. I had never been into fashion and never visited Bristol; as long as there were no holes, I wanted to get going. The boat had been a let down and so had not been able to set sail immediately.

Despite my itchy feet, I put on a brave face, but even with the officials carrying pistols, I wanted to throttle someone. Frustrated by the officials, plus the realisation that a contest between them and I might lead to bullet holes, my argument with them lost steam. However, as the days went by, fratricide moved nearer and nearer the top of the agenda.

Norman had already secured the title of Captain Ahab and yet all the whales, including the son of Moby Dick, lay out in the ocean, while we languished in the soulless marina, connecting with real people only in the shanty town and when we went out each evening; but even this treat was beginning to pall.

Firstly, once you had chicken and fish two nights running at the Cabana, there was nothing else on the menu. The novelty of eating on benches with the charcoal and flagons of wine stacked up on the far wall wore off very quickly.

You could not choose who sat next to you.

My brother, for all his scintillating conversation, was too exhausted to talk further, as was I. Eating a meal in silence is like listening to pop music without the drum or an orchestra without violin and piano; it just doesn't feel or sound right.

Our one trip to the transport cafe where we ate quails was both worthwhile and satisfying, but it was deemed too far to walk just for decent food and the walk back had been horrendous. The Victorians used to say: "after lunch rest a while, after supper walk a mile", but two miles was excessive even for the most passionate of nineteenth century pundits.

Finally, after much bureaucratic wrangling, filling of forms and photocopying documents, we got clearance by the port officials to leave harbour. Our next visit to the local store was to be the last, so we went to the bank, took out some money and bought plenty of honey, along with bread wine and a noxious local spirit which came in the same bottle as our paraffin.

There was no electricity on board, so we had to use hurricane lamps, filled from what looked like a stretched, clear wine bottle with a plastic stopper. Cheese and beer made up the rest of the list.

We had our priorities.

Butter was a luxury and would have melted. This sailing boat travelled lightly and swiftly; having no larder and no fridge meant that our stores were limited. Our range was three days at sea, maximum. Fresh water was supplied from a fifty-litre plastic Jerry can filled with fresh water from the harbour master at a cost.

Coffee and tea had been brought in bulk from home along with a single jar of English apricot jam, heavy on the sugar, light on the fruit. That was that. We had six bottles of paraffin (we bought one daily to increase our stock).

We added the spirit bottle to the two we already had, and the case of beer complemented the three cases we had on board. There were twenty-four bottles in each case, but they were tiny bottles, quarter of a litre each.

We had several litres of lemonade, too. It was rare that we would drink alcohol on its own, because in the heat the effects are more concentrated.

Our mooring fees paid on Thursday 20th; we were ready to leave. Eleven days after our arrival, I had insisted we go. Preparing for departure involved more sorting through, the paint tins stowed carefully, just in case we had time, at a later date, to finish the job. Waterwitch looked white and right on one side, and like a camouflaged World War One cruiser on the other, a disruptive pattern of greys and whites.

I counted three shades of undercoat and I would not even have attempted to count the smears of filler that broke up the outline of that particular side. It was truly a disruptive pattern. We set sail on the ebbing evening tide, five days after the originally agreed departure date.

There was a light wind and we goose-winged it past the customs men who waved as we went. I wanted to give them a gesture, but as we sailed past them at two knots it would have looked faintly ridiculous.

How uptight and urbanised I was when we started. After our ordeal, I became one of the most relaxed and grateful people on earth, a few steps down from a priest.

Once out in the ocean, the wind picked up and we sailed gently and majestically into the open sea.

Finally, we were sailing, even if it was slowly. It was an ideal time for my brother to acquaint me with the boat. I tried to show my knowledge, gleaned from a Royal Yachting Association course.

'So, you're in charge of the jib,' he said.

'Okay,' I agreed, 'I'll fasten it to the forestay and haul it up.'

'That's right, the hanks, those small clips, attach to the eyes in the sail; a bit of a fiddly job, but it shouldn't take too long. Make sure that the sheets aren't tangled.'

The sheets were attached to the clew of the jib, and they would haul the jib from one side to the other when we changed direction.

I had to make sure they were not coiled because they were hauled in from the cockpit at the aft of the boat and gave us the power to turn. The jib was the first piece of canvas that caught the wind when you changed direction; if the ropes became snagged the boat might lose the wind and just drift.

'Where are the winches to haul in the sheets?' I asked, perplexed.

'This is a basic boat. See those brass cylinders, the drums, you put the rope around those, one turn only and they click. Draw in the sail until it's almost taut - you cannot let go of the rope until the sail is as trim as can be, then fasten the rope in those teeth underneath. The drums only move in a clockwise direction, so you have to wrap the rope around in a clockwise fashion.'

It seemed simple enough to me.

'Then I fasten them between those two grips,' I asked while one hand pointed at two teardrop-shaped wooden blocks fastened to the gunwales, underneath the copper cylinders. They were parallel but tapered towards each other and they had wooden teeth on them to grip even the slipperiest of ropes.

'Only when I have brought the boom around,' he replied.

The mast and boom formed the right angle for the mainsail and the mast formed the hypotenuse. The foot of the sail sat in the groove of the metal boom, the base of the triangle.

The mainsail was furled around the boom when not in use. When used it was untied, then fastened by clips on to the main mast halyard, a steel wire that was hoisted up the mast by a single rope, a pulley, allowing you to hoist the sail up and down.

There were two hooks which you wrapped the end of the rope around, one faced upwards, the other downwards. This encouraged you to fasten the rope in a figure-of-eight fashion around these hooks. If the weather were good, the sail would be hoisted to the top of the mast. If the weather was gusty then the sail could be hauled three-quarters or half the way up the mast, this was known as being point-reefed.

Running from the mast to the beam were the shrouds, steel cables that gave support to the mast. Similar cables known as backstays ran to the aft of the boat. I was getting to know all the little bits of the boat. The beam was the centre of the boat, its fattest point. Before I had called it the middle and once, I knew the name, I could not wait to mention it.

'What do the shrouds and backstays do, apart from support the mast?' I asked.

'Nothing, except provide a line for us to run up the courtesy flag, which we will have to change from Portuguese to Spanish once we enter Iberian waters.'

'Are they that strict?'

'All countries are, it is maritime law after all, a sign of respect.'

'I see,' I replied.

'I believe it was the British who started it, something to do with territorial waters and who commanded them. I should think most sailors have forgotten why we do it. We can hang our washing from the shrouds, which is handy. Even jeans dry out very efficiently after a few hours tied to the shrouds - the De Nimes flag.'

We laughed, but the lesson was not over. He pointed to the port deadeyes at the bottom of the port shroud, a block of round, flat wood with an iron band running around its circumference. It was pierced with three holes to feed a lanyard through it.

Norman continued.

'The bottom of the shroud is made fast around the upper deadeye. The lower deadeye is fastened to the gunwale and cannot be detached. If you pull on the lanyard, the shroud can be tightened in really bad weather.'

'I shouldn't think that we'll have any bad weather, so why worry?'

At my comment, my brother looked at me quickly and then away, changing the subject to the operation of the mainsail.

'The mainsail works in the same way, but the dead-eyes of that are attached to this steel bar that runs along the front of our sailing bench. That bar is known as the sailing horse.'

He pointed to a bar that ran along the middle of the bench and that was curved at each end, the metal disappearing into the wood of the bench. It looked as if it would take a lot to separate the two, as much as it would take to detach the bench from the skeleton of the boat.

A compass stood on the outside lip of the stairway into the cabin. There was a bench with a sailing horse that ran a foot and half along the front to which the mainsail dead- eyes were attached. A wooden tiller arm protruded across the top and over the back of the sailing bench and that was that. The gunwales were made of mahogany. The patina and varnish had faded over time; they were now grey and to this the backstay shrouds were attached, as were the hanks for the foresail. Outside the gunwales on the slopping deck were the drums, the windlasses.

'So, I sit on the bench and steer, pull in the jib, then set the mainsail by pulling on the dead-eyes.'

'Exactly, don't touch the shrouds; you have to really know what you're doing,' he warned. 'Once you decide to turn...'

'Come about,' I corrected him.

'Once you decide to change tack, you call out, 'jive, ho,' turn the tiller, loosen the deadeye and let go of the jib in that order. I know others release the jib rope first, but I don't. As you come about the boom dead-eye will slide along the pole.'

'The sailing horse?' I asked for confirmation.

'Yes, but only once you have the jib trim do you start to haul in the main sheet. If we are sailing together, the responsibilities are the same - you handle the jib and I'll handle the mainsail.'

'That seems clear enough; by the way, what is a stanchion?'

'Every wire on the boat is either standing or running rigging. Stanchion just means an upright support.'

'So, it is a support for some of the metal wires or ropes on the rigging, then?'

'That's right, put simply. You'll get used to all the different ropes and wires in no time. Then the only other pieces of equipment that you have to worry about are the anchor and the ropes to tie up the boat.'

'We call them painters.'

'Yes, sailors call them painters. We have ropes down below that tie the fenders to the boat.'

'The fenders are the rubber buoys or tyres attached to the boat to stop it scraping against the harbour wall or other boats when it's moored up in a proper berth or dock.'

'Okay, you know something about sailing, but not in this boat and not on any racing boat.'

'I see.'

'Anything else?'

'Are we going to tack at some stage today?'

Once I said that I thought, in all innocence, that my brother might have thought I was still trying to be clever. No such luck.

'Too little wind, I'm afraid; we'll have to motor sail from here. You can take down the jib and stow it, there is a bag in the forward cabin on my bunk.'

'Sure.'

'Get out the Genoa instead, it's in the canvas bag.'

'What about the racing jib?'

'That's in the blue nylon bag, but it won't help much. It's not the strength of the wind, it's the direction.'

'Oh.'

I sauntered down below to get the bag.

Popping my head out of the forward hatch to judge where to throw the bag, I squatted down, clasped the big bag around its circumference and, with a mighty effort, raised the heavy canvas through the lip of hatchway, against which I rested it for a moment. Then pushing it from below, I eased it on to the deck.

Using my arms as leverage, I hauled myself up through the hatch and next to the foresail. As I hauled her down, I uncapped the brass bulldog fasteners, the hanks, from the forestay.

Those bulldog clips were brass and as old as the boat, but the springs inside them that made them snap shut were as effective as ever, so you had to watch your fingers did not get snagged in them. My brother had already released the jib sheets.

With just the mainsail up we were going to rely on that and the outboard motor, which we could strap to the port side of the boat.

We had limited petrol, but the British Seagull engine was built to pre-war specifications, which guaranteed reliability. My brother rummaged round under the stern deck housing while I took the tiller. Eventually, he found the small, robust engine and strapped it to the port side by its bracket. Although the engine had a very little power, it could move our three tons of boat through the water at four knots, effectively doubling our speed.

The motor chugged and we smiled. The adventure had finally begun. It was still light and with our sunglasses on and heading southeast, we kept a weather eye on the sun as it sank slowly in the west. Our plan was clear. Sail from Vilamoura into the channel at Faro, the Praia de Faro, skirting the marshes of Cabo de Santa Maria and sailing along to Olhao.

Once there, we would moor that night off an island southeast of that fishing town. Apparently, the island was teeming with yacht crews and the bar served delicious food, great beer and was owned by an old English sea dog who had tales of the Caribbean seas and stories of adventures in the Mediterranean.

From there we would shadow the coast of Spain until we reached the island of Ibiza. That was all well and good.

However, as we approached Faro it became clear that unless the wind picked up to eight or nine knots, we would have to rethink our elaborate plan.

The drone of the motor and the fading light reminded me of my preconceived ideas.

The perception I had had was of sunlight and speedy progress, a comfortable boat heeled over as it approached the twelve-knot mark.

I would have to be patient.

The point I was aiming for as I held the helm was a speck in the distance. Perhaps we could have walked there more quickly, but we had to take the rough with the smooth, or more especially in our case the rough with the rough. It was early evening by the time we reached the shallows that signified the entrance to Faro. My brother was at the helm, and he had debriefed the crew at five o'clock.

Silencing the engine, he announced with triumph that we had enough wind in the sails to make the use of the motor redundant and that we were doing almost four knots. Waiting for me to be suitably impressed led to a long silence. What I wanted to know was: when would we get there? As if wounded by my need to know our ETA (Estimated Time of Anchoring), my brother went into the various logistics of moving such a small, wonderful boat along the coastline.

With much reference to her heritage, and lineage, the speed she could and would be able to achieve in the right circumstances, he made it abundantly clear that we were far from these ideal conditions. This boat liked the open seas and felt constrained by these narrow channels. With my rudimentary knowledge of sailing, I felt we might consult the chart and see if there was a shortcut.

Unfortunately, I was informed that on my brother's trip to London there was not a chandler in the land that had the prerequisite navigational maps to hand. They could be ordered and dispatched within twenty-one days, by which stage we would be in Ibiza. I found it hard to argue the logic behind this, but as a privileged first mate I was allowed a peek at the Michelin road map, which we were to use until we got to Gibraltar.

In the dim light, I became fascinated by the coast road that hugged the shoreline and succumbed to its allure. Surely, it was a pleasure to drive along.

The upshot was that we would sail through the early evening and with luck and a flowing tide we would be in Olhao by nine o'clock, already anchored, having battened down the hatches and we would have two beers on the bar by nine thirty.

I had looked over the chart, enquired as to our average speed and observed silently to myself that this was a hopeful scenario.

Sensing my distrust, my brother had informed me that the wind would be picking up soon.

Apparently, this part of the coast was notorious for its strong winds. One thing we had to watch out for was running aground. That was something we could not do. As if to illustrate his point, the flags fluttered in the new wind. Waterwitch had lain on the sea floor for months when she ran aground before. Armed with this knowledge, I was pleased to be sent to the front with a plumb line to take soundings.

It was getting chilly, but I still wore shorts. I had a navy cotton sweater on which had a collar that I turned up. I could feel the hairs on my leg stand up, but it was a pleasant cooling feeling. We were on a tight tack and close hauled so unfortunately, we could not take advantage of the gust. However, we were overtaken on the port side by a windsurfer whose path was ideally suited to this wind. Skimming past over the barely undulating waves, he gave a nonchalant wave and a cheery Germanic

'Hello.'

My brother was understandably incensed. It was the fact that a windsurfer had overtaken him that annoyed him so much. I, too, was perturbed.

Surely, we should be going faster, but if we had done it would have necessitated several tacks and the channel was not wide enough to complete them, so we bobbed along as the wind got fresher and the sun, disappearing into the west, ceased to warm either of us.

We were too busy to brew a coffee. Lashing the tiller and lighting the primus was too dangerous with the prospect of turning into the wind to avoid a sand bank. I was well aware of our six-foot keel creeping along underneath the water, while I took depths of seven, nine or ten feet.

When we entered the channel, we were sure that the tide was carrying us along.

In fact, it was only the wind.

The tide was ebbing, and the light was fading.

However, we had made it into what seemed a deeper channel and this allowed my brother to light the hurricane lamps and switch on the navigation lights. There was a pathetic glow from the rusted oil lamps - the wick had not been trimmed and a black oily smoke eased up to the tin chimney, clouding the already dirty glass. You wouldn't want to read a book by that light, let alone use it as a warning lamp.

We started to pick up speed and swapped positions. The lights of Faro glinted in the distance. A warm welcoming sight, but we weren't heading there. We were heading into the night. I lashed the tiller for a few minutes while I dressed properly for the cold night air. Jeans slipped over shorts and a windcheater. My brother had kept his stowed under the tiller and was wearing them now, along with some warm-looking sailing trousers. The cotton in my jeans seemed to absorb the dampness in the air and I wished that I had equipped myself more thoroughly for this journey.

When discussing this trip neither oilskins nor night sailing had been mentioned. How far away all this was from the pleasant holiday in Greece, at Easter, two years ago; never sailing beyond six o'clock, on shore tied up at our moorings by six thirty, showered and in the taverna by seven thirty, the warming wine that we illicitly drank, added to the warm evening breezes.

I shuddered with the cold and the remembrance, as I stepped back on to the ever-darkening deck, lit only by the pathetic, black oily glow of one hurricane lamp. In the sombre evening, I could hardly see the details of my brother's face at this stage. He was becoming a shadowy form on the foredeck.

He swayed like the Grim Reaper, as he set the line into the water and raised it up to the torch, hanging from the forestay, which set an eerie pool of light just in front of his feet.

Up ahead we could see a cruising yacht, twenty-eight foot or maybe more, a floodlit deck, brimming with high power lamps beaming across the water in front of it. Ours were the smallest navigational lights I had seen; theirs were like beacons. The water around them was floodlit, like a stadium, Albert Speer would have been proud, and the boat was reflected in the glow.

In the case of our boat, even the white side was shrouded in shadow, the navigational lights, which ran off two small batteries, were the size of an indicator lamp, hardly visible a nautical mile away. This boat, on the other hand, was lit up like a Christmas tree and could be seen from other countries.

We heard the thud of their big diesel engines, and we could see they were drinking hot coffee. I have never been an envious person, but that night I was visited by the green- eyed monster of jealousy, theirs was a luxury cruiser; ours was camping at sea.

A strange spot for a picnic and rather late, I remember thinking, but it was Ahab who saw the trouble; the poor people had run aground. Being Irish, but living in England, there was a danger of becoming more English than the English. My brother demonstrated that whimsical notion that night.

We were flying the Red Ensign and we would abide by British Maritime law that states you should never neglect a boat in trouble. As he strolled back to get the loudhailer, a rusty, green metal cone, with a stirrup handle, I heard the engines rise in pitch, rev and then there was a churning sound as the propeller was engaged.

The crew of the other boat were trying to reverse off the sand bank. We were close enough to see clearly now, in their lights, not ours, and I watched as the muddy brown water spiralled underneath their stern. The propeller seemed to be stuck fast in the marsh.

'Ahoy there,' that's really what he said, 'Are you in a spot of trouble?'

'Ja, we are stuck,' said a Germanic voice.

That, and having seen the German windsurfer, convinced me that we were witnessing an invasion of German tourists. They might have been Austrian; my German dialect has never been good nor has my ability to distinguish between German and Haut Deutsche.

'Oh,' my brother said, pretending he had only just noticed their predicament. 'You've run aground,' sailors are so insufferably snobby, you did not get stuck, you ran aground, 'We'll tow you off.'

The German smiled and then saw our boat; his smile evaporated, and his mouth widened in disbelief.

'Throw us a rope and we'll have you off in a jiffy.'

It was not clear to the Germans what a jiffy was, but they had obviously been trying to manoeuvre out of their position for some time because he shrugged. How easily people accept help when they are desperate.

'Throw us your stern rope,' my skipper said confidently.

This would be interesting to watch. We were doing around four knots. Their diesel engines had not shifted the boat, yet we would try. The German was weak with frustration and too tired to argue. He gathered up the rope as we passed and threw it to my brother, now stationed at the main mast stays.

Grabbing the mess of rope, he strode calmly to where I sat and attached the rope around the nearest windlass, which would have had the jib rope around it if we were on the opposite tack. The rope became taut. The windlass clicked twice in the clockwise direction as he wound the rope around, and there was a creaking sound from our poor old boat.

If ever she were going to break up it would be now.

A sucking sound came from the bow of the German boat, her engines idling, but it was not necessary for the diesels to become active. Their propeller shaft had been stuck in the mud, too.

We came around the back of her and she swung around and off the bank, both boats floating. With pride, our skipper unfurled the other boat's rope.

'You should be all right now,' he said cheerfully, and I felt a note of condescension in his voice. A grateful 'thank you' came from the two men and choruses of 'danke' from the two women. Whilst basking in this newfound glory we hit the bank.

It was no great thud.

We just stopped and glided on to the shallows. One minute I was almost glad that we were there to help and not in some bar with warm lights and a warm fire, but in the next moment, the bubble burst. My brother stumbled. It was a good job he had been standing with his legs apart and arms akimbo, like Peter Pan or Errol Flynn, otherwise he may have landed in the water. The rate at which we hit the bank was so slow that, as it was, he regained his balance and composure with consummate ease.

The Germans noticed this, the indignation of it all, the agony and ignominy. Before we could establish whether we were stuck fast the German had hailed us.

'Now it is our turn to help you.' The captain called; he emphasised the 'you' as direct revenge for the condescension my brother had showed them.

Deftly he threw his rope back and my brother tied it to the same place. I loosened the sails. Perhaps we could tack at the same time, get on to a better beam and start to really move, although I noticed the wind had dropped yet again. It was lucky we had the good fortune of having someone to get us off.

The big diesels growled, and the propeller burbled in the water, and we drifted off the bank as easily as we had got on to it. We were extremely grateful and shouted our thanks. I thought my brother was going to say, 'you're so kind', or 'do come again', but we contented ourselves with choruses of danke and danke-schon.

We were young, free, and international. The slate was clean. We had rescued them; they had rescued us.

We came about, a nautical term for turning around. Sailing majestically towards both our victims and saviours we decided we could tack at the entrance of the channel we had just been up and send the boat along the course that would bring us finally to Olhao.

It would waft us to the warm bar with friends we had yet to meet, a roaring fire and ice-cold beer to quench our thirsts. I dreamed of allowing my brother to row the tender back to the mother ship and collapsing contented in my bunk. All I wanted was warm food, cold beer, and a lavish sleep.

It was not to be. As we approached, we noticed the Germans had managed to get their boat lodged on the sand once again. My brother leapt into action, this time with our rope. Nevertheless, the Germans were adamant they did not want to spend the evening with each boat freeing the other in turn from the quagmire.

They shouted across that they were all right and proved it by reversing serenely off the bank. In the meantime, we narrowed our wide tack and headed for the stricken ship. The ship started to motor away, and we hit another sand bar. This time we hit it with a thud due to such a superb speed on that stupendous new tack.

The Germans waved.

I am sure to this day that they were aware we once more needed their help, but they ignored us.

This situation would not be tolerated in the Baltic, Barents, or any other sea. We called after them and their hearing, which had seemed so acute all those minutes before, failed them. To this day I can see the skipper of that vessel waving and wishing us goodnight.

We could hear him, and he was downwind, how could he fail to hear us? Cursing our luck and the lack of Christian charity, we secured the boat with anchor and stowed the sails. The talk over a warming cup of coffee laced, in traditional naval style, with a generous tot of brandy was all about the ungrateful and un-gentlemanly skipper of that boat.

The fact that he was German never came into our castigation of his character, the fact that he had ignored our pleas for help and flouted all maritime and humanitarian laws did. My brother, the excellent cook that he was, cooked us supper, what he called his 'one-pot-wonder'. This was so called because we only had one saucepan and it was a wonder, we could cook any decent meals in the one pot.

It was then we realised that our mooring was closer to Faro than we imagined. Not Faro town, but Faro airport. The late-night rush was on, and aircraft engines screamed literally a hundred feet above. Trying to sleep in a flight path is no easy task, particularly when the planes seem about to hit the mast.

As we sat waiting for our food to cook, the deafening sound of aircraft pierced the night. The boat shuddered and I could feel the shock waves of sound reverberating around my body. I wanted to sleep and yet I was hungry, I wanted peace and yet every twenty minutes another winged beast flew overhead. We waited for the one that would take off our mast.

Chapter Five - Hanging Around, Having Run Aground

The first few planes were not so bad. They had a good height and they had approached the airport high above our marshland home, but the next six or seven were coming in low. We hurriedly ate our supper, still complaining that if we had not been so helpful, we would not be in this predicament, deciding that no one of that calibre should be let loose on a boat. Conversation in a confined space when nothing is happening tends to be limited and repetitive. Even the simplest slight is magnified and mulled over again and again.

A sounding after supper, to complement the one beforehand, assured us that the tide was no longer ebbing. It was reassuring to know that we would not sink further into the swamp. If we sank too deep, our weight would embed us in the quagmire, and we might not get out. The rising tide would then flow over us rather than lift us out of the swamp.

After all our hard work, it would be a shame to see the boat drowned in a marsh. It was decided that we would have to wait four hours for high tide and that sleep was the best course of action. My complaint that it might be difficult to sleep within a stone's throw of one of the busiest European airports met with a broad smile and the offer of a copy of Erskine Childer's book, *The Riddle of the Sands*. Apparently, the book tells of two men in the Baltic who constantly ran aground. I pointed out that I knew where the Baltic was and if I had wanted a holiday like that I could have gone there or, for the same weather patterns, sail a dinghy on the marshlands of the Fenlands.

How I regretted ever reading Swallows and Amazons as a child. That book glamorised sailing for me and led to my involvement with wind and water. If only I had left it to the professionals. I was young and naive, cold, shell-shocked from the bombardment of aeroplane noise, yet I had a full belly, a steaming cup of coffee, dry warm blankets, and shelter of sorts. Life was not so bad after all.

I flicked the cigarette I had allowed myself into the still water. We had both brought local cigarettes the first week, as they were a quarter of the price of those at home and you soon became used to the tobacco in Sagres, the Portuguese brand.

We had become so used to them that we were smoking forty a day and, in the sunshine, we hacked and coughed with bronchitis. It had been decided we would give up at sea but acknowledged that we may need a few packs for the first days. I looked at how many cigarettes I had during our first day at sea.

From a full box, I now had three left. It was so easy to light up with our petrol lighter, knowing we had enough petrol on board to guarantee, at least, that our lighters would always work. The monotony of drifting along the coast had meant that my first few days' supply had gone in an afternoon. I was tired, so I finished the last swig of brandy and hoped that I was not taking the first watch.

'Well,' I ventured, 'we're out of the harbour.'

'We're still afloat, just,' my brother smiled.

'Do you think we'll make Olhao tomorrow?'

'We'll be there for lunch, no problem.'

'I hope so.'

'We've just had a bad day.'

'It can only get better, right?'

'Of course, I reckon it will take four hours to reach the island.'

Who's going to do first watch?'

'No one, we're in a shallow channel - no one would come down here in the day, let alone at night. We're quite safe.'

A plane roared overhead, looking like it was going to clip the mast. Our dim navigational lights would be unseen from the air, I assumed.

'We'll both get some rest and move out early in the morning,' Anton decided.

'I'm off to bed.'

'See you in the morning,' he continued, 'I was hoping we might drift off with the current but that's not happening; I'll put the anchor out and set the alarm for high tide. We should be able to get off then.'

'Fine, sleep well.'

'I will.'

I noticed him helping himself to another shot of brandy. We were using the disposable plastic cups given to us for our drinks on the flight. He was generous with his measure someone must have jogged his hand; the glass was three quarters full.

I was not worried. People on the continent seemed to drink far more than at home. I was not a regular drinker, but abroad people often keep up with the local alcohol intake. I had not quite adjusted to this yet.

One generous glass and I was numbed and exhausted. In the cabin I slipped off my deck shoes without untying the laces, tore off my jeans and shorts, peeled off my jumper and T-shirt, slipping naked into the cold cotton of the lined sleeping bags.

Sitting up I threw my clothes on to the bunk opposite and draped two of the synthetic acrylic blankets over my legs, then pulled up the top two corners, bringing the fold up to my chest. I curled into a foetal position, unconcerned about not having brushed my teeth. I reasoned that I would brush them doubly well the next day. We had showered twice a day in Vilamoura, but one day without washing would do no harm. We were camping, after all. I was content to think of the shower that I would have on the island, east of Olhao.

My head lay on the pillow and my eyes closed, I could feel my head spinning pleasantly and could hear the lapping of the water against our wooden hull. I was safe and secure and asleep almost immediately. By now I was used to the dampness in the cabin. I would air my clothes on the deck railings the next day and change into something I had packed in my holdall. Over two weeks into the trip, I still had clean clothes to wear. I was pleased that I had so many pairs of underwear, but worried about how we would wash our clothes now that I was down to my last two pairs.

It was morning somewhere in the world when we awoke next day, but for us it was still night. The airport was in silence, the lights of Faro glowing brighter in the clear night.

Each holding a boathook, we moved to the front of the boat.

'Right,' said my brother. 'Just push your boathook into the marsh and we'll punt this thing off.'

The anchor chain was loose. We were held by the mud bank and nothing else. My boathook squelched in the mud and splashed the water as I raised it.

'Together, one, two, three,' came the order.

Holding our palms over the top and leaning heavily with the other arm, we pushed our lances into the bank and heaved. A sigh came from the front and the boat started to drift off We were free. My brother laid down his boathook and hauled up the anchor as we drifted backwards off the mound. I was ordered to the stern to take up the tiller. I unleashed the rope and pulled her hard to the port and the boat swung around drifting on the eddy currents. We moved down the channel, and I straightened her up. Silently, like commandos, we eased along the widening stretch of water to the mouth.

My brother took soundings and when we were at a depth of fourteen feet, he turned off the torch and picked up the anchor. Tossing it over the side, the splash pierced the night and some marsh birds squealed at the disturbance, their panic echoing in the silence.

'Right, back to bed. I'll do the rest. I'll put the sea anchor out, at the stern, and that will stop us spinning in the night,' Anton assured me. We had merely moved the boat into the deeper water of the channel and now we could go straight to sleep.

'The alarm is set for the next high tide; I don't feel able to take her through this in the dark.'

A nod from me showed that I concurred with his view. My bed was warm now. I had only slipped on my shorts and a cotton jumper. It was cold on the deck and even after less than ten minutes in the cold, damps night air, I longed to be back in my cocoon, asleep.

Hardly had I curled up and dozed off than I was awakened again. This was all I needed. Six hours had elapsed and yet I still felt that I was suffering from severe fatigue, the sea air had left me quite exhausted; yet I was under twenty, fit and lean. I obviously lacked stamina.

In truth I knew why, we were up early and in bed late. Before I had left, I had been to a party on the Friday and Saturday nights. Staying up all night had been easy. After all, I was going to have three months to recover, but I had not managed to catch up on my sleep and I felt it now. It was sunny, but not warm, a cold breeze made the stanchions crack, the shrouds jingled in their housings; the Ensign fluttered, our own wind vane.

I wiped my eyes and scratched my chin. Shaving in harbour was fine, but out to sea I would not be bothered. Indeed, this was a dangerous manoeuvre, which could result in a cutthroat experience, or at least duelling scars all over the face. My brother was sporting a blond beard, and, within a few weeks, I would have one too, I could shave in Ibiza.

Taking a quick wash, splashing the water from the Jerry can into a plastic bowl, I wondered when I would be able to have my next proper bath. The showers at the harbour had been adequate and the pipes had warm water in them. From now on, there was cold fresh water from our jerry cans and soap, or the sea and sea soap, specially formulated to lather in salt water.

Looking over the edge and feeling the cold against my arms, I decided to stop at just cleaning my face. My towel was damp and musty smelling, as was all the gear in the boat every morning. It was why I despised camping, getting into soggy clothes.

As a child I had been spoilt; warm folded clothes came straight from the airing cupboard, and always made you feel cosy.

The kettle was on the boil, so I made us some coffee, rinsing out the dirty mugs with the hot water before adding instant coffee and dried milk. Sugar was a luxury, so we both did without.

Sipping our beverages, we sat next to each other on the wooden plank, which served as the cockpit seat. The tiller sat between us, and I rested a toot on its wooden arm. I let my other leg dangle.

I hugged the cup and my knee, looking across at the marshland. The airport was well camouflaged; Faro was practically invisible now the lights were off.

It stood beside the sun that was rising, a blurred outline on the horizon. I had not combed my hair and I felt the wind ruffle it gently. Sipping the hot fluid, I looked around for any sign of life. If this was a wildlife haven, then they were keeping a very low profile. I craned my head from left to right; there was nothing but flats and water. We were totally alone and from what we could see, in the middle of nowhere.

Our road map of this country would not include where we were. It was lucky we had stumbled upon this enclave, but we did not want to be here, and we were not sure how to get out.

I was hungry now and we decided to eat before pulling off the bread was soft still and the apricot jam delicious; another cup of coffee and a cigarette topped off the meal.

The food was good, the location peaceful and calming, the sun was beginning to climb and even the wind seemed less chilled with two cups of hot liquid in our bellies.

The impression may have been given that our voyage was of an eccentric or foolhardy nature. This was not the case. My brother was and is a fine navigator; he had a good compass, sextant, and other hand-held navigational instruments.

Like sailors in the Second World War, we had all the basics, except for a wireless transmitter and radar. He could judge our speed and the distance we had travelled extremely accurately, and he could plot a course second to none. Any sailing depends on different factors, that is why it is considered a dangerous and thrilling sport, even if the danger is only of capsizing a dinghy in safe waters.

Tide and time wait for no man; currents change, and winds whip themselves into a frenzy or gently stroke your face. Variables such as these affect any voyage.

Our first outing had been most unfortunate. The wind was not playing our game. She blew us gently when we wanted force five. The coastline was unforgiving, no separate sand and sea here, more a mixture of the two, clay soil resisting the progress of the water that wore it away. With all this, the sea dumped its cargo of sand against the soil and formed sand banks.

We were equipped for ocean sailing; the boat and her crew did not stand a chance in this bog. A canal boat with its shallow hull was more suited to these channels. It was, however, too late to exchange our vessel. She was in unfamiliar waters, and we needed to take her home, back on to the ocean waves, where her free spirit and long mast would be given free rein.

We set off hopefully, Waterwitch and my brother straining to get free of this shallow sea. I had been imbued with an unhealthy cynicism, which I kept from my brother for fear of upsetting him. We had wanted to go from A to B and now we were at C; there was nothing I could do.

I had been impatient both to be at sea and to get to B. I was in their hands, and I would row along with them, sail side by side. So, there I stood, in my damp clothes, watching the murky water for any sign of a sand bank, my boathook in one hand ready to fend off any outcrops that we came close to. There was little we could do about taking soundings.

We had to follow this channel. The wind had decided our direction for us as well as the beam on which we would sail. It was a strong wind, and we did not need the engine. If our keel struck an outcrop underneath there was nothing we could do; we would deal with that eventuality if it occurred. My mission was to fend off any danger from landmasses to our port bow. The starboard side was clear, and we raced on; we were ever vigilant and primed for any sudden contact.

We still had an hour before the tide went out.

When that happened, if we weren't out of the swamp, then we would have to close haul the sails and punt our way through the shallows.

We both hoped this would not be the case, Waterwitch had been knocked around enough over the last sixteen hours. She had rescued a fellow damsel in distress and been abandoned by her younger and stronger counter-part, to wallow in the shallows and miseries of her outrageous fortune.

Chapter Six - The Open Sea, the Ever Free

Soon we were free from the swamp and out into the open sea. We held our course south, southeast for an hour, before tacking back and heading east into the true entrance of Olhao. We clipped along merrily and within three hours we could see the navigation lights of the harbour, red and green, lit even in the dusk, that demarcated the entrance to the harbour. We had had lunch on the move. I was galley boy and made some salami sandwiches with slices of cheese, each sandwich being a quarter of the remaining stick of bread, which was hardening nicely.

We were allowed to use the rest of our fresh provisions as our destination was so close. There was still some hard cheese left and we had tinned food to keep us going for three weeks. My brother ate his sandwich at the helm, and I ate mine sitting on the windward side, spray splashing my face. I had brought out two beers and we clamped the bottles between our knees as Waterwitch lurched determinedly through the rising breakers. This was sailing. It was a little overcast now, but it was fairly warm. The wind was not icy, but we wore our anoraks.

We had not quite made Olhao by lunchtime, but we still had six days until my other brother came to join us for the trip from Portugal to Gibraltar. The wind continued to daunt us. We made swift progress on one tack and then scant progress on the next. Eventually, at about three o'clock, we were preparing for our final approach to the harbour. It would entail sailing up a wide channel to the north-west of the harbour and then turning about and heading for the harbour, passing the entrance on the same tack, and heading for the island, perhaps making several small tacks on our passage there.

All we could see was the harbour wall and getting there was our objective. Once we were past, we would set another course. I took the helm. The salt air made my lips dry, so I licked them, enjoying the saline flavour.

My arms felt more burnt than brown. They had not stung like this in harbour, but I looked at my arms and could see a dusting of dry salt on them. The wind was cool enough to make the blond hairs stand on end. It was bizarre, my arms were hot, but I still had goose pimples, salted goose bumps.

'Now you see that buoy on the port side, the red one at eleven o'clock. Set a course for that,' the Captain told me.

Ever dutiful, I steered for that buoy, aimed the bow of the boat right at it and kept the tiller swaying slightly against the waves. We were heeling over slightly with the wind. My brother felt we could use a better jib, a racing one for our dash past the harbour and so he went below to rummage around. I saw the hatch above his cabin open. Before leaving he had told me we were doing five knots and that the compass reading showed a bearing of 355 degrees. I looked down at the compass, up at the buoy and eased us back from 345 to 356 degrees to compensate.

The buoy started to disappear off and along the port bow, so I pushed the helm gently away from me. We hit several waves and then the compass read 343 degrees and the buoy had disappeared behind the bow. I pulled the tiller gently towards me and we started to head along at 355 again.

For ten minutes, I kept her on course. My brother's head poked up through the hatch again.

'Are we at that buoy yet?' he asked.

'Getting nearer,' I replied.

It had seemed like we were getting nearer, but in fact we weren't. I couldn't believe that it had taken so long. Perhaps our speed was not correct. It showed three knots. The wind had dropped noticeably, or had I just got used to the howling and flapping in my ears? My brother fed the bright racing jib through the hold and on to the deck. I knew what his question was, and I hated to give the answer -we were no closer to the buoy now.

'Oh, you bloody idiot!' he cried from inside. I was glad I was there for him to take his frustration out on, as glad as I was that I had not booked a flight to Kenya.

Blood is thicker than water even if the water is a bit saltier.

'Can't you do the simplest thing? All I asked you to do was steer for that buoy.'

'But I am steering for the buoy, our course is still 355.'

'Then why aren't we there?'

'I don't know.'

'I should have done this myself, he hissed. He was furious. I was about to offer him a cigarette when he turned on me and glared. 'I need a drink.' He scuttled downstairs into the cabin and came up with a shot glass and a bottle of the local firewater, stopped with a cork. I quite felt like a drink myself after that tirade, but I felt it was his prerogative to have first shot. After all, he was the one in a bate. I hadn't seen him so batey since we were children. He wasn't angry, like adults are he was batey like children are.

Melanie Klein would have had a field day with her theories of transference. We were not making the progress that we were meant to make, and therefore it was not fate or bad luck, but my fault. All that I had done was to try and steer the course given to me. He bit into the cork and wrenched it from the bottle with his teeth, then spat the cork at my feet, perhaps expecting me to pick it up.

I was busy though, steering course 355 degrees. He looked at me again with narrowed, piercing eyes. I pretended not to notice, looking over the port bow at my target, still a small speck in the distance.

'Oh, my God,' he exclaimed, slamming the bottle down on the roof of the cabin and wiping his mouth, 'Bloody paraffin.'

In his haste to get a dose of alcohol, he had not checked which bottles were which; a sniff would have told him. He had swallowed a whole delicious mouthful of paraffin down his gullet. I felt so sorry for him that I could not laugh. I said nothing but looked terribly concerned. He looked at me, reading my face.

'Are you okay? Drink some water.'

'Water, bah, where's the brandy?'

'Where you left it last night,' I replied tersely, waiter service was not on offer. Sure, enough it was under the tiller, and he reached out and took the bottle, unscrewed the cap, and took two thirsty drafts, the second of which he swilled around his mouth and gargled in his throat. I decided against offering him a cigarette. The flame from the Zippo could well trigger an explosion. I had enough problems without an incendiary device on board.

'Give me the tiller,' he ordered, speaking softly, but with menace.

I almost said, 'Say please', but that would have been churlish. He had suffered enough by swallowing the paraffin. For ten minutes, I watched him sail the course I had. Every so often he glanced up to the sails to check they were full and back over his shoulder to check our speed.

'I can't understand it,' he said eventually, quite calm now.

'Nor can I, the buoys can't be moving.'

'No, but we can. What if the tide is coming out at three knots and we're travelling at the same speed? That would account for it.'

'I hadn't thought of the tide at all. My experience has been in Portsmouth Sound in dinghies, it's so deep that tide doesn't come into it. In Greece, the tide is only a matter of inches.'

'Well, that's the answer. We've a strong wind in our favour.'

I thought; where have I heard that before?

'With luck we should make it through the harbour channel and into the bay on one tack; we have to try it. We have no choice.'

'I'm up for it, on one condition.'

'What's that?' he asked.

'You don't have another drink until we reach land.'

'We'll be too busy for that, help me with the racing jib,' he ordered, a smile playing on his lips, like a pirate about to attack a treasure ship.

He lashed the tiller and slackened the foresail sheets. I went forward and undid the jib halyard. The foresail slid down the cable. I allowed the jib to fall slowly and as each section passed me, I unhooked the hanks and furled the sail.

As quickly as this happened, my brother was clipping on the racing jib. He clipped the bottom end to the forestay, on the prow and then, gave me the signal to hoist.

As I pulled on the halyard, he was already fixing each hank on to the halyard. The jib billowed with wind as I raised it. He was back at the tiller by the time the sail was fully hoisted.

The mainsail had kept us steady, and we really started to move as the wind filled the new sail. We healed over as I folded, bagged, and stowed the old jib, throwing the bag through the hatch and on to the bunk in the forward cabin. I closed the hatch and hung on to the mast, sea spray splashing up on to my feet and thighs.

Chapter Seven - Olhao, Ahoy!

It was late afternoon on a cool day. My jeans that I had intended to wear occasionally had become a dirty uniform. I wore a dry sweater, and despite the cold, I felt warmed by exhilaration and hope as this proud vessel did what it did best and was designed to do - raced.

'Ready about,' my brother cried.

I trotted unsteadily to my position beside him, almost slipping on the sloping deck.

'Jive, ho,' he called when he was satisfied, I was ready.

Releasing the jib as he pushed the tiller away from him, the boat came about in a wide arc. The main sheet was released as we commenced our turn and the boom swung round as we started to point in almost the opposite direction.

I pulled hard on the jib sheet and the sail came around on to my side of the boat. The wind ballooned the nylon and satisfied with the course and the fullness of both sails; my brother told me to pull the sail in a fraction more.

The windlass drum clicked twice, and I forced a part of the remaining rope into the teeth of the clam jam cleat, which was just in front of and below the windlass. He held the tiller as he instructed me on how to trim the mainsail.

The wind was howling in our ears and the spray from both sides of the boat splashed into the cabin space. We were moving now, and the harbour was getting closer and closer.

Nothing could stop us now.

Olhao was a fishing port, commercial through and through. The early morning boats had tied up long ago and the evening fleet would have left a few hours ago. We could see no ships and they would not be back in this area until nightfall drove them back to safety.

The drifters were slow, lumbering ships and we would be able to outrun them. Besides, the tide was ebbing fast, and they would stay out until it flowed again. My brother was pleased, and I was relieved.

'We're doing nine knots. This is terrific. I'll slow down to about six as we get to the harbour. You'd better get forward and look out, there might be some banks up ahead. Get the anchor ready. We'll drop it once we get past the port. The island is not far away. We'll either have enough speed to sail straight there or we'll row there in the tender.'

'Aye, aye skipper, I shouted merrily, the pirate mood was taking hold of me too, now.

I grabbed my jacket from the cabin and slipped into it as I made my way to the bow. I felt elated, watching the water rushing by, foam-topped waves, lapping against the mahogany. The sails overshadowed the Sitka spruce deck. I moved forward ready to take up position.

Again, twilight was coming, but it was an hour off. The dimming light and cloudy sky made me feel colder, but even if those grey clouds told of storms, we would shortly be in the bar, eating hot food served on a proper plate with salad and chips.

The boat cut through the waves, rearing slightly.

The waves were rising now as the wind picked up more. I waited to be told that we had achieved ten knots. We had to case off from the wind to clear the harbour as we approached the wall.

The current was flowing out, but still, we didn't want to get too close to the rocks, especially as there might well be areas of eddies.

A sand bank was directly opposite the harbour wall and a dredging ship was anchored there, scooping up the mud from the seabed and depositing it via conveyor belt into the hold. The harbour needed to be dredged daily to keep the fishing boat channel open.

This was not always the case.

The town had been a fishing port for many centuries, but now the new harbour wall with rocks stacked against it to act as a breaker and the deposits from the sea had made for a tight channel. Larger fishing vessels had also changed the profile of the channel.

We had the choice of either a pell-mell dash through the channel, with the danger of hitting the harbour wall or the dredger, or alternatively, easing off our course and sailing majestically though at five or six knots.

After our earlier experience, we erred on the side of caution. I stood at the bow railings, looking over the side, as we came through the channel. On either side there was a sand bank invisible at high tide but now ominously present. Each minute more of the sand was visible.

The water was draining from this area and quickly. We had ten feet either side, so there was little chance of our striking those banks.

Having no idea of how far away the island really was, my brother, seeing our situation, instructed me to put down the boathook and pick up the anchor. I stood pressed against the bow railing, my feet apart, almost like a figurehead from an old man of war.

The railing reached a few inches below my knee and my shins rested on them. I looked forward to the day when I could sit on the bow holding on to the railing as we raced at ten knots.

For now, I was contented with the wisps of spray that soaked my trousers and slipped off the nylon of my skiing jacket. It was waterproof and warm; I was pleased it had been cold enough in London for me to wear it on the flight. I did not mind my jeans getting soaked. As long as my torso was in a cocoon, the extremities could be a little damp.

However cold it was out here in Portugal, it could not compete with the cold front that had come to England in May, making it feel as though the country was still in February. For the first time since we had left Vilamoura, I felt happy.

This was what I had come to do, sail through the elements. I pictured the warmth of the bar in my mind's eye. As we sped through the channel, I wondered at our swift progress.

This was a side of sailing I had not seen on this trip. So far, we had drifted quietly along, now we were motoring. It was a glorious strong wind in our sails. Five knots does not sound fast, nor does ten, but when you are up in the prow of a boat as it cuts though the water, canvas alone pushing you on, you feel you are flying.

The racing jib with its brash colours and nylon skin contrasted with our grubby beige mainsail. Its fullness drove us on even more efficiently. The canvas mainsail was taut with wind, too, and straining; the aluminium mast that had replaced the old wooden one was creaking in its wooden housing.

Ahead of the mast, the jib, a perfect triangle, did not flap a bit. It was at full stretch and hauled in tight. The sounds and smells of the sea aboard a yacht, nothing could beat that feeling. The sight of water passing by underneath and the port revealing itself more and more, the broad bows of the dredger becoming clearer all the time; I was on cloud nine.

Then, it happened.

There was a thud like a distant drumbeat, and we stopped dead in the water. I was caught off guard and became unbalanced, the heavy anchor adding to my inability to regain control.

How I managed not to end up in the drink, as sailors call the sea, I shall never know. I had hit both shins hard on the metal, swayed back and forth, the anchor dragging me to and fro like a weight on a pendulum, but by the fifth sway I had steadied myself and I slipped the anchor on to the deck, letting the chain slip through my fingers as the anchor came to rest on its side.

Perhaps it was because my legs were bent slightly that the shock was absorbed, like skiing on moguls. Both legs felt bruised from the hard contact sustained by the railings. It was the least fleshy part of my legs and I winced.

'Are you okay?' my brother called.

'Fine,' I lied, "what happened?'

'It looks like the keel hit a sand bank; the tide's pretty low.'

'What now?' I asked.

'Over the side. We'll have to take down the sails and secure the boat or we'll topple over.'

I had the jib down in record time, furled but not stowed. My brother was dealing with the mainsail. As I slipped off my jeans and took off my shoes, he had tied the canvas around the boom. He too slipped out of his oilskins and was wearing swimming shorts. We peeled off our T-shirts together.

'Right, we go over the side, each with one of these.' He was holding the thin, steel cable, the halyard that went up to the top of the mast. 'The first thing we do is secure the boat by the mast. Untie your anchor at the bow; I'll untie the one at the stern. Attach it to the end of your rope and that should hold her. I don't know how deep the keel is in, but we need to spread the weight. The mast is aluminium and if we can keep her upright it should keep the pressure off the keel.'

We went to work and the metal wire from the top of the mast was connected to the anchor. Our mast would be like the tier of a suspension bridge.

The tension would stop the boat from lurching and snapping off the keel. We would have to secure the anchors well if we did not want a broken ship.

'Okay, once in the water, swim out as far as you can and plant the anchor deep. We can winch in any slack from on-board. We'll wedge some planks of wood and the boathooks against the hull later.'

I jumped with the anchor; my knees bent. There was a small splash and I stood up. The water was below my knees, and it seemed to be trickling away like water from a bath when the plug is pulled.

To see the tide ebb at such an alarming rate was a very worrying sight. Every second more of the seabed was revealed. It is best observed from a distance, not in the thick of it.

'Don't swim,' my brother called, 'Run.'

"I thought it might be deeper,' I called back as I scurried over the beach, through puddles and across compacted sand.

Soon the wire cable became taut. I planted the anchor securely and ran back to the boat, darting around the other side. My brother was already at work wedging wood under the hull; I hoped he had spent almost as much time digging in the anchor as I had, but the taut wire above our heads confirmed that the boat was suspended ninety degrees vertically.

We could not see the keel and did not want to. The water was now only a foot and a half deep and we had no way of judging by how much more it would fall. The boathook was wedged in the sand under the hull in the middle and two planks were similarly supporting the aft and bow.

My brother pulled himself up aboard the boat and I went around the other side. Handing down the planks and boathook to me, he smiled. 'We're in deep water now.'

'Up the channel without a paddle,' I suggested helpfully.

'That's an idea," my brother replied, ignoring my poor attempt at a joke. 'We'll use the oars from the dinghy as well. We've got two pairs, just in case.'

He smiled, but I didn't feel like smiling back.

"That's a relief, "I mumbled, not sure if I wanted to make anymore failed attempts at humour.

I secured the starboard side, quite happy to be out of the boat. The paddles were given to me, and I was directed where to put them, a few feet away from the boathooks.

'You can come up now,' he called. I would have rather not, but it was lonely on the mud flat. I heaved myself up off our little beach and into the cockpit. The wood had a hollow echo to it as I walked over to the cabin to look inside. No cracks in the hull that I could see. My brother was still tightening the steel cables that held the anchors. Perhaps we would not fall over after all.

'Right!' he exclaimed.

He kept saying 'right' although.

Everything seemed so wrong.

"What do you want me to do?" I volunteered, ever the willing cabin boy.

'This is the story. The keel's six foot and we can't see how much is stuck in the sand bank. As the water is about two feet deep, we can assume we have four feet of keel embedded.'

'The water is only one and half feet deep, now, that makes four and a half,' I commented.

'Quite the mathematician.'

'Thank you.'

'So,' (thank god he didn't say, 'right'), he explained, 'we have little choice. There are two possibilities. The water will drain away completely, and the boat might then keel over, so we can't leave it alone, we'll have to have someone to send up a flare. The other scenario is that the tide will come in and the keel is stuck fast, therefore we will sink as the water rises and the boat does not.'

'In that case you stay with the boat, and I'll walk to the island.'

'It's a bit more difficult than that; we're on a bank now but there's water from here to the island. It's quite a deep bay. The only danger is here where the mouth of the channel has been silted up. I know where the island is, and you don't. I'll row and get help; you stay here and look after the boat.'

A quick rummage around in the aft hold, which was just space under the aft deck, and he found the spare oars. Apparently, they were kept in case of loss of one of the other oars or to row Waterwitch along. Although that sounds strange, I had moved her with one hand, so beautifully did she cleave the water.

Sometimes I felt she would sail on our breath if we asked her, despite her three-ton keel and heavy wood. That keel now held her, but there was a danger that the weight of the boat above would split the keel or shore off the bolts that fastened the keel to the rest of the vessel. If that happened to be the case, I would be the only one on board and if she capsized, I might well end up with more than a few bruises.

I hoped the steel lines from the mast would hold and not snap. I did not relish waiting on our improvised suspension bridge, particularly if one of the anchors worked loose.

Reluctantly, I helped him unleash the tender that was strapped upside down on the aft deck. We had quite a struggle lifting it off and down on to the beach, then, carrying it to the water. It was getting dark now and, in the twilight, we lit our hurricane lanterns, which we had put inside the boat.

My brother filled them each morning and I held mine up to light the cabin. My brother tied the lantern to the side of the boat. I hoped by now I would see the lights of the bar on the island.

I saw nothing.

Chapter Eight - Alone in the Dark

It was becoming dark, and I watched as my brother rowed away, the dim lamp lighting up his hands, arms, and face. All I could hear was the sound of paddles beating the water rhythmically and my heart breaking. My feet were still in water. I could feel the sand drifting though my toes. The water was surprisingly warm; it was almost body temperature.

The dredger was silent, a distant mass; a white light on a mast and a red one near the bridge; it seemed deserted. The crew had most probably gone ashore hours ago, by foot. I held up my lantern, watching the light disappear. I put the lamp on to the deck and clambered up into the still boat. I could hear the wood creaking and I looked from the cockpit into the cabin. It would be warm and out of the wind.

I went below lighting another lantern in the cockpit. Before he had left, my brother had turned on the navigation lights, then secured a lantern to one of the jib's halyards and hoisted it up as a warning and a beacon for the rescue party he was going to collect. With a heavy heart I unfolded the chart table and used the lantern to help me look for something to read on the bookshelf that was screwed to the cabin wall.

Later, I sat on the bunk opposite my bed, reading *'The Riddle of the Sands'* by the light of my hurricane lamp, which now glowed and flickered beside me on the chart table. It was the only light that I could see on this dark night. It would be a long wait. I knew that, because even when I had got on to the boat at nightfall and looked for the lights of the island, I could see none. Listening to the creaking of wood and the howl of the wind is an unsettling experience, especially when you know that you are balanced on a knife-edge and that the ground in which you are stuck is a constantly shifting mass, that may well, in the space of even an hour, drift away, leaving nothing.

Sand was a wondrous thing. Solid and supporting, it could hold three tons of boat; sifting and drifting it would hold nothing, would let slip its grip, as easily as it gave up grains to a passing wind or the whim of a current.

I was tempted to get the alarm clock from my brother's cabin, but I could tell he had been away a long time, simply by the number of pages I had read, the stiffness in my body and the weakness of the lantern flame.

My eyes needed to rest, my body needed to stretch, and the lantern needed more fuel. It must have been three hours since he had gone and apart from shifting a little on the bunk, I had not moved. I felt it was time to stretch my legs and make a warming cup of coffee. I trod gingerly over the boards.

They sounded hollow, no longer buoyed up from below by the water. Even the water in the bilges had lost that resonant timbre; the bass was replaced by a new wood sound, the noise of planks before they are put into place.

This feeling of dislocation was increased when I slid back the cabin hood and looked out around the boat. The whole shell reverberated with air, not water, and it felt like being on a plinth or in a glass jar. Unlike a glass jar, there was a feeling of trepidation. One false step and the boat could veer forward or aft, and in doing so disturb the balance in the rigging.

I pictured the boat bowing, twisting, and falling on to the now larger beach. From my vantage point it was impossible to imagine that we had once been at sea.

The moon had risen now and off into the distance, I could see its whiteness reflected in a pool, the same pool from whence Norman had departed, but its body had shrunk even further back.

There was water there at the end of my sight, but what was beyond I could not tell.

Turning to look into the shadows, I could only see sand. There might have been sea beyond, but it too was dark. I could see no reflection of the moon in that direction. The shadows of clouds hung oppressively overhead. It was as eerie as any horror story. I was totally alone, totally stranded and terribly cold.

Despite my predicament and my sore bottom, I was enjoying the book, which was a spy adventure set before the First World War. Our boat had much in common with the protagonist's boat, carrying virtually the same equipment, but they had a radio, and we did not. I felt alone, but confidant. I made my coffee and even imagined I heard my brother return.

Then, I started to figure things out, I was the night watchman; waiting for him to return was completely fruitless, a useless presumption. Once at the bar he would have eaten and drank. No one would have wanted to leave. Besides the boat had a caretaker on board, who could look after things and be blamed for any mishap. Thus, he would spend the night sleeping soundly in a bed. Clutching my coffee, I slipped into my bunk, reached over, grabbed the book from the table and read.

After two pages, I realised the light was even dimmer, so I got up and brought another hurricane lamp in, hanging it from the galley nail. That improved my reading light and I determined to let the other lantern burn out through lack of fuel. I was contented now. I no longer needed to be vigilant.

Once I had finished my coffee and read a few more pages, I would snuggle up and go to sleep for the night. That is pretty much what I did.

It must be said that the irony of reading The Riddle of the Sands while myself aground was not lost on my youthful mind and the writing of Erskine Childers was so gripping that I became immersed in the book, no longer aware of my perilous position. I read on way beyond the time when tiredness would have dictated sleep, the book was so gripping.

The next morning, I was awoken by Norman who was busily thumping about in the cabin and walking noisily over the deck. The resonant, watery bass had returned to the boat. Could it be we were afloat? It sounded as if we were, slightly, anyway.

'Where the hell have you been?' I asked.

'Hi, Finn,' he said cheerily, 'listen, I'm sorry, no one would come out at night to help me and the next high tide at daylight was this one. We've just arrived. We've checked she's secure."

"Thanks," I mumbled sleepily.

"Do you want to help me get the planks and boathooks in? George says he'll try and row us off, but we may need someone in the water to push off and collect the anchor.'

'What will you be doing?' I asked.

'I'll be at the helm. It's the most dangerous position. This stage is crucial. She could capsize or simply fall to float. I have to wait until the tide comes up.'

I was far from convinced and told him so. I could behave like a spoilt brat; I had practised a lot as a child.

'I've spent all night on the boat and now because of the tide, I have to leap out into cold water, while you stay dry in the most dangerous position. The most dangerous position, matey, was on this boat last night. I'm staying put."

"Okay," he agreed, trying to appease the truculent beast I had become.

We'll soon know if the boat's keeling over and the two of us can pull the rigging in. I'll take the starboard side and you take the port. If we float, then we can release the wires holding the anchors and your friend in the dinghy can row the anchors in from their positions. None of us has to get wet. I read about that in the book you gave me last night. It's amazing what you can learn when you're abandoned for eight hours or more.'

My brother wisely said nothing.

A bad bate or a morose mood needs to be fed by carbohydrate and I managed to find a small hunk of bread, stale, mostly crust and the last of the cheese.

I could smell the bacon and eggs and coffee on my brother's breath, so I did not offer him anything to eat. He could have brought me a bacon sandwich or even a croissant and jam. Sensing my mood, my brother went up into the cockpit and looked around. He spoke briefly to his friend George who had appraised the situation outside and was collecting the boathooks and planks. At the same time, he asked my brother to put the kettle on. George was an experienced sailor who now owned the bar on the island we had been heading for.

By the time I had finished eating and Norman had finished washing the spare cup, George had bounded on board.

'Hi, Finn, sorry not to have got here sooner, but I was on the mainland until a few hours ago. I only got the note that you were stranded when I got back. I woke your brother, fed him, and brought him here. I brought you a croissant, it will keep you going until we get something hot inside you later,' he explained.

Ever word was like a pearl.

He handed me a brown paper bag and inside was a beautifully baked croissant with cheese in the middle, the mere sight of which made me salivate uncontrollably. I put it down though while I made the coffee. I could wait a while longer and it would taste better with a brew.

'Thanks; I'll eat it with my coffee. How many sugars do you take?' I asked.

'None,' he replied.

'That's good, we're fresh out.'

'I'd better take it black, too, hadn't I?' he laughed.

'It's better that way.'

'Wow, it's cold today. Your keel is stuck fast, Norman, you must have hit that bank at some speed.'

'We did,' he concurred.

"You've cut right into it, and you won't get any further through. You've made it through the gooey stuff. I like the way you've rigged up the anchors, that wire is good and strong and is most probably supporting the boat right now. The tide's coming in, it's been coming in for three hours."

"I understand," I lied.

"The last bit will be the most impressive. What I propose is we wait here- within the next twenty minutes we should be free. We'll have enough water for Waterwitch to float on and I'll take the tender around the back and drag you out the same way you came in. When the boat floats the anchors will loosen. Keep them taut until you're sure she's afloat. I'll be in the stern, and I'll signal you.'

'Okay," I sighed reluctantly.

'Once she's afloat kept one anchor taut and winch yourself off the bank with that anchor. If you loosen the starboard rigging, then I can row out and get the anchor for you once I've pulled you off the bank.'

'Sounds good to me,' my brother said.

'A brilliant idea, have you ever read The Riddle off the Sands?' I asked.

'Once a long time ago; Why?'

Our friend was surprised by my inquiry.

'Just wondering. Drink your coffee while it's hot,' I replied, smiling at my brother for the first time that day.

Chapter Nine - Ever Onward

There is a tide in the events of man that if taken at the flood leads on to happiness...

It was truly amazing the way the water came back into the channel, just flooding upwards, rising all the time. Earlier we had managed to walk across puddles that were rapidly filling up or mounds of damp sand, all three of us choosing the least damp route, to pick up the tender. It was made of heavy wood and the three of us struggled with its ungainly bulk. It was not made for carrying, but we managed to walk it to the stern of Waterwitch.

Now, we could see the extent of the problem. Part of the boat was submerged; part was above the water. Visible to all of us were the two feet of barnacled hull that was painted with red iron anti-fouling paint, something I had been sure I would never see until the boat was in dry dock back in England. Then, there was two foot of keel, heavy dark metal, dripping water like sweat, a mossy skin splattered with seaweed and one or two seashells, determined lichens, obviously liking this spot.

Waterwitch looked vulnerable. Just like a beached whale, it was still unclear whether the tide that came would be her deliverance or her downfall. Whales are sometimes lifted off a beach with the help of a flowing tide; on other occasions, the currents push them back. Waterwitch was still wet, but the sun would come soon and dry out her hull; the swollen planks would contract, and she would separate, leaving the boat full of leaks.

Worse still the fishing fleet would be setting sail and Waterwitch would be in the way. We floated the dinghy in some water that spiralled into the sand. We were all barefoot, wearing shorts in the hope that it was going to be a sunny day. All of us were cold, but none of us would admit to each other that we were.

We were hard sailors, Atlantic sailors; we were tough enough to survive a chill morning wind. The hairs on our arms and legs, together with the wind, ruffling our matted hair and making our ears red raw, showed how cold we really were.

We left George in the boat. He visibly shivered but smiled at us. He had a sweater on, and the water was coming in fast. He'd soon be rowing which would warm him up. I took the painter and walked as far as I could with it.

Norman got up into the boat using a pair of rope steps we had hung out over the side that morning after coffee. He trotted up them and threw a short piece of rope to me. It was the rope we used to make our springs in harbour, and I tied it in a reef knot to the painter of the dinghy.

Then, he called out to me and hauled the bow mooring rope over the side and towards the dinghy. I stepped to one side as the heavy hemp uncoiled a little behind my feet. Picking it up off the wet sand meant fishing for it.

Already the water had come up an inch and this was the high point of the sand bank. I helped George secure the rope to the seat in the boat. There were only two paddles, but they were arranged in bulwarks. I offered to help him row, but he said I'd be needed on board to release the anchors and my weight might help the boat's bow move off the sand bank, so I returned back to the boat.

The water was rising and by the time I put one foot on the ladder, my ankle and an inch of shin was covered in water. It was as though someone had opened the sluice gates on a dam.

Lifting up the rope stepladder, I stowed it and readied myself for action. The boat rose off the sands, floating majestically on the calm water that covered the sea floor more and more. It was a dramatic event. The dredger was silent, a hulk to our port, but you could see even that heavy vessel rise, as more and more of the sand banks were obscured. There was no great rush of water, just a calm drowning of all that had been visible that morning.

Within a range of ten metres, three metres of water had suddenly appeared. It did not even take quarter of an hour to do so. The fact that we had afloat amazed me.

Surely, the keel buried so deep should have stayed in the sands as the water rose up above the boat. But the sands had released us more easily than they had entrapped us. Both George and my brother were being cool, but I think they were stunned too, by our luck and our boat's strength, in equal measure.

Subsequent to that, the quiet sail from the channel to the island was unremarkable. We were close-hauled and the wind was a gentle coastal breeze. It took us almost an hour to reach the island. It was not as close as either my brother or I had imagined, and it must have been hard work for him to row that far.

As we sailed on, he revealed to me that he had rowed for ten minutes, anchored the tender, and walked towards the lights of the bar tor twenty minutes. The wind hardly drove us forward and I suspected that the currents of the rising tide got us to our destination sooner than if we had merely sailed there.

It was ironic that the tide that had kept us from reaching safety now pushed us there when the wind could not. We anchored and rowed across to the island where we ate and had a beer. I had a cooked breakfast; they had rolls and jam. I deserved an extra beer and I got it.

Chapter Ten - The Eye of the Storm

I can now return to the storm because it was when we reached Olhao that the idea of my sailing with Geoffrey first reared its ugly head. We had to await my eldest brother's arrival and we would not be sailing for a few days. Therefore, when my brother noticed an acquaintance from Vilamoura in the bar, he mentioned that I was both green and also hungry for some sailing experience.

I had no say in the matter. I had been sold into galley slavery. There was no need for my consent, nor was it asked for. I was made to feel beholden to this person on first sight because he was willing to take me sailing.

Even at the time it seemed a disappointment to be going back to the start of my journey and not seeing new places, but I did need the experience so I could not argue. Besides, my brother and I had been living in each other's pockets for almost three weeks and two people in a confined space for too long could not be healthy. That is how I rationalised the situation at the time.

You already know what my brother was up to. He knew this chap was an incompetent skipper and that I was unlikely to come back from this voyage alive.

Now he was guaranteeing his inheritance. It was a plot by both my siblings to share the house and, if I can use the nautical expression, leave me high and dry.

It was so cunning; send me sailing with someone that even I would believe was good at his job. I may be cynical, but when I saw the yellow oilskin jacket, the wind-burned face, and a dark, rich tan, and a brow and cheeks fairly wrinkled with saltwater lines, I thought this had to be an expert captain, a commodore amongst sailors.

 The fact that he was looking after someone else's valuable boat convinced me further that this was a man of integrity and a respected and valiant member of the sailing community.

That his name was Geoffrey neither decreased nor increased my respect for him; lesser men may have been swayed by a name, but I do not put much sway by it.

I did have an Uncle Michael, though, who was charming and every Michael I have met since has been charming. Equally I dislike the name John and all those with that name I have found either totally abhorrent or not worth commenting on.

This is purely personal, and I look forward to the day that I may meet a kind John and a Michael I can despise and thus confound my experience up until now.

Anyhow, we were anchored off the coast of Olhao. The island that my brother had raved about was indeed small, a few shrubs, a wooden jetty and a bar.

Apparently, the customers had all moved on, either for the Mediterranean and summer cruising there, or off to the Azores and on to the Caribbean, though this would be their winter and most of those off in that direction were to be refitted in the West Indies for the Caribbean summer season.

Geoffrey was at the bar with my brother, they knew each other from the occasional wave and brief chats in the marina at Vilamoura. Geoffrey was telling my brother of his planned trip back there. In my brother's eyes I was still too green, despite two fortnights sailing around the Greek islands.

I was also far from indispensable, particularly as we were to await the arrival of our elder brother, meeting him as soon as he had notified the local post office by telegram of his flight details.

I was not needed to support my brother in his drinking habits - he was perfectly capable of getting stupefied without my help, and it was with trepidation that I realised the bar bill was being run on a tab and the drinks were not being paid for immediately.

A tab is dangerous because once money does not have to be found for the next drink, drinking is no longer a matter of struggling to afford to get yourself drunk, but a simple means of becoming virtually catatonic. My brother was equal to this temptation, as he was equal to trying any form of temptation, be it in alcoholic, tobacco, or any other form.

I was of a similar disposition, but I had to be removed from the scene under the premise that Geoffrey could teach me to sail.

The idea was sold hard.

I needed all the experience I could get. The fact I had more dinghy sailing hours than my brother had in proper yachts did not count, of course.

The fact that we would be headed for the Mediterranean and I was getting experience in an ocean, when we would be sailing along a sea, confused me. I felt just like someone sold into slavery. Geoffrey, if I had my way, would have to sail his brute of a fifty-footer on his own without my help.

I wondered where the rest of his crew was. Had they jumped ship? And how much had I cost Geoffrey? Uncharitably, I felt that my brother could be easily bought, a few beers knocked off his tab and I was thrown in to help sail, a convenient and lucrative deal.

Even if money or favours had not changed hands, my brother was storing up very good brownie points. I feel it was more than that, but the waves do not reveal their story, unfortunately.

Whether I was sold or offered for nothing, I felt my services were more beneficial to Geoffrey than they were to me, despite my inexperience. After all I was capable of following orders and allowing Geoffrey, through adhering to instructions, to be in two places at once.

My skills at coffee making were, almost, world-renowned and I could make a delicious sandwich too, given the right ingredients.

I knew when I wasn't wanted and my idea of fun was not to be in the bar for three days, hearing for the tenth time about some transcendental experience a friend of a friend had suffered on another boat. I had come on holiday to sail and that was what I intended to do.

Our imminent departure allowed me to take an early night after a light supper of chicken sandwiches. The fowl was fresh and the seasoning light; the bread was soft, doughy, and salty, just how we sailors like it. Anything that reminds us of the open sea is good. Watch any fisherman with a saltcellar and food.

I was glad that Norman was rowing me home, or at least to my bunk. I had quite enough beer to feel both content and tired.

My brother had just got a taste for it, I could tell. I wanted him to have more, to have a good time. It was just that I had to be up in the morning to help Geoffrey sail to Vilamoura.

So, I was pleased to see him rowing off into the distance somewhat unsteadily and not quite maintaining the straight path he might otherwise have taken.

He was cheerful and relaxed; I think he preferred ownership of a yacht in harbour - there were no incumbent responsibilities. It was only once one set sail on the sea did the whole situation involve such nastiness as responsibility. I think he worried about me too much.

Chapter Eleven - Before the Storm

At dawn I stood naked on the deck, stretching in the cool air, and watching the sun of a new day rise. I was alone. Only three vessels sat at anchor in the calm bay, they were: Geoffrey's, one other and Waterwitch. No one moved on the other two boats.

They were battened down, looking as if they were deserted. I had slipped from under my sleeping bag cover and straight on to the deck. As I lifted my body from my bunk, I heard my brother snoring loudly. He must have got back late.

It was my own special time now. I was on my own, alone, truly alone, the only person up and the only person on deck. I could have danced the hornpipe and all others would have slept on.

Instead, I climbed on to the port beam with the shower bucket and our Jerry can of fresh water that we had filled the previous evening. There was no longer pressure to conserve supplies as we could fill up again from the plentiful and un-metred supply of fresh island water from the bar.

I poured the cold water from the container into the black, rubberised plastic bucket, heaved the bucket with both hands above my head and tipped the contents down over my head, allowing the water to cascade over my hair and face and the front of my body.

I repeated this process with some fresh water, but this time I tipped the water over the back of my head and down my neck, over my back and down my bottom. The last remnants of the bucket eased down over my legs.

Again, I filled the bucket and tossed the cold invigorating water over my chest and then straight over my back.

This was my first wash since leaving Vilamoura and I was determined to make it a good one.

Although we had been out of the marina for two days, we seemed to be remarkably clean.

Wearing shorts and a T-shirt meant we kept cool. It was only when we put on our musty clothes that we noticed any unpleasant odours. Otherwise, we got used to each other's aromas.

Neither of us had any deodorant; it was all back to basics, but a wash, with soap, generally left us smelling sweet. On this morning, deprived of my wash for two days, I treated myself to an extra dollop of shampoo and scrubbed hard at my scalp.

It was already warm. The rising sun started to heat my body or perhaps I was getting warmer through the fact that the chilled water had now run off my body. The absence of a cold wind surely helped. It was uncanny how still it was. I remember my feet being cold, but I didn't mind.

I was so invigorated by the feeling of complete abandonment and the comforting bubbles forming on my head that I was put in mind of my sister washing my hair all those years ago and all those miles away.

It was bliss to feel clean again. I lathered the rest of my body with the soap that I had brought out with me, which I guarded jealously once I had seen that my brother only had a bar of 'Fa' soap from Spain.

There I stood, legs apart, completely uninhibited. There was no reason to be self-conscious, no one would see. I was alone with nature. Bending over, I started with my ankles and soaped upwards to my scalp where shampoo and soap met. Then, I put my soap back in the travel dish and sat down on the cabin roof, a difficult exercise covered in soap. I, then, washed my feet and sat watching the rising sun spread orange over the horizon, I was near enough the water container to reach it, tip it over on to the deck and on to my feet.

With my feet rinsed and the soap on the deck flushed away, I stood and raised the remains of the water over my head and shook the plastic Jerry can over my head and shoulders. Water chugged out of the small opening, falling in brief torrents, over my shoulders or head. Showering had never been so much hassle, so much needed and so much appreciated.

I gently padded around the boat, letting the water drip off me and walking as if there was just the boat, the sky and myself in the universe. I had left my towel hanging outside the cabin, draped over the bench seat in the cockpit and I wrapped it around my waist.

It was one of the mildest mornings we had experienced and one of the few that was not accompanied by a damp chill. The air was completely still and the sky a hazy summer blue. I brewed some coffee.

My brother had lent me the alarm but had left no instructions for me to reset it. I presumed he would be having another relaxing day- that is, having fun, while I went sailing with someone

I did not know and whom I did not trust. But this is what sailing around the world is all about and it is especially concentrated, like the culture, in Europe. I had some idea that he had been involved in strange affairs in Holland and England, but that was all I knew about my new captain.

He was twice my age at least, but he also had a reputation as an experienced and competent skipper.

I poured hot water on to some instant coffee granules and towelled my hair dry as I waited for the boiling water to cool enough for me to drink. I had taken the whistle off the kettle and put it on top of the primus stove, on a low flame, before having my wash.

My brother would have been extremely annoyed if he had known that I had left a gas bottle lit and unattended in the cockpit of a wooden boat, but this simply added to the delicious luxury of such a project.

The coffee was extremely welcome, as I had been fairly cold in the night.

It was, after all, still spring and the temperature dropped dramatically without cloud cover to keep in the heat. We had two nights of cloudless skies, plenty of clouds on the horizon as far as sailing goes, but no cumulus or stratus to keep us warm during our trying night times.

A shower is a shower, but I would always prefer a hot or warm one. That morning the fresh water had seemed particularly cold.

Once I had filled the kettle, drenched myself and rinsed myself off, all the water was gone. We had two Jerry cans on board, so my brother could use the other one for his coffee and wash. He could refill both easily. They were a bit cumbersome loading in and out of the boat, but he would manage or get help. I had been wicked using up five days supply of water in one, but I felt I had deserved such indulgence.

Out of almost three weeks in Portugal, I had been sailing for three days, a day a week. I could manage twice as much sailing each weekend at home in England. I had all the drawbacks of living on a boat, with little of the compensation for doing so. I wanted to sail all the time, make progress to our goal and to reach Ibiza, even then it had a cachet, and I was to learn that destination had a well-deserved reputation.

Drinking my black coffee, I considered my lot. The sun was shining, it was a new day and things would improve; plus, I had just had a lovely wash. Thoughts of steamships heading to India in Victorian times made me realise how lucky we were. I considered those poor women stuck in hot cabins, barely cool at night, with only a sponge and a glass of water to keep them clean day after day.

'I may not enjoy going back to Vilamoura', I thought, 'who wants to return to the place they have left if they are on an adventure where new discoveries are expected?' but I reasoned that at least I could have a hot shower there.

These were the sorts of creature comforts that I craved after barely two full days at sea. Sipping my coffee in the cockpit, I started to think of food, but we had none, so that was immediately off the agenda.

I actually heard the alarm clock in the boat twenty feet away because it was so still and quiet. There was no bird song or gull cry, which I always expected, and the absence of these sounds makes me feel uneasy; a bad omen, except in France where they eat the small birds so there are none left to perform the dawn chorus.

Having had quail for supper two nights before, which could have been and probably was robin, it was quite possible that the Portuguese had similar habits.

How were we to know? On reflection, I felt that I was only over-reacting. How often we ignore their inner voice, listening to logic and not our primeval protection mechanism. If only I had listened or stayed in bed or overslept.

Instead, I swigged the rest of my coffee and changed quickly into summer clothes, navy polo shirt and cut-off denim. I put my feet into a pair of slip-on navy deck shoes in the time that it took me to grab my flip-flops and sweater, putting them into my holdall.

Already, I knew that it could get cold out there, at sea. No matter how warm and wonderful it was close to land, nothing had prepared me for the coldness and dampness of the Atlantic Ocean. A cotton sweater was no protection against the rain.

Our tender was tied to the side of our boat; a bowline looped around the mainstay and fastened to one of the clam jams cleats.

After my coffee, I rinsed my mug and prepared to leave. As I did so, Geoffrey came up on deck and waved to me. I rowed across with my bag and he informed me that he had met two hikers who had nowhere to stay.

They were asleep below and quite prepared to make up the crew on our voyage to Vilamoura. Apparently, they were heading west to Lagos, which sounded reasonable to me. I stowed my bag on the cockpit deck so as not to disturb them. He woke them with the starting of the engine and we motored on our anchor chain as close as possible to Waterwitch. I fended off his boat from ours and leapt across to tie up the tender dinghy, so that my brother would not be stranded on his boat. Geoffrey held the boats close together to allow me to tie up the tender and leap back on board.

Once he released his grip, we drifted away from my brother's boat.

On this modern boat, the anchor was on a motorised winch, and we were hauled back by the chain to directly above the anchor. We drifted forward releasing the anchor from the seabed.

The sun was rising all the time, sending shortening shadows of the mast and hull across the sea of the bay. Geoffrey engaged gear and as the motorised winch hauled up the free anchor, we moved onward towards the open sea.

Avoiding Olhao, we circumnavigated the island and headed southwest towards a different channel. I had lost count of the number of channels in the marshland around Faro.

In no time, we had prepared the sails and we chugged through the sunlight of the straits. It really looked like it was going to be one of the sunniest days since I had been here, a real August day in May.

I was allowed to take the helm while Geoffrey battened down the front hatch, unpacked, clipped, and raised the jib. Together we raised the mainsail and it hung proudly from the mast, a gentle wind pushing the boom to the port and filling the sails.

Everything looked good.

A clean, bright boat slid majestically through lake-still waters, driven by a strong breeze that billowed the clean, white sail. The propeller at the back disturbed the channel waters, rippling them and sending out a wake.

I caught a distorted reflection of the boat in the water; it was a quick glance to see how still the water was. I could not believe that it was so calm. As we cut through the sea, the waves hardly lapped against our hull.

Behind us there was the biggest sun I had ever seen and the clearest blue sky, a scene from a glorious summer's day. I sat with my face towards the sun, basking in its warmth. A chilled wind came drifting in from the ocean, but I ignored it.

Sheltered in the cockpit, it merely ruffled my hair. The sun's radiance and warmth made all the difference. I had almost persuaded myself that, in fact, it was warm that day.

The engines were cut, and we sailed on a broad reach towards the waiting ocean.

Suddenly up ahead we saw the entrance to the channel.

Two lines of white stone from shore to shore, but in the middle, two lighthouses marked an exit, providing our escape route. One flashed red and the other flashed green. We headed for the starboard light. It was phenomenal. In front of us was a grey sheet draped as far down as the white wall, a grey silver sky; there was a fog waiting for us on the other side of the sea wall.

Then, as we sailed closer, we saw the wall of water that stood at the harbour entrance; foaming, rounded, as tall as the sea wall itself, it rolled just outside the entrance.

None of the waves broke through, not one bit of the tempest crossed the line into calm water; it was as if an invisible line had been drawn from one lighthouse to the other. The storm waited for us outside the harbour, like a cat waiting for its prey.

I looked at our skipper and he looked at me.

'Shall we turn back?' he asked.

'I don't know, what is it?' I replied. I had never seen anything like it and, judging by his shocked look, nor had he.

'We'll go on,' he determined. There was a cheque for him to collect and a bank for him to cash his cheque at. The turning around had been academic. I may have had to sponsor him and his two friends in the bar otherwise. "It doesn't look good.'

He needn't have bothered telling me that, I could see for myself.

'Is that a wall of water?' I was incredulous.

'Yes.'

'We should turn back.'

'It's too late now, we'd never make the tack.'

As if to back him up, we hit the first of the shock waves, and rolled over it, still sailing away from the sea wall. Within quick succession, we hit three more waves; the first was three feet, the second, five feet and the third, ten feet. We smiled at each other. We were amazed that we had crested each wave.

'We'll just have to let the storm take us,' he told me. I smiled, but the next wave was bigger, and we landed on the other side of it with a thud.

The next wave picked us up and threw us deeper into the melee. A big boom signified our dip into the next trough. On the next surge we flew through the air and the boat landed on its keel, having floated four or five feet in the air, no longer in water.

There was a tremendous crash.

The metal cabin doors flew open into the cabin, slamming into the overhead lockers that were the cupboards, providing a view of the girls still nestled in sleeping bags on each of the two bunks. They were dozing before we hit the first wave, now they were awake, upright, and alert.

I watched as every tin and pot and possession spilled from the cupboards. The louvre doors clapped against the shelves, sprung open again and allowed the tins to flow out. The boat rolled to port and the rest of the contents of the cupboards, on the starboard side, spilled on to the cabin floor. The boat rolled to starboard and the cupboards on the port side emptied.

The girls had been lounging on their bunks when we hit the water so hard; instinctively they had curled up and covered their heads.

Miraculously, none of the cans that rained down on them actually hit them, although two or three bounced off the bunks before thudding on the deck. The rest along with other stores had showered straight on to the cabin deck. It was like witnessing an earthquake or a tornado.

Upstairs we tried to secure everything as the rain pelted from above. On the first wave we had smiled at each other, a mutual, 'that was a bump!' we signalled to each other with a, but our smiles vanished on the second bump, the crash that reverberated throughout the skin of the ship.

We were all shaken by it, particularly the lurch from side to side when we landed. The keel was bolted on to the hull. That style of keel had been known to snap off before now.

I was not sure when this boat had last been serviced, but within days of arriving in Portugal, I had heard of bolts shearing off in bad weather and the whole boat capsizing.

Our original journey should have been about two hours; from Olhao to Praia de Faro past Quinta do Lago, Vale de Lobo, Quarteira, finally to the marina at Vilamoura.

Instead, within the space of six hours, we passed all these points: Acoteias, Fatesia, Olhos de Agua, Balaia, Oura, Sao Rafael, Armacao de Pera, Gaivotas, Sra da Rocha, Centianes, Carvoeiro, Ferragudo to the Praia da Rocha, before reaching safety.

We were swept on by the storm to a small fishing village called Vau, outside Portimao. In all the races from Vilamoura to Portimao, the fastest time has only ever been eight and a half hours. We were two hours further east, along the coast, to Olhao and we had done the whole journey in six hours, despite our boat being rigged for cruising, not racing.

That was how powerful the sea was and that was how quickly we raced along. At Vau, a decision to try for shelter was reached. Geoffrey suggested we give it a go, even though it would be dangerous.

The girls were too ill to be vocal. They were not sailors; they had not become accustomed to life at sea and even Geoffrey had been ill over the side four or five times, twice spectacularly and the rest just bile.

No one could tell you why I was not sick; I just wasn't, though I might have felt better if I had been. Perhaps it was my love of the fun fair and stomach-churning rides that made me so resilient, but six hours on a fair ride is enough for anyone and that was what it was like.

It was I who reassured Geoffrey that his decision was sound and that entry into Vau should be attempted.

Whether it was because we were out of the eye of the storm or whether the storm had abated, we didn't know, but we were able to gain control of the boat.

The mainsail was hoisted, but only halfway up the mast, close-reefed; the wind was still gusting, and we motor-sailed into the shelter of the harbour. Getting through the narrow entrance of the fishing port was a difficult task and we were almost swept into the port wall. Once inside the walls, the sea was choppy but manageable, so Geoffrey took down the sail, while I held the helm.

We swapped places while I stowed the sail and we tied up. I leapt on to land with a painter in hand, secured the front and ran to the aft to catch the rope Geoffrey threw at me, which I tied to the dock rings. The boat eased itself against the harbour wall, resting on its fenders that sighed as they were crushed between harbour wall and metal hull.

I felt like kissing the ground, but instead I waited for the other three to join me on the quayside.

We walked to a cafe, the German girls wearing their rucksacks, all of us dressed in the same clothes. Still dripping, we sat down inside on wooden chairs and drank coffee liberally fortified with brandy.

We were all relieved to be alive and no one spoke.

Eventually, the Captain broke the silence to tell us how bad a storm it was, not that we needed telling; neither did we want to be reminded of the voyage.

He had promised them an interesting trip; an adventure and it seemed then that his words were the epitome of English understatement. The girls finished their coffee. I assumed they had only accepted the warm drinks because they were so cold and shocked.

Geoffrey was keen to keep them with us. They were equally as enthusiastic to be as far away as possible from the situation, the sea and from Geoffrey and me. It was with embarrassment that I realised that they had lumped me in the same category as him. It was not he they wanted to put distance between, but us, yet I had done nothing to them.

Despite an offer from our illustrious Captain for them to stay on the boat and be taken back to Vilamoura, they grabbed their rucksacks and bade us farewell.

I asked where they were going next, and they shrugged as if to say, 'anywhere away from you two and a sea view'.

It would be the last time they would hitchhike on a boat. Lifts would only be accepted from cars or trucks from now on. They had been made wise at twenty. They waved us goodbye, heading for the nearest hostel or the bus station.

We decided to leave the boat overnight.

She could not possibly dry out in these overcast conditions, but we had had just about enough of the sea that we could take. It was difficult to walk back on land because we had got used to the roll of the boat. The effect of the brandy did not help. Neither of us had eaten for six hours.

We looked like a pair of drunken sailors as we ambled along, trying to steady our feet. Perhaps that was where the girls were heading, to get something to eat. They were both well built and had a Germanic appetite for food. It may well have been the first time in their lives that they had not eaten every three hours. I could not think of food.

We gathered up our bags, so that we would have clean clothes, and hitched a ride in a truck up into the pine forest above Portimao. The smell of eucalyptus filled our nostrils. I had bought some cigarettes in town, but I was saving them for the meal.

We had phoned Geoffrey's local friend and stopped off at a store to buy a couple of cheap bottles of white and red wine, the type with a plastic closure and no label. Later that evening, after a hot bath followed by warming wine and chicken stew, we retold the tale of the storm to end all storms and we chuckled at the enormity of it all and that we had survived.

That night, as I lay in my bed, a pleasant stupor blurring all my senses, I realised with dread that we would have to sail the boat back to Olhao. I did not have enough cash to get a bus; my passport and travellers' cheques were on my brother's boat. That was that.

Waking early the next day, I showered and dressed quickly in the kitchen by the warmth of the stove.

Geoffrey's friend and his wife were up already, and they offered me a cup of coffee from the pot on the stove. My head was throbbing, and I was still tired, so I accepted readily, thanking them for thief hospitality.

They chatted with me as I dried my hair, rubbing the towel back and forth over my head, from ear to ear. It was an effective and quick method, working in a seesaw motion; my hair was dry within minutes, and I was ready to drink the much-needed coffee.

Chapter Twelve - Reunited

We sailed off that morning, just before noon. We had arrived in town early, gone for coffee with a friend of Geoffrey's who owned a bar and then headed for the port.

The tide was high in the harbour, but by the time we made it down to the port and cleared the mess ready for sailing, the tide was beginning to ebb, so we began our journey, drifting out on the receding sea.

It was still choppy out there, white horses on top of wild waves, which as far as I was concerned might as well have been the size of Trojan horses. To say I was nervous was an understatement. The wind was very strong still, gusting towards the coast.

We were half-reefed, half the mainsail was up, and we had a small, red jib flying, yet we keeled over at an alarming angle and one or two gusts sent us over the point.

The point was just before capsize, the theory being that when sailing you reach a certain angle of heeling that cannot be increased because if the wind blows enough to take you towards overturning, the hull will have edged over enough to shield the sails from the gust; the wind simply spills out of the sails, and the boat will right itself In other words it was impossible to capsize, the wind brought you to that point, but the hull would save you once you reached that point, the keel and hull preventing the wind from giving that extra push.

Boats did capsize though. The Torrey Canyon had apparently; so, had catamarans with their added stability and supposedly absolute safety. The fact that the Kon Tiki, a raft, had made it across the Atlantic did not enter the equation. After our experience, you believed in the exception not the rule.

You respected and even feared, for the first time, the power of the sea, that force that had driven you over an eight-hour racing course and beyond in six hours.

The boat heeled over, and I lost my nerve, turning the tiller so that the wind would drop from the sail.

The Captain understood and took the helm with a sympathetic look.

I had been churlish to blame him. He had done his best and that is all you can expect from anyone. Taking hold of the tiller, he sailed much more gingerly than I had just been doing. Perhaps his added experience and years at sea had helped him to read and feel the wind more effectively.

I felt seasick, and vomited violently into the water, feeling the spray lashing my face, my mouth a foot from the water, as we were still heeled over. It was ironic that I felt ill on a relatively calm day, when on the previous day even the Captain had been violently sick, the girls had spent the voyage vomiting, yet I had kept control. I alone out of us four had been fine.

That following day our hikers were most probably cramming food down their throats for breakfast, instead of spewing food up. The Captain looked fresh and well and much less pale than he had done on the day of the storm. Here I was, too scared to be ill before, brave enough to allow myself a feeling of fear and nausea now.

I lay down below, the classic cure, but inside the cabin with the rolling of the sea, I felt worse. Perhaps it was a hangover. I wished more than ever that we were in the Peloponnese or cruising the Ionian Islands. My experiences in the Greek islands had never been like this. The wind died a bit as we sailed.

We kept close-reefed, our red jib and white sail halfway up the mast, a testament to our caution and trepidation. I came up on deck, feeling immediately much better, but also feeling sure that I would throw up once again. Whilst the skipper made us some coffee, I took the helm again.

There was hardly another boat to be seen. We hugged the coast, not leaving more than two miles between us and safety. It was reassuring to know that we had the lifejackets.

Even though they would make a pathetic buoyancy aid, we were not afraid to use them. The storm had prevented us from going this close to the shore and now, although it felt less like sailing and more like boating along a river.

I felt more self-assured and less nervous. I was annoyed that after so many delays we had to go into Vilamoura proper. Most visitors would tie up at the entrance and walk to the post office or the harbour office for news or information, but we had to be tied up in the marina for no other reason than that we would be visible to others, so that they could come and see our illustrious Captain if they so wished.

The way that he talked about it, I thought the cheques in the mail would be equivalent to a minor pop star's royalty. Instead, he had one cheque, small, judging by his pursed lips as he struggled to read it without glasses. He was pretentious, but at that moment I could read his mind. He'd hoped for more.

Then there, was a letter from the owner of the boat countermanding something that had been written in the letter, which had accompanied the payment. Both letters seemed short and inconsequential.

It seemed a long way to come for a cheque, which he did not even bother to cash and for a letter which I managed to ascertain from his garbled mumbling concerned a situation occurring in late August or September.

Plenty of people had their mail sent down to them in Olhao and vice versa. It would have been simple to have these correspondences similarly dispatched. It would have saved us both a lot of trouble and discomfort to say the least.

The experience that I had just undergone had been humbling and certainly helped me to appreciate how precious life was, what a gift it was and how lucky I was. In fact, I mused that it was my good fortune that I had not become a fisherman or sailor.

However, I felt that to say I had gained experience sailing was, in fact, a spurious claim.

I had gained experience of fear and facing death, ignoring danger as best one can. To me that was not sailing experience. That was what tuna fishermen in Newfoundland and Alaska did. They had to work hard and fast in extremely cold, slippery, and difficult conditions to bring us our tinned seafood. If you lost a friend over the side, they had less than three minutes alive in those treacherous waters.

Thankfully, the danger, like rigging in the North Sea oil fields, carried its own reward, a large pay packet, danger money, but money, nonetheless. I was doing all this danger stuff and daring escapades for free, a bizarre situation, but one I had to grin and bear.

I had done fairly well on the food front. Geoffrey's friends in the mountains had packed us off with so many sandwiches that they lasted from breakfast until suppertime. I could not complain, I was getting food and lodgings; Geoffrey was good to me, he didn't let me starve.

We spent the night in the marina, Geoffrey in the forward cabin, myself on the still damp cushions in the lounge, but the sea was calm and the sound of the water lapping against the hull lulled me to sleep. The next morning, we set sail on the high tide. There were no problems from the customs men and harbour officials for this vessel.

Three days late, exhausted both physically and mentally, we spied the two lighthouses, which had somehow held back the sea on the day of the storm.

The water level both inside and outside the harbour wall was the same height this time, no special effects. It took an eternity to sail back up from there to the island. We could not use the motor because we had used it too much on the day of the storm and the owner gave only a small monthly allowance for fuel.

Luckily, the wind had driven us along that day, or we would have used up twice as much fuel. So, we sailed majestically back into the channel. Once we were inside, the wind dropped and we were cruising very slowly, more like drifting. With horror I realised that my brother's boat was not so bad. It seemed to take less wind to move her and get her up to speed.

I thought that an anchor might have been thrown over the stern to slow us down, but on serious reflection, I realised tide and wind were not our friends that day.

We arrived back at about ten fifteen. My brother had already left and was heading to collect our eldest brother. I was alone with steel boat's captain, but I was not able to socialise with him beyond a quick glass of beer. I bought him a glass of beer, but he refused to sit at a table with me, preferring to stand.

I had stood about as much as I could on our voyage and I felt, perhaps unreasonably, that he who pays the piper chooses the tune or at least where we sat or stood. He, obviously, had his favourite perch at the bar, always in the same position, so that anyone who sought him could find him there.

I was tired and wanted to sit down, so I feigned exhaustion, and concocted a story, which was less fact than fiction, about my situation before I came out, and how hard my brother had worked me, I carefully added a section where I mentioned that I had wanted to rest, yet my brother had volunteered me for an assignment, helping him to sail his steel boat.

Not, in order to protect his ego, that he needed help, I added.

Charitably, he mentioned how useful I had been, using words so bland and clichéd that it sounded, almost, as if he had said, 'We couldn't have done this without you.'

That was enough for me, I was being put up as a ship's mate in this person's eyes and yet there was no one else that I could more readily despise.

Perhaps, I was being cruel, but this guy had endangered my life, coerced some teenagers to come with us and impressed me, as a teenager myself, more with his cowardice than his valour.

If he was half the sailor that he purported to be, he would have listened to the weather forecast the previous evening and saved us all a lot of suffering.

I managed to convince him that he should take the next ferry to Olhao to see the fish market and get provisions.

Despite the length of time, he had allegedly spent on the Algarve, he had never been inside the fish market. I thought this incredible, as I felt sailing should bring you closer to the people, not further apart.

Traditional sailors generally took umbrage at new marinas and apartment complexes along the coast simply because they eroded the simplicity of their life, the 'back to nature' feel. The real core or spirit of anywhere was the atmosphere that the local people brought to that place; marinas took this away.

Geoffrey embraced the whole idea.

They were clean and convenient and brought more people, more opportunities for him to take advantage. I learnt about this through our numerous conversations, his stories, and the odd remark in the hills above Portimao and on the boat.

That was the type he was and, being an innocent and having such high ideals, I was extremely disappointed in this man's sense of humour, sense of honour, and his ideas of right or wrong. I could not wait to be reunited with my brother.

After his beer, Geoffrey decided to go off to the port, to take my advice. There was no reason for me to join him and I relished the idea of having some time alone. I had declined his invitation, saying I needed to catch up on my sleep.

The bar owner was, intact, in Olhao that day and the Portuguese barman, although speaking far better English than any member of the sailing fraternity could speak Portuguese, was not suited to long dialogue. Geoffrey was prepared to engage him in conversation, but only in that which involved a subtle wit and ready repartee.

This was lost on the English people that he knew, so it was bound to fall flat on the indigenous audience, whether it was one person or a whole village. What counted was having an audience that could appreciate innuendo. Luckily for me I could feign innocence and the barman could, truly, plead lack of knowledge of the English language.

So, I left him trying to explain to the barman what an actress and a bishop were and what the actress and bishop stories meant. The latter was obviously the harder part of the task.

Our tender was tied to the jetty. My brother must have rowed ashore in order to catch the ferry to meet our older brother, so I rowed it back to the boat.

Dumping my sailing bag on my bunk, I collected my bedding, taking it forward to the master cabin. I undressed, threw my clothes into the now-bulging laundry bag, and then collapsed in a contented heap on a foam mattress in the forward cabin.

It was a relief to get out of my clothes, which had become decidedly grubby. I had decided that my hard bedding was more like horsehair or hard fibre, but my brother's bed was divine - thick, soft foam.

I snuggled up in my sleeping bag and blankets. Being at the nose of the boat, the mattress was much wider. For the first time on board, I could roll around with abandon. Once curled up under the covers, I dreamt of warm weather days, sailing, and sunbathing abroad, riding on a boat along the Thames or picnicking in Richmond Park. These various visions soothed me to sleep.

I awoke at three o'clock that afternoon, starving. It was then that I realised that I had not eaten all day. Normally it is difficult to keep me away from food in any shape or form, but obviously in my state of exhaustion, sleep had, for the first time, become the paramount priority.

Dressing quickly in clean clothes, I looked around on deck. It was mid-afternoon, I had expected Norman back with our elder brother and food. There was no sign of them. I was already quite used to the time keeping on this voyage.

I knew that my brother had flown in on the morning flight, so I expected them either at around two in the afternoon, that day, or two days later, one or the other.

I had no opportunity to go to the bank. They were shut in Portimao when we arrived and had not been open either of the mornings, we set sail. The ferry was the only communication between the island and the mainland. As a result, I had spent most of my Portuguese money, expecting that we would be in Spain by now. I only had some pesetas and travellers' cheques in large denominations.

Luckily, after a thorough search of my clothes, I found that I had possessed enough currency for a small meal and a large beer, or a small beer and a large meal. Life was not so bad, and I was not so poor after all.

I rowed happily to shore.

My first disappointment was that the bar had run out of local beer, and they only had a more expensive import. It was a beer I could not highly rate.

The local brew was much nicer. It was not to be had, sadly. I could cope with this, but unless I wanted to drink Fanta, I would have to make that choice. I could not afford a bottle of wine and spirits were left to those of my brother's age or older.

I was limited in my choice of food as well. There were sandwiches, soup and bread, or snails and bread. I was utterly fed up with bread and processed cheese and chicken, so I plumped for the snails.

I adored escargots with rich garlic butter and parsley. Sitting on a wooden chair, at a scrubbed wooden table, I downed half of my beer before my meal arrived, just in time because I had eaten three of the four pieces of bread that were meant to accompany the meal.

A bowl of shells swimming in water was placed before me. I took one out. It was hot, the broth it was swimming in was warm, but it was not a green colour, more like consommé.

Worse, there were no fatty globules to suggest that any butter with or without garlic had been put near this dish. I tasted the consommé, it was salt water, I tasted the snails, and they were bland and rubbery.

My Portuguese was not good enough to complain. The owner was most probably picking up a few crates of local beer as I ate and, perhaps, he had ordered more snails.

I was next to one of the most thriving fishing villages on the whole Algarve and even perhaps Portugal, yet I was reduced to eating snails in salt water.

They were small mangy things, but I had no change for another beer, just enough for the tip, so I wolfed down my lunch as best I could. I must have been a peculiar sight. There I was with a toothpick, pulling out these flecks of food, trying to chew a pip-sized mollusc while pricking the next. If I had been timed, I could not have emptied those shells faster or filled my face less well. I saved the half piece of bread until last.

The snails had been too salty and but for my extreme hunger, I would have left them, so it was an immense treat to sit with the last mouthful of cold beer washing down the doughy bread. I dreamed of butter and Cheddar cheese and bacon and wished that I had enough money to buy an omelette.

I wanted to be in Spain, or even to go to the bank, but the ferry from the island came and went at the behest of the bar owner. Both he and the pilot of that small wooden boat, with its outsize outboard motor, were over in Olhao, most probably the pair of them having just completed a slap-up fish feast.

I wondered where my brothers were and knew that as long as there was a bar open and time for another, I could wait well beyond the cows coming home, the banks closing, the shops shutting, and my credit being refused at the island bar.

I hoped they were happy. I had almost died, then, hoping to come back to the bosom of my family, had ended up alone, destitute, disheartened, deserted, and disappointed.

I had survived the shipwreck, but now I was marooned on my desert island. I was tempted to renew my friendship with my brave pilot of the storms, but he and I had not been brave, and the wind and water had piloted us.

I was not hungry enough to beg food off him. He had been generous and fed me in Portimao and on board. I couldn't face being on that boat again. The yacht looked pretty secure.

He was either sleeping or ashore.

My rumbling stomach disturbed me, but it didn't warrant disturbing him. I was about to walk back to the tender now that it was beginning to cool, and evening was approaching when I heard the Mercury engine of the ferry. Then, when I looked out to sea, I could see both my brothers standing up in the prow.

At the helm, the dark Mozambique pilot stood also, his head bobbing as he tried to look between the shoulders of the two figures to get a better look at Waterwitch. Typically, they had not even considered that they might be obscuring his sight.

That was my brothers, considerate and thoughtful to the last. I did not mind. This meant a decent meal and expensive beer, which in quantity could make up for its lack of quality. Most importantly of all, I was back with my family. What- ever they did, they would always be my brothers and I felt good about that. On balance I was lucky to have such fine brothers.

All negative memories of either of them disappeared, Norman had not wished to send me to a watery grave, he had just wanted me to have some fun and learn some more. I was sure of it now. What a nice guy, I thought, inviting me along on this adventure and then inviting our other brother out to join in, we would be: 'Three Men in a Boat, the boys together, a few, a happy few, a band of brothers.

This was what adventures were made of.

We would sail out into the ocean blue, just us three. That was the plan, but Murphy's Law suggests that anything that can go wrong does go wrong, and our trip was no exception to the rule or to that law.

It was with great satisfaction that I saw the arrival of my brothers, particularly as I had faced what I myself considered a life-threatening experience, upsetting at the best of times but made more poignant by my tender years. I was a mere teenager and teenagers traditionally smoke and drink and generally take risks because they suffer from the wild delusion that they are invincible and unstoppable until a disaster happens.

I had recently had my humbling experience. I had seen death and faced her beckoning finger and her cold clutch; and somehow, I had slipped from her grasp, but only just. It had been a close-run thing and I was glad. I needed to share my story with someone anyone and my relatives would do.

I had shared the experience, exhausted the topic on an eight-hour voyage with the only other person left on board. I wondered where the girls were now. It was time to relate the story to other parties. The Portuguese barman had never set foot off land, except to take the ferry to the bar on the island, so it was no good telling him. Besides his English ran to six or seven types of drinks that were available from the bar and regularly ordered.

My Portuguese was poor, my Spanish passable, but given that we were not yet in Spain, it did not help. I had ten stock phrases in several languages, but all concerned food or drink and did not stretch to a description of my sailing adventure, more's the pity. I stood on the dockside ready to welcome my brothers. I felt that the boat, which I could hear better than I could see, would contain my brothers. It was the hope that they were on board that made me wait. As the ferry neared, I could see their £lees. Norman was tall, tanned, and thin, the sun had coloured his mousy hair, streaking it with blond highlights. Patrick was shorter by an inch or two, almost ashen in his paleness, but of the same slim build. I was the beefy one, tallest and broadest, youngest but looking the eldest, a high forehead giving the illusion of balding. The other two had low brows.

I took the bow painter when the African driver threw the rope to me and, my brothers, the only others on the ferry, fended off from the dockside as best they could. I tied the· painter and held my hand out for all three passengers in the craft and they all hoisted themselves up off the boat with my help.

I was there to assist their landing as much as they had been there for me on numerous occasions, helping me to ride a bike, learning to drink, teaching me to ride a motorbike and not to drink too much. The pilot smiled and wandered off to the bar and my brothers shook hands with me.

My eldest dropped his bag and hugged me as if we had not seen each other for years, when in truth I had seen him just before I had left, which did not seem that long ago to me. Since having been half-starved in India a few years previously, we had allowed him to be over-emotional at greetings and departures. He had stared death in the face himself, starving in the streets of Delhi, after being robbed, penniless until money could be transferred to him.

Then, he had returned to England with a black beard, a gaunt face, scruffy clothes, and a dark tan. Now he was clean-shaven, wearing ironed shorts and T-shirt, the mark of a married man, the razor-sharp creases forming starched rectangles across the white top and blue shorts. His skin was the palest white, like milk, no hint of even a bit of red. Too many English winters and too few sunny holidays. When we greeted each other, my hand looked like mahogany; his looked almost like old ivory.

'How are you?' he asked beaming.

'Fine, you two have obviously stopped for lunch.'

'Norm dragged me into one of these bars downtown, just an opening in the wall; superb sherry, lovely local wine from the barrel and tremendous food, you know the type of place I mean?'

'Oh sure.' I could still taste the salt water of my snail stew, could almost feel them swimming about in my rumbling stomach.

'Patrick hardly recognised you, Finn. I saw you from the boat and waved madly. He asked who I was waving at, I said Finn, and he said ...'

'That's not Finn, that's an old man!' Patrick laughed, and then noticed I had lost the plot and explained. 'Your blond hair looked white from far off, and with the blond beard and the dark tan, I thought you were some Portuguese fisherman.'

'Oh, I see. How was your trip?' I could not share the hilarity that they both enjoyed.

'Fine, we took a cab from Faro to Olhao, took us no time at all. I'll get a plane back from Almeria after a week.'

This was extremely hopeful as Almeria was on the southeast coast of Spain and it had taken us all this time to get remotely near the Spanish border.

'Good, welcome aboard.'

'Talking of which, where is the boat?'

'She's over there,' Norman pointed proudly.

'She's a beauty, isn't she?'

'Yes,' I stammered.

These two had cash and with cash came beer and with beer came peanuts or tapas, and I was hungry enough to be agreeable to anything.

I wanted to finish by saying: 'She looks beautiful from a distance but wait until you have to spend the night on her.'

She was nice from far but far from nice.

If I had been more honest with myself and the rest of the crew, I would have voiced my doubts that we could have reached even the Spanish border, just beyond Tavira, our next port of call, by the end of the week. Perhaps he had bought a return ticket just in case.

He gave the impression that he was flexible and that his time was our time tor a week. Norman noted this; now he had two subservient crewmembers to manipulate. Having two of us meant that we could do some night sailing; our watches would be quite short, and our time off-duty would be increased. This meant he could stay up drinking for longer as his recovery period would be increased.

The ferryboat's engine started with a cough, the noise of its thumping pistons disturbing our conversation.

Norman told me that the pilot was off to collect the boss. He waved at us as he roared off It was hot in the sun, so we sauntered over to the bar. Several beers, snacks and hours later, we all piled into the little dinghy with Patrick holding on to his case. Water started coming over the gunwales and so I climbed back on to the jetty and Norman rowed Patrick to the boat.

After lighting the hurricane lamps and deftly throwing up our guest's overnight bag, he came back for me.

We were all in an exuberant mood. I had told them my story and they had been suitably impressed and shocked. Stories of the storm had swept the coast like an aftershock from an earthquake, echoing the storm's intensity.

The power of the storm had been so greatly exaggerated that it seemed a miracle that I had survived. Norman had been sure that we would have made it to Vilamoura before the storm or have found shelter in the marshes around Olhao and Faro. The storm had been bad, but the publicity had made it a hurricane. Even Norman with his experience around the Canaries had only ever been in a storm half the strength of the purported conditions.

Even if the storm was half as strong as people said, (which I favour, being always one to underestimate rather than exaggerate) then I was still way ahead of my brother. Suddenly, the respect he had for me had risen a few notches. I had done well.

Starting the week as the whinging crewmember who once under way could not reach a buoy, I was now the hero who had stayed with the ship when the captain had lost his nerve. I was the daring crewmember who had fought the sea through such a bad storm, the only one not to be physically sick.

My self-esteem was on a high. Unfortunately, there were no damsels to share the stories of my daring escapades, but I would remember the events to impress them, and my brothers had enjoyed the tale.

Once on board, we prepared for bed. Our eldest brother brushed his teeth with fresh water, something my brother and I found amusing. We would just gargle with our last mouth full of brandy or coffee, last thing at night, then brush our teeth twice as rigorously with toothpaste without water the following day.

It was so sweet to see him put water in a cup and walk out on to the deck and spit over the side.

I pictured him coming back inside and changing into flannelette pyjamas with a paisley pattern on them, making sure the top button was done up.

Instead, he slipped off his clothes and climbed into the sleeping bag, which had a nylon lining. I chortled as he slid around in the cold material, trying to get warm. My sleeping bag had a cotton lining. We had left a sheet for Patrick to put inside the bag, but we had forgotten to tell him. He was quiet after the initial shock, so I decided I would tell him in the morning.

We bade each other good night and I turned off the valve on the hurricane lamp.

The cabin hatch was pulled back to let the air in, although it was not that warm on this particular night. However, the sky was Prussian blue and only a few white clouds puffed by the stars were bright and I thought to myself that things could only get better. What faith we have when we are young.

Tomorrow would be another day.

It was the lull after the storm. I dreamt that night of sunny days and strong winds; of our journey eastward into the welcoming, obedient Mediterranean with her lake-like predictability and lack of tides; of the sun that always shone along its brilliant sun-drenched Costas.

The previous summer I had been in Malaga, and it had rained only once. The Atlantic with its winds and tides from the four corners of the world was far too wild and unpredictable for me. I wanted a holiday.

I had paid for that, yet so far, I had painted and cheated death on a helter-skelter, surfboard ride that I had not even booked. Things would have to improve, or I would have to take shore leave, permanently.

Just above the doorway, to the port, an inch or two below the cabin roofline, there hung a brass bell. This was presumably for ringing in foggy weather, though we never used it despite the fact that when we had run aground in Faro, the dawn brought a thick mist with it.

We had enough fog to warrant taking it in turns to ring the bell, but we had eventually decided that there would be little shipping in the flight path of an international airport and that it was much warmer in bed. Therefore, the bell had never been used and was purely decorative.

Perhaps it might work as ship to shore communication, but without fog, the bell, which the Captain himself polished every day, to a gleaming mirror finish, was redundant.

Elsewhere on the boat, there were bits of brass and copper and other metals made green by the saltwater or through sheer neglect. For all I knew vital screws were not merely coated in saline corrosion but worn right through with internal rust; but at least the bell shone.

I knew the keel and mast were steel. The mast was painted with grey anti-fouling paint to resist rust and what I had seen of the keel seemed corrosion free. However, it was the bits in between that worried me, the parts you could not see.

Despite all these forebodings, when morning came, nothing worried me.

The sunlight spread a morning glow into the cabins. I acknowledged morning's approach by looking upwards, out through the hatch, closed my eyes again, curled up into a ball and turned my back on the morning. I was sleepy still, warm, and comfortable, for the first time that I could remember; I was waking to a cabin that was not dew-ridden and humid.

Perhaps the weather was changing, and summer was finally here. I smiled at the thought, but my eyes remained shut, my head still heavy as though I was about to sleep rather than about to wake.

Then, the bell went, clanging like the hand-held bells they used to ring at Victorian Reform Schools. It was thoroughly unnecessary and very annoying. We were the only boat in the bay and the people at the bar, even if they had heard the bell behind the steel shutters, would be in such a deep alcohol-induced slumber that only the depth of their snoring would be affected.

'Wakey, wakey,' Norman called down, blocking out the sun behind him for a moment.

The whistle of the kettle, letting off steam, assaulted our senses. Coffee, now there was a thought. For the first time since we arrived, I was served coffee in bed. It may have had fat globules floating around it because of the powdered milk, but it was the service that counted. I knew there had to be a catch.

There was.

'I couldn't get any bread yesterday.'

I thought: 'You didn't because you were too busy drinking.'

'So, we'll have to wait for lunch when we arrive in Tavira.'

'What about Olhao?' I asked.

I was determined to have my most important meal of the day and what was more, I could cash my traveller's cheques. I hated relying on my brother for cash. I hated relying on anyone, but him especially because I was a guest on his boat.

'Fine,' Patrick said. 'I never have breakfast anyway.'

My ally had already sided with the opposition. Was he not aware that Ahab would take this as another show of weakness to exploit? It was us two who had to be strong against him and persuade him; we could not allow him to divide and conquer us. It was important we stood together on all issues and showed our solidarity. Therefore, I had to agree with Patrick despite my own wishes.

'That's fine,' I said.

The Captain of our ship was amazed at my lack of mutinous murmuring. Impressed by my new-found loyalty to him, he was too shocked to wonder why I had not complained or whinged. I knew that I could store up my complaints for when we were alone. For now, we were one big, happy family, enjoying our holiday. It didn't matter what we each called it. Patrick had married an American girl and therefore called it a vacation; Norman honestly referred to it as a trip; I was deluded enough to refer to it as a holiday. Perspective is an amusing subject to contemplate.

We set sail almost immediately. It was a fair wind and a full tide and wisely our skipper had decided to take advantage of both.

Once our coffee was drunk, we dressed and came up on deck.

In fact, I dressed, grabbing jeans and top from my store of clothes, stuffed into my bag, which was wedged into the shelf above my bunk. Patrick took more time to extract a neatly folded scoop neck T-shirt and navy starched shorts from his fastidiously packed bag.

I had a linen bag, which kept damp or dirty clothes; my sailing bag had clothes tipped into it from when I had flung everything into it before the trip. That was my idea of packing. I delved deep for clean socks and underwear, grabbing my other clothes as I did so.

While our landlubber brother eased himself into both the day and his clean clothes, I busied myself with helping my brother to prepare for the off.

The jib Genoa bag was already by the foresail halyards. He was busy untying the laces that secured the sail. He had attached the bulldog clip snap hooks of the sail on to the halyard and hoisted the mainsail by the time I had similarly attached all of the jib.

While he went back to the tiller, to make final preparations, I silently hoisted the Genoa, our largest jib.

I knew we had a window of opportunity and that we should set sail as soon as possible. No orders were given. None were needed.

The sight of the canvas flapping loosely on the boom signalled that it was up to me to raise the jib, then the anchor. Patrick came up from below, squinted at the sunlight and awaited instructions.

'Empty the kettle over the side and take that and the gas stove down below; put it on top of the cooker,' the Captain ordered.

The cooker was a paraffin pump affair, popular on boats in the 1930s, which had not been used since then as far as we knew. It stayed on-board, defunct, as no one could work out how to jettison such a well- mounted part of the fittings. It was a useful shelf, having a depression that would hold the kettle and a well that housed the gas bottle when we were sailing.

I could not see Patrick's face when he was given the order, since I was hauling up the clammy, cold links of the anchor chain. Wherever we docked there were always strands of seaweed, which I had to pull off before I let the wet chain slip into the forward hold.

It was a manual job and one that I wanted to hand over to our new shipmate as soon as possible. I hated getting the slime on my hands. Tugging on the chain gave us a little momentum and the boat, riding on its anchor, started to move forward.

Patrick popped his head up and was about to step into the cockpit when my brother asked him to get his sunglasses from the main cabin. I think he realised that we wanted him absent because it was not until we were well underway that he dared attempt to come out again.

I heard the creak of the port windlass as my brother pulled in the jib rope and, as usual, I helped to push the empty canvas of the foresail around to the port side. I returned to the chain, which proved easier to pull up, hearing the wind fill the jib with a reassuring thump. The anchor no longer held us as we had passed over it. Now instead of harnessing us to the seabed, it dragged underneath us.

The boom came around with a clank as the deadeye hit the end of the sailing horse. Working hand over hand, I pulled up the anchor chain. Free of detritus, it slipped through into its housing. As we sailed on, the anchor gushed water as it broke the surface, a steel spade with two trowel-type forks. It stood suspended from the prow as I locked the chain into one of the brass clips that lay on the deck.

Once clipped into place it was a devil to undo, but it meant the anchor chain was held in a vice-like grip even in the roughest seas. It was an ingenious device consisting of two parallel converging strips of brass.

You dropped the anchor chain into the back, and you could only release the vice by pulling the anchor chain backwards and upwards, raising it out of the clip. Such technical details would be explained to our new shipmate, but not now. He could weigh anchor when we arrived in the next port. On a starboard tack, hard on the wind, the sails pushed out to the port side with the breeze blowing in a north-easterly direction, we slipped sedately towards Olhao.

'I've got your glasses, can I come up?' Patrick enquired from the depths of the cabin.

'Of course, you can; it took you an inordinate amount of time to find them,' said the Captain.

Patrick just smiled and handed them over. I was standing on the beam deck, just above the cockpit on the port side, holding on to the main mast shroud, hidden by the sail, and watching out for the boom. I called to my eldest brother.

'Patrick, you had better put a towel around your neck, the sun is strong out here, even if it is hidden in a haze. You've got to keep your neck covered, have you got any collars to your shirts? You'd best wear them and keep them turned up to protect the neck, especially with that short haircut.'

'Don't worry, I'll be tine, I've put sun-block on,' he assured us.

'Have you blocked your ears?' I asked.

'Why, are you going to say something I don't want to hear?' he laughed.

'I meant put sun block on your ears.'

'Don't worry, I'll have a tan like yours before I go.'

'It has taken us a month to get this far and the first week we used sun-cream everyday. Didn't we?' I said, appealing to the skipper.

'Even I did, Patrick,' Norman replied. 'Huck Finn, here, had been to Spain for three months, along with a trip to Spain in February, so he has a good base and I've been out here solidly since January. You'd be crazy not to cover your neck and wear a hat too, I don't want you getting sunstroke.'

'Don't fuss, neither of you are wearing a hat.'

'But we did,' I explained, 'until we got acclimatised. You'll have to drink at least a litre of water every day as well; it seems cool on the boat with the wind, but the sun dries you out just as effectively.'

'I've been to India; I know about sunstroke.'

'Good.'

'I'll be fine, don't worry.'

Of course, he wasn't, by the end of the day, his neck was burnt and so were his ears. He had to wear a hat and a damp towel around his neck inside the collar of a long- sleeved shirt for the rest of the trip. His burnt neck and arms must have been painful, but he got no sympathy from either of us.

Our course meant that we only had to tack once or twice in the channel. The wind was not that strong, so we drifted past the flat lands, admiring the church and the farmhouses, drinking beer. My brother, now helmsman, sat on the bench.

Next to him, with his legs jammed between gunwales and sailing horse was Patrick, in full sunlight. Being tanned already, I also sat in the sun, legs hanging over the starboard gunwales of the cockpit, leaning my shoulder against the cabin wall, with my arm draped over its roof.

When we did tack, we simply shifted our positions to the opposite side of the boat.

We had got up at six thirty in the morning and had not made it out of Olhao until nine thirty. It was Saturday 29th May. We had arrived on the 8th. It was the beginning of our third week in Portugal and we had not even made the Spanish border. I doubted that we would reach the east coast before the end of June. We were expected in Ibiza by 1st July.

We would have to sail extremely well to make up for lost time.

Symbolically, my brother handed the helm over to me when we approached the harbour walls. I steered the boat between the lighthouses and into the open sea, but I was not the least bit concerned. I could have no feelings of trepidation with both my brothers on board.

Once out to sea, we even let Patrick take the helm, and gave him a lesson on keeping the sails trim, using the compass to keep a course and the best position for holding the tiller. It was with great satisfaction that I saw his difficulty in guiding the boat over the waves. I too had suffered from too light or too firm a hand resulting in over-steer, so that we were off course, or under-steer which resulted in us losing wind from the sail. She was a difficult boat to navigate.

I was glad to see someone else having similar problems, from the point of view of both empathy and self-confidence. My brother had made me feel inferior because I found her hard to control, but here was our guest having similar and more exaggerated problems than I.

It was a pleasure to see our host bite his lip on several occasions and almost flip at other times.

Progress was slow, whoever was at the helm, we had to accept that, but Patrick had a useful morning of induction. He saluted my consummate ease with the wooden handle that formed our tiller. I admitted that it had taken some time for me to become even this adept.

Neither of us could compete with the gossamer hand of the owner and we all knew it. From the first we included Patrick in all the events on board: tacking, coffee-making, checking our speed. When I took the tiller, my brother took Patrick for a tour. Sailing in its raw form seems simple and there is little knowledge needed. You have to know that wind fills the sails. If this is not the case, then you will drift at best.

There are two sails, a mainsail, and a jib. The jib is there for power, like first and second gear in a car to help you move off and to help you corner.

Only once you have cornered correctly, found the wind, and kept it in the billowing triangle, can the boom move across and give extra speed, third and fourth, maybe if you are lucky, even fifth gear. It is important to know that left is port and right is starboard, starboard has two 'r's in it and is therefore, doubly, right. Port is generally left until the end of the meal. Port is left.

Once these basic facts have been mastered then it can be 'plain sailing'. Often a course is followed to reach a point and remembering that wind has to be in the sails it is, as a rule of thumb, necessary to zig- zag along.

A straight line is often impossible as it is necessary to have the wind to either side, so that the boat can move forward. To have the wind coming behind, or worse still towards you, is a maritime nightmare. If the wind is coming directly towards you, then you are in trouble.

Try flying a plane with a nose wind and no engines. A boat needs a tail wind, but one that will catch the sails. If by some navigational fault, or by a change in wind, or the need to go in a certain direction necessitates having the wind behind you, then there is only one thing to do.

Sinking the boat is not an option, nor is abandoning your ship.

Gull, or performing a goose-wing is the only solution. This involves loosening the boom ropes and swinging the mainsail as far as possible towards the mast, keeping it there by using a spinnaker pole, or in our case, by jamming a boathook under the boom and resting it on the deck.

You won't get much more than a seventy-five-degree angle, often, but it might be enough to nudge the boat along. Meanwhile, the jib goes out in the opposite direction, that is port mainsail, starboard jib or vice versa.

This is pushed out from the bottom corner, again suspended on the end of a spinnaker pole, or in our case, a second boathook either wedged on to the hull or held by hand in that position. Hence the jib and sail are on opposite sides and the wind fills each to some degree, resulting in the appearance of a goose flying, wings outstretched, although the jib looks much smaller than the mainsail, so strictly the goose has one short wing and one long one.

It may sound complicated, and it is. It is also worth mentioning because, for the last part of our voyage, the sail up the channel to Tavira town, that was what we had to do. There was too narrow a space for us to tack in any direction and too many sand banks to avoid or hit depending on your viewpoint.

The channel was designed for motorised shipping and not for sailing boats. You could motor sail up the channel with no difficulty if your engine worked. It took an age to sail up that channel, but with the three of us on board it did not seem so bad.

I was beginning to enjoy both my brothers' company.

It was in fact the first time we had been on holiday without our sister or mother, not necessarily both, but one or the other. My middle brother and I had been to Spain when the elder had left home and we were mere young teenagers.

The eldest had given up coming with us when he started his business. I was nineteen, my brother Norman was twenty-one, my sister who would be joining us in Ibiza was twenty-three and then there was a gap.

My eldest brother was thirty. Our parents had been travelling around a lot when they had given birth to Patrick and had waited until they were more settled before considering further children.

Hence it was always vaguely amusing to see my brother, the Captain, order our eldest brother around. I was youngest so it was okay for him to scream and shout at me and forget his manners, but with his elders, even if they were not as competent at sailing, Norman was extremely polite.

For a less confident and more sensitive soul, he would have appeared to be upsettingly polite, but I was made of tougher stuff I could bend with the wind like the reed, the intransigence of an oak leads to its demise in a storm.

There was no way I could be top dog on this voyage, but I did not want that. Without having studied psychology, I knew that it was wrong to blame me for most eventualities, including bad weather and ebb tide and to expect me to do everything, except polish boots.

For me there was safety in numbers, and I dreaded the moment when Patrick left, and I would be on my own.

I could quite understand how some people fall out on holiday; the close proximity, the realisation that they don't really like the person they are with.

Imagine being stuck in a confined space with people who were relations, yet to be convinced that you liked or even cared about them.

Life may be a big rowing boat on a rough ocean, but even if you row together, it does not help if you are all rowing in the opposite direction.

I make this sound so black when in fact it was grey, well, charcoal. In truth we laughed a lot, and I don't think it was nerves. We really enjoyed each other's company and we loved each other as only brothers or sisters can.

Some people may think that each of us may have admitted that we could not stand each other's guts and it was only because none of us was willing to walk the plank or scupper the sailboat that we made it from Tavira to Gibraltar, but it was not true, honestly.

There could not have been a happier crew in any of the oceans or the seas around the world. I had loved my brother for so kindly inviting me on holiday, hated him for making me paint the boat without pay and without prior agreement and hated him more for the unscheduled delays.

But I loved him for the food we ate, the skilful way he sailed the boat and got us off the marsh when we had run aground and his obvious navigational skills.

I loathed him for the fact that he had made an error and forgotten to include the tide in his calculations, an offence I could have lived easily with if he had not transferred his anger at himself on to me.

My respect for him increased when we sailed for Olhao but met an all-time low when he let me alone on his boat, knowing it could have fallen over at any time with me in it.

We both could have gone for help, got some food, had a decent night's sleep and a cooked breakfast. I could hardly thank him enough for almost sending me to my premature, watery death.

Being alone on my return was not pleasant, particularly as I had had to learn about my brother's absence from the barman who kept the key to the padlock that secured the cabin hatch.

There was no note and no money. Pennilessness and loneliness combined in a cocktail of misery. Who needed friends? I told myself repeatedly that I was glad to be on my own.

Chapter Thirteen - The Three of Us Together

I had more mood swings in that first month than a manic depressive has in a decade, but once the beer flowed, so did my feelings of bonhomie and goodwill towards my fellow man and crew members. The more I drank, the more positive I became, and the less the degradation I suffered.

This was further improved when we ate snacks before our main meal, followed by a proper fish supper, grilled on the barbecue outside a bar as the sun went down.

Then, only then, did I feel at one with my fellows.

This was life and I could be with no finer people. Neither of them had been deliberately malicious, they had just been unthinking or thoughtless, spontaneous, or reactionary. None of their deeds had been premeditated.

They had not thought things through, but just as that was true, they meant nothing by it and had my best interests at heart. Part of their immense quality was their spontaneity.

I truly believed that and when they offered me a brandy at the bar on the island off Olhao, I was so overcome by their generosity that I almost accepted, forgetting that they had most probably drunk a litre of spirit while I sipped beer and slurped snails. Again, they had not thought it through, brandy on top of beer, a guaranteed hangover. Not even I would mix the grape with the grain.

It was only thinking about it later, when my head spun in bed, that perhaps they wanted me to have a hangover. It might keep me quiet. I dismissed this thought. We were the Three Musketeers, all tor one and one for all, all for fun and tun for all.

The first day was successful, lots of coffee, lots of wind and we sailed sedately. Norman became excited that we were making such good progress.

'We're doing six knots now,' he said proudly as if we were doing one hundred miles an hour on a motorway. 'We touched seven knots just before that.'

Neither of us had the guts to point out that, since the wind had picked up, it was strange that we were going a whole knot slower. Something was going awry, or someone was doing something wrong. He sounded as if we had broken some land-speed record. At this rate one of us would have to swim ahead with a red flag to stop us from going too quickly.

Even with my limited maths, I had worked out that six knots was less then ten miles per hour and that we had seventy miles to cover.

I had realised that we would not have lunch before eight o'clock that evening and to most people that was suppertime.

The trouble with Norman was that his days were so long and when you were on watch, the nights were consequently very short. We both sounded suitably impressed, Patrick more so because, as we later found out, he had thought that we were doing seventeen and sixteen knots.

We had just been through a few hours of my brother barking orders. Hoist that, tighten that, non-stop, until he went hoarse, and we both felt it was only fair to be agreeable in case we endangered his vocal cords in lengthy explanation. We quite enjoyed being the crew and the fact that we were never asked to do anything politely mattered little.

Even making coffee or boiling a tin of soup for us to drink out of mug had its bonus- it kept us out of the wind. It was his ego trip, and we were sharing it good-naturedly. We tugged our forelocks and showed our consent by the odd 'Aye, there, Captain,' or 'Aye, Aye, mate, avast ye,' with a thick Cornish accent. Between ourselves, when we were at the bow, we joked about sighting Moby Dick and how Captain Ahab was the finest master of a schooner ever born.

This was holiday entertainment.

We were creating our own adventure by plagiarising other seafaring experiences and any literature with which we were familiar. Above all we were having fun and making progress!

One commodity that Patrick brought from home that we welcomed, with the same enthusiasm as a child receiving chocolate in the Second World War, was cigarettes. It was not that they were a luxury item and out of our reach financially. It was not that the South African tobacco contained in British American Tobacco's cigarettes was superior to the blend from that in Sagres cigarettes.

It was, merely that we had given up at sea to save our health.

However, because we had a guest on board, who was so generously offering tobacco products about, it would have been rude to refuse his generous offers of cigarettes, churlish to make him feel awkward or uncomfortable for being the only smoker in the boat.

We were, above all, gracious hosts and if it meant putting ourselves out slightly, or even greatly, then so be it. I think our intake of coffee must have increased tenfold, at least, in those few days, simply because a smoke of any kind meant a cup of coffee to go with it. Some people favour tea and cake, some milk and cookies, some coffee and chocolate biscuits.

We, as a family, favoured coffee and a cigarette and why not? Lent was long gone, and we had only given up cigarettes for health reasons.

Yet, we were benefiting from the negative ions in the sea air. Having lived in London all our lives, with a diet of lead pollution, smog, and carbon monoxide, it was decided that smoke from cigarettes was hardly more detrimental.

In an urban situation, a cigarette is just another noxious gas in the atmosphere. In rural areas, cigarettes disturb the purity of the air; in alpine areas, it restores the balance between toxins and pure air. At sea, the dryness contrasts with the damp air, the fire's warmth with the cold water; the incandescent glow with the impenetrable darkness of the opaque sea.

So aesthetically, as well as politely, we had no choice but to smoke these small pipes of peace, set fire to the cylinders of cigarettes, draw on the poison poles of politeness. It was also our duty to look as if we were enjoying the experience.

This was rather like the situation one imagines when presented with a plate of sheep's eyes.

One would have to pretend it was one's favourite dish, that they longed to try it or have it again, like roast beef and Yorkshire pudding or lamb and mint sauce for the English, hot dogs and apple pie for the Americans, frogs' legs, and escargots for the French.

The only problem for us was that we enjoyed our cigarettes as much as any Englishman enjoys his lamb and mint sauce; the flavour was exquisite, the smell was as enchant- ing as freshly brewed coffee and baked croissant straight from the oven for a Parisian.

It was the best pizza, hot dog and hamburger in Detroit, the best Lebanese, Ethiopian and Mexican in Washington and the greatest granola in California.

Basically, it was the best of all worlds in one and it came in a tube with a cork at the end covered in a brown speck- led paper. It was carcinogenic and unhealthy, unwise, and anti-social, killed as effectively as anything else, limited your life span, but made your head spin and your heart pound.

It was the most dangerous and unhealthy thing to do. It was so easy to get hooked.

You spent a fortune, which could be spent elsewhere. It was the devil's drug, the most highly addictive drug in the world, guaranteed to make you ill or to kill, depending not on your constitution but on your luck.

To us it was a wonderful invention.

It was too difficult to refuse.

Chapter Fourteen - Patrick, My Friend and Ally Against Ahab

For myself, I was immensely relieved. Each of my brothers was trying to outshine and outdo each other in order to be nice to me. It was bliss. Norman tried because he did not want to be seen as the bully that he was, and Patrick because he genuinely felt sorry for me, having come on the voyage, and having a further two or three months on board, depending on my luck and how quickly we could get this vessel to harbour in Ibiza.

That was the agreed stopping-off point and a handy stage for me to either sign up for the voyage from Spain to France, through the canals and thence to the Channel coast, or retire.

My temporal desires were amply supplied, with alcohol from Norman and tobacco from Patrick. However, our living space was cramped. My bunk, and Patrick's for that matter, was five feet long and two feet wide. It was curved along the lines of the hull and lay below the water line.

There was only a space of three feet above it and it had one of the thinnest foam-filled mattresses in the world. The bottom of the bunk was a foot from the cabin floor, underneath which were the bilges - they smelt terrible. Our skipper had the fore cabin and space.

The only refuge was on deck and that could be cold at the best of times. In other words, it was like living in a small, rather unpleasant tent. There were compensations.

Norman made up for his misdemeanour twenty times before the event and twenty times after. It was not a problem. Compared to those I have subsequently met who blame all life's disappointments on others, my brother blaming me once was trivial and yet I devote so much time to it. The reason I do so was that, as a teenager, it conflicted with my sense of fairness.

Also, life on board a boat concentrates all experiences, from the cold you feel on deck at nights to your perception of events.

Life is very complicated.

You start life expecting everything for yourself and then you are told to share. You are encouraged to be open and friendly to strangers when you are a baby and yet as soon as you can take care of yourself you are discouraged from any friendliness to any stranger.

In fact, others are so ingrained with such thoughts that a smile can really be disarming and disturbing. After a time in the country as a teenager, I returned to the city with easy rural ways. I greeted old couples with a cheery: 'Good afternoon'. In return they registered horror and scurried away.

Chapter Fifteen - A Sailor's Life For Me

Sailing is about hailing, being friendly, saying hello, calling to each other over long distances, ahoy, and all that. As you don't often meet strangers at sea and you have run out of things to say after a day in a confined space, you yearn for a new face, a new voice. You want to see something different rather than buckets of water or oceans of sea. A sailor's life can be extremely lonely even with a crew of over seventy.

In the weeks of preparation before the voyage, Norman and I had talked about life, the universe and, indeed, ourselves. This brought us closer together and bred a mutual understanding. This was important, nay vital, as without this, we would have throttled each other on the first day at sea and Waterwitch would have drifted on alone.

Patrick understood the situation. He was the guest and he had to divide and conquer, to avoid both of us turning on him. He, after all, had not been sailing before. He was, to all intents and purposes, a landlubber.

He had been to India, which made him hard and tough, but he was not erosion-proof; he had not been storm-hardened. Frankly he was wet behind the ears as far as sailing went.

We already had so much experience; we had almost drowned.

In comparison, we were like Achilles dipped in the river Styx while he was dry. We had the experience. He still slept with the light on as far as we were concerned.

It was therefore vital for him to make a good impression and we both enjoyed the attention. Of course, it was also a diversion. We finally had someone else to talk to, but this was someone who was more frightened than ourselves. He was less of a yachtsman, too. His lack of experience made us both superior in that respect.

However, he was the most senior family member. Perhaps he feared we would make him walk the plank, knowing that we had no plank. We must have led him to believe it was a possibility or otherwise he would not have treated us with such civility.

What a difference a day makes. I was suddenly having all the breaks. Here I was the dishwasher, head bottle-washer and dogsbody, tail, and snout; then along came a third party and I am treated royally. Captain Ahab treats me with respect because I could side with Patrick and gang up on him.

A mutiny of two is as perilous as fifty if you are only one. Then there was Patrick, with whom I sympathised because I too was not a bona fide, proper sailor, yachtsman, or crewmember. Ahab was closer to saint than sinner in yachting terms and I was close to sinner in comparison to Norman.

Therefore, Patrick naturally warmed to me, to avoid a tongue-lashing and meagre rum ration. A lesser man would have taken advantage of the situation, but I, if modesty will permit me to say, adapted maturely to the situation. I merely basked in the attention I was receiving from both brothers. Individually, I had never had so much respect.

They did not quite fight over me, but they did do their damnedest to win my favour. I had a constant supply of duty-free cigarettes by the carton-load from Patrick, lest he lose his landlubber ally. I had brandy, beer and wine from the boy-scout barman, Captain Ahab, who was always well prepared.

I felt like some young poor pretty young filly that two old nags were fighting over, both prancing around the field to impress me. It was a small field, and it took little to impress this filly. Booze and fags were reward enough. My loyalty could be brought for such cheap commodities.

I wanted our voyage to go smoothly, as did everyone else.

Let the sea or scenery provide the drama.

It did not have to come from us.

It should not come from us.

It could not come from us.

Some people have to manufacture drama to make life more interesting. We were quite prepared for a quiet time and for nature to supply the excitement. If she did not, then a relaxing time was paramount. Our agenda stipulated relaxation; nature's adventures were extrapolation.

What I failed to realise at the time was that both my brothers were basking in the same sun, wallowing in the same glory as I was, but from a different perspective.

Captain Ahab was saying to himself exactly what I was saying, how noble he was not to take advantage of these two inexperienced crewmembers for their sakes.

We were a trinity of harmony.

We all needed each other, Living in such close quarters, we survived by remembering cardinal rules.

We were one of the most obliging and most polite crews on this planet. It was important to each and every one of us that we behaved so and that we treated each other with such wonderful respect.

We were after all on holiday, a fact that we failed to realise until our brother came out. His presence pointedly reminded us that this was meant to be fun, that life was a bowl of cherries, not olives or salty snails.

Tavira was hot and the source of immediate food and provisions for the journey. Therefore, it was attractive.

We could match Norman's lunchtime drinking any day, it was more sedate. After we had lunch at two, we decided to go back to the boat after three too many brandies and ended up staying the evening in the same port even returning to the same restaurant to savour their food.

A different choice of food this time but the same, light white vinho verde and one too many brandies. We had such a good evening, I cannot recollect how we got back or who rowed our tiny tender, but I do vaguely remember getting my jeans wet and finding it highly amusing. The fact that I awoke with my jeans hung up by the cabin doorway to dry and a damp towel by the bed, led me to believe that it was I who had steered the boat.

Ever ready to volunteer, it could have been me who had sat in the precarious and dangerous pointed end of the boat, while they rowed from the middle or at the back. Either way, water had lapped over the side and made me damp, yet I could not remember having got to bed, let alone drying myself.

I presume it was the Spanish brandy on top of the wine that brought about this state of affairs. Yet it could quite easily have been diesel fuel and methyl alcohol for all the difference it made to me. My dear brothers, in no fit state to rise, let alone sail, just seemed to moan, or wail.

Their suffering made my whinging seem insignificant by comparison.

I was dying to set off and sail around the Mediterranean.

Ahab had sailed enough, and he longed for the company of shore people, my brother and the shore bars as opposed to the rigours of the sailing bar - lighter fuel mixed with home-brew.

Patrick had not had enough of the sea and hardly showed any interest in expanding his knowledge. It was the diversity of our approaches and our expectations that made the voyage such a success. There was no competition to out-sail each other or outdo each other. We hadn't the time for that nonsense.

Norman had seniority in the forecastle, Patrick in years; I was best suited to preparing breakfast, croissants, bread sticks with cheese or apricot jam which seemed to have a new layer of mould on it each morning.

Patrick would prepare lunch, cutting the swollen tomatoes and the warm cucumber, then the partially melted breakfast cheese, which, accompanied by some tinned pilchards or tuna, counted as a feast. We had cheap red or white wine, bilge temperature.

Supper was the highlight either a meal ashore or one of Norman's one-pot-wonders.

If Norman had not been possibly one of the finest sailors since Magellan and Columbus, one who could navigate by gut and stars alone, he would have been a superb chef, a Michelin star gastronome, rather than a Michelin map captain.

We travelled by sail, directed by CGS (Compass, Gut and Stars), but we marched forward on our stomachs.

Our equipment was sparse, but we did not need more than a Calor gas cylinder with a collapsible steel frame screwed on and our one serviceable saucepan.

Through mixing pastes and herbs, kept in a special rack, like a doctor's herbal medicines, my brother produced the most delicious sauces, into which he would pour canned beans, or tomatoes or baked beans, letting them reduce, followed by tinned fish of any type or tinned meat.

After mixing the ingredients, he allowed the pot to bubble for a while. Then we would have a perfect meal.

The trick with the one-pot-wonder however was to boil fresh water and cook rice or noodles or pasta in that water, drain over the side, using a colander, which was miraculously part of the ship's inventory, and serve on to one of the four plates on board. Then, the sauce and meat or fish could be prepared and the starch dish from the plate could be mixed with the vegetable and protein part of the meal.

This was not the Hay diet, separating constituents for each meal: a carbohydrate meal, a plant products meal, then, an animal products meal. This was food combining, not separating, but with the herbs and spices, pastes, and powders, ground leaves and sprinklings, the meal tasted superb.

It was a wonderful concoction, washed down with a cocktail of complimentary drinks, beer, wine, and spirits. Even on the occasions when our drink was gone or we preferred to drink lemonade or fresh water, the meal was sublime. By adding either beer or wine it became more than that and by adding both to the meal it became heavenly.

The two things I remembered my brother for were, one, that he is a superb cook, and two, his continuous attempts to murder me throughout the voyage.

Chapter Sixteen - For Gibraltar, I'll Be Bound

The morning of the 30th, Pentecost, we set off for Gibraltar.

Making progress was our common goal. The strangest thing of all was that the wind, water and Waterwitch magically co-operated with us. The wind blew in the correct direction from the south and at a reasonable speed.

The water moved from almost dead calm to slightly choppy and no more. The waves seemed to move in our direction too, willing us on. The sun shone and the storm clouds stayed away. In fact, the stratus stayed away too.

A more puerile crew might have played 'spot the cloud', but we were too busy enjoying the sun, trimming the sails, plotting the quickest and most efficient course, steering a steady tack.

All three of us were busy; our senses strained to detect a change in the profile of the hazy land mass ahead, looking for a lighthouse or some other landmark that signified that we had reached the Spanish coast, something to tell us where we might be, what progress we had made. We could hear the swish of water against the hull and had the speed metered in our brains.

Like an engine driver knows the noise his train makes at a certain speed, we knew the sound the hull would make at seven, eight and nine knots. Often, we would turn with disappointment at a lull in the wind that sounded a slow-down.

Our ears were pricked for these sounds, our eyes peeled for sight of vessels or navigational clues and our noses sniffed the air, to check it was a warm, dry breeze blowing which brought fair weather and fair winds. Our sense of touch was brought into play when one trimmed the sail, pulling on the rope or easing it off to help the sail billow, another held compass in hand, keeping it steady, or the ruler on the map, and the third kept his hand upon the tiller.

The last and final sense, taste, was catered for by the flavour of success, which we could all feel on our lips and savour on our tongues, that of successfully moving the hulk of wood along the ocean waves at such an incredible speed.

The keel was angled, the sheets pulled in tight, and water rushed by, lapping at the gunwales, threatening to spill over. As much as the boat was threatening to capsize, it would not happen, not in these calm seas.

It was then that the three of us realised taste was the most important sense and sensation, but it needed more stimulation.

The charts were put away.

We lit some cigarettes and brewed some coffee. We had been professional sailors for ten minutes, serious, focused, positive, purposefully, and professionally steering a course. We needed a break - the senses had strained for long enough. Nicotine and caffeine were the two watchwords; these were the commodities we would much rather have fill our senses.

We maintained our speed, dropping one knot, an eighth of our speed, which we could live with while we smoked, drank coffee, and chatted for ten minutes. It was a long smooth tack, to the southwest, on a broad reach.

We had gone far out to sea on the other beam, a favourite tactic of our Captain's, shadowing the coast. Then we would turn about and come back heading northeast at the most efficient angle of wind to fill our sails.

It was as if we were blanket-stitching along the coast of Spain. Now that we were on the home course, the morning had almost gone, and we hoped that we could get in another tack after lunch so that we could complete our 'W' in port by nightfall. That best describes our course: a 'W' a day kept progress at bay, you might say. It was, in actual fact, a brilliant strategy.

As we moved southeast along the Spanish coast, it allowed us to relax as we waited the two or three hours before we could get a reliable fix on any of the features on land. When we reached Spain proper, the lack of undulations and definitive landmarks proved to be a flaw in this plan. As it stood, we lived with it.

We could slack off slightly and talk and joke, and the best bit was that we could allow one or other to have a rest. We would all get up together and have a breakfast briefing, which entailed descriptions of what ached, what was stiff and sundry other complaints.

Then, after the open forum, a competition for the best or most original whinge, we had breakfast prepared by myself, often accompanied by swearing as I cut myself with the sharp knife, due either to the motion of the boat or my own bleary-eyed carelessness.

Then we decided who wanted to go back to sleep and whoever it was retired for an hour or two, waking half an hour before our break for coffee and a cigarette at eleven. It was very civilised, except the Captain who was on call and could only lie down once he had set the course, both outward to sea and inward towards land. We were to follow a compass direction, a nautical heading.

Since the compass lay on the cockpit deck, the crewmember at the tiller only had to make sure that we were heading in that direction and if we veered to the east we corrected to the west and vice versa.

After much practice and a lot of veering, we could all steer a true course, give or take a few degrees. This might have meant a tack sooner rather than later but was not as serious as steering ten or twenty degrees off (though there were several opportunities for such a mistake). Having the ultimate responsibility, my brother could always be relied upon to sort things out.

That night the Captain and I went to bed early. I was to perform the night watch and he was to take the dawn patrol. We left the novice in control, steering a straight course in co-operative seas. As a treat I was allowed the front cabin, Norman taking my bed, in order to be close at hand in a crisis. During the night Patrick started shouting for the Captain. His shouts woke me. I rolled over, but all I could see was Norman asleep in the bunk. Patrick tried again and this time the Captain responded. At first, he sat bolt upright, hitting his head on the ceiling of the boat.

Then, realising there was a crisis, he tried to jump out of bed, only to find that he had fenced himself in with the storm board, a two-foot-high planking restraint that was bolted into both the head and the foot of the bunk.

We all used the flap to prevent us from falling out of the curved bunk when the boat was at an angle, it was second nature to lift it and lock it.

My brother rubbed his sore head.

Patrick was still in a panic in the cockpit; so, he jumped out over the board, painfully catching his shin, then fell flat on the floor that covered the bilges. Finally, he picked himself up off the floor, knowing that Patrick was worried and that I was asleep in the front cabin.

It was imperative he continued his attempts to get up on deck. Patrick was green and therefore had the ability to run aground or steer into the wake or path of a tanker, all equally dangerous and potentially fatal.

As he got to his feet, he hit his head on the ceiling again. He staggered forward and head-butted the hurricane lamp, almost starting a fire with the lit fuel that spilt on the floor. In pain and barefoot, he stamped out the lit fuel.

Then, as he made for the cockpit, he tripped on the steps and banged his head on the wooden hatch, which sent him reeling down the stairs.

Having recovered enough to re-attempt the ascent into the cockpit, he tripped on the lip at the top of the steps, ending up splayed out on the cockpit floor in front of Patrick, only to be asked which star was the Pole Star and where should it be in relation to the boat.

Norman was not pleased to be disturbed or injured, but he explained the various groupings of stars over a brandy and cigarette. The stars do look wonderful when you are far out to sea.

Being on duty for four hours when you are captain, bosun, lookout and navigator is tough work.

Pulling in the sails to keep them trim, foresail and mainsail, keep on a compass bearing, look out for ships in front and behind, all this adds up to an action-packed time, busy and frenetic. It is physically and mentally draining.

Concentration throughout is total and paramount.

The wind changing or great tides altering, or your grip loosening on the tiller as you pull in one of the two sheets, could alter your course completely or even slightly and then, instead of going to bed an exhausted heap at the end of the stretch, you risk explaining what happened during your watch and why we were in a different spot and how we had lost the plot and why we would have to change our heading.

There was then the danger of having reduction in one's tot. I would imagine it is tantamount to flying a helicopter without a co-pilot.

You have a very sensitive joystick, which is equivalent to the rudder; you have two foot-pedals that are equivalent to the mainsail and the jib; then you have your compass and speedometer.

If you can accept the analogy of helicopter and sailboat and suspend cynicism, you can appreciate that as the pilot of the helicopter flies, he has someone navigating or a course plotted to stick to.

We had this, but our speedometer was a line out the back, which told us how fast, or in actual tact how slow, we were going. We called it our log. One had to crane one's neck without altering the course of the rudder and affecting the compass reading, simply because we were meant to pursue this course at a certain speed for a certain length of time.

The wind can whip itself up and die a death within minutes, the current can push you one way one minute, the other the next; flexed muscles can ease due to fatigue after ten minutes or two hours.

Sadly, the concentration can wane after fifteen minutes. One's sight can be distracted by the phosphorescence; or a dot on the horizon; or a full moon's light behind; and the shadow of the sail in front. All these factors have an effect and can affect the course you take. All these failings need to be made correct. These variables can put you five miles off course, when it is all too late for any kind of remorse.

Once you are eight kilometres from where you should be, you might as well be ten, and if you are ten you might as well be twenty kilometres off course. My fondest memory of this rough guide to sailing was that night, the watch after Patrick's.

Most yacht crews are in harbour by nightfall, showering and having supper, ready for the following day of cruising.

Not us.

If other boats were the rental cars of the oceans, then we were the back- packers and we rode and hitched a lift on the same waves as the juggernauts of the sea. This was the Orient Express compared to the baggage wagon.

We longed for a bath, a shower, not having to hang over the sides or use a bucket each time we went to the loo. Our heating system was layers of sweaters or blankets, along with rubbing your hands together.

At night, your lights are the moon, the stars, and the phosphorescence. Civilisation is marked by the shadow of land off the port bows, but occasionally there is more, for example, when you enter the major shipping lanes.

Congestion is minimal, that is until you reach a large port. Sailing through Cadiz was such an experience. Monsters, shadowy steel hulks break up the horizon, navigation lights, are green and red eyes in the distance. It was my watch, and we were on a course that would bring us past Cadiz and on, tacking northeast after our night run southwest. The wind was strong, but warm, a veritable sea breeze that filled the sheets, sent the halyards shaking and the bow breaking though the surf.

The spray spun off the hull as we heeled over, gunwales centimetres from the foam, still white in the night. I checked our wake and the speedometer; we were doing nine knots. It was quite frighteningly fast. This in itself was danger.

Would I be able to maintain this speed, or would I lose the wind in the sail? Would a gust force us over to the point of near capsize?

I was perturbed by either eventuality. There was more - we had to pick our way through these immense structures, like islands dotting our path. There was always doubt as to whether they were at anchor or on the move. Sometimes in a car you can see a plane, but if you are moving fast, the plane seems to stand still. Such was the sensation on board Waterwitch.

A small miscalculation on my part and we could end up drowned in the wake of a moving tanker, at the very least shaken and stirred by the experience, if not overturned.

There was nothing for it. I could feel the wind in my hair, and I knew I had to steer the course given me. It was my duty. I was still shaken by the storm, and I had heard the usual horror stories of yacht meeting ship, and these were some ships.

It was a skill steering the boat in front of the tankers as they lumbered along: too slow and the wake would ruin your run and possibly all your fun, too fast and you could misjudge the distance, hitting another tanker.

I had no experience with this particular skill, nor did I particularly wish to test it, but test it I did.

Still, she ran on, and more and more of these massive shapes revealed themselves.

Those at anchor we passed by metres, looking up in awe at their cathedral proportions, black bows, and hotel sterns with an expanse of deck too broad and too long to take in. These immovable obstacles had to be avoided, yet this visible danger was nothing compared to the moving monsters. These made such scant progress that from a distance they seemed at anchor.

In all respects they were similar to those at anchor: accommodation lights burning yellow-gold, navigation lights green and red or just green or just red depending on the angle at which you approached them.

It was akin to trying to walk over three carriageways of a motorway, without stopping. It was four-fifths luck, one-fifth nerve. There were literally hundreds of ships heading for Cadiz and we were cutting through them, like a battleship working its way cautiously through a minefield. We had thrown caution to the wind, however. We were running downhill with the brakes off, running red traffic lights.

I was wearing a sweater and a strained look. My foot tapped the tune that filled my head, the Doors pumping through the headphones of my Walkman. My feet rested on the gunwales and my arm leant on the tiller.

I peered over the cabin at the next hulk. We were converging. This second tanker was moving and, disturbingly, heading for the same point as I was. There was no way I was going to disturb either of the other two.

They deserved their rest and I, in turn, could have mine later. The adrenaline surged through my veins. We had been in the shipping lane for thirty minutes and my concentration did not allow me to notice my body shivering or my need for nicotine. We were getting closer and closer; the shadow of the ship's hull hung over me like the sword of Damocles.

I was doing nine knots; they must have been doing ten and still we came closer. I saw the point where I wanted to be, and I noticed that it was about to be obscured by the nose of the tanker.

 I could turn the tiller and luff long enough for us to let the tanker past, but then the wake would rock us and capsize us. It was sink or win. It was the most dangerous game of chicken I had played, simply because I knew the lookout on the tanker would not even notice our tiny navigational lights and the hurricane lamp on the deck would be obscured by the phosphorescence in the sea.

There was no way the tanker captain would lose his nerve. He relied on his radar to pick up large shipping. The braking distance of a tanker is a few nautical miles in any case.

They could run us over and not even notice.

Quoting maritime law that sail has right of way over motorised shipping is pointless when you have not been seen in the first place. I held fast and prayed the wind would not fail me. On and on our two bows raced.

Within a minute I was under her bows and through the other side, I saw her big black beam and heaved a sigh of relief Keeping the tiller steady I dared to look back and watched this moving mountain of steel glide by.

I knew what was to come but I also knew what to do. I pulled the tiller slightly towards me. The wake would come from the tanker, but our stern would face it. Sure enough, the first wave picked us up like a hand and we surfed along it. Just as gently as it picked us up, it dissipated and let us down, as did the second and third.

My experience in the storm had been useful after all. I trimmed tiller and sail and moved on to the next obstruction. This one was silent and still, I could make out an open door and a person coming out to smoke, a small figure way above me.

The steel hulls thinned out gradually, but I still had to judge their heading, their intention, and our best course. The compass told me that we were still on the right tack.

The North Star was still where it should have been and the only problem, I could see was that the tape had run out on my Walkman. It was safe enough for me to remedy this and so I flipped sides.

Leaning back on the tiller, I grabbed the soft pack of Sagres filters from the bench beside me, flicked my silver steel Zippo and drew on the lit tobacco. It was good to be alive. Checking my watch and our speed, I relaxed for the first time on that watch, content to know that I had another hour to go before a warm cup of coffee, laced heavily with brandy, marked my passage to my bunk and bed.

I looked forward to a long luxurious rest.

It was a shame that no hot shower or warm bath awaited me. It was so cold I would most probably sleep in my clothes, but it did not matter. I had moonlight music and a perfect view.

The cloudless sky, the full, swollen, risen moon, stars dotting the horizon and the North Star burning bright to the north-east, just off the port stern and the blue-black, inky water contrasting with the midnight blue sky, alive with sparkling phosphorescence, gleaming more brightly in the light of the silvery moon.

The others lay secure in their bunks, oblivious to my game of rushing, not Russian, roulette. My shoulder muscles ached, and my arms felt tense, but above all I felt immensely relieved. We had gone for broke, and we had made it. It was a calculated risk, but this was living life on the edge, man and boat against physical elements and other dangers afloat.

At that stage I was very proud of myself but pride, as everyone knows, comes before a fall.

PART TWO

Chapter Seventeen - From Cadiz to Gibraltar

Once past Cadiz it was safe going and we cruised. I was relieved, before the sun came up, by Norman. I simply never heard the alarm, still listening as I was to another tape, although the batteries were almost entirely exhausted having been used constantly for the past however many hours. It was beginning to irk me somewhat that Cat Stevens seemed to be singing at two beats to the bar when he should have been singing at four.

My frustration ebbed with the appearance of a blond mop of hair, just under my line of vision. He was holding a mug and I accepted the proffered caffeine. The coffee offered was hot and black. It was time we headed for shore to get some milk that was for sure. I took off my headphones to allow us to chat while I drank the brew. Halfway through, Norman took the tiller. From then on, he was in charge of the rudder.

He told me about Patrick's progress. The novice had several hours of experience at the helm, determined to master the night technique. My brother trusted his progress enough to leave him, but with strict instructions to wake him whenever he encountered problems or had strayed too far from the given bearing.

Neither of us were allowed near the log; we had to make a mental note of our direction to enable calculation of the next heading and readjustment if we had veered off course. It was mostly my brother who set the course and trimmed the sail for optimum trajectory.

All we had to do was hold it on that bearing, a difficult enough task. That night the sea had been very calm, no trace of white horses or choppy waves. It had been a pleasure to take control, the bow making light work of the gently moving mass of water. It was a breeze.

We had ideal conditions, a strong wind, steady not gusting and as flat a sea as one is likely to encounter.

This was night sailing for real, using the eight hours of darkness to put some nautical miles behind us.

It was possible to clear about seventy miles, thirty-five to forty on one tack, the same distance on another, on a map we would have cleared forty to fifty miles of coast.

Our zigzag pattern was not as efficient as linear progress, but it was an achievement anyhow. Norman was well wrapped up against the cold; the air was cool, and the wind was cold. He wore a jumper, some corduroy trousers, thick socks, sailing shoes and his yellow oilskin coat.

It was useful having a third person, with two you are constantly alert for four hours, then asleep for four; with an extra man on board, you could increase your sleep to five hours. You needed it after concentrating so hard on speed, the sails and direction, let alone other shipping, unfamiliar lights and just keeping your tired eyes open.

The extra hours left over before your next watch could be spent reading or relaxing. There was no joy in sleep and work, sleep, and work.

The sky was midnight blue, and that was roughly about the time, too. I shared a few words with Norman, smoked a cigarette while he smoked too. I was cold, just wearing my sweater and nylon ski jacket. It was the constant inactivity, sitting for hours on the bench, barely moving. One arm had most of the exercise. It was only when the hand got cramped that you would shift to the other side of the tiller, but this made navigation difficult and steering awkward.

You needed to be able to see over the cockpit clearly and only in the corner closest to the water could this be effectively achieved. I had really had enough of the briny fresh air and being on deck, so I drank the coffee as quickly as the heat would allow.

Tossing the cigarette butt into the phosphorescent water, I drained the cup, making sure our course was clear to our new navigator, reporting our speed and bearing, but not our intended destination.

Our destination was not a tangible place. It was in fact this bearing until four o'clock in the morning, eight bells. I was told not to worry and to get some rest, I could not argue with that. My brother would let us know if he had a problem.

There was no reason why he should, we had let the coast and our heading would take us further out to sea. To get to my bunk took twenty minutes. This included five to change and a few to swill my mouth with brandy.

I was going to spit it over the side, but I swallowed it instead, not wishing to waste any, at the same time saving the fish from getting drunk.

Finally, with tired limbs and mentally exhausted, I slipped the towel from around my waist, unzipped my sleeping bag and curled into a foetal ball in order to get warm, a difficult manoeuvre on my bunk, with its curved sides, but I had bolted myself in.

I was snuggled up well within seconds and the oblivion of sleep could not have taken more than a few minutes more to wash over me. Tiredness had taken its toll. I was exhausted by sleep deprivation and extreme concentration.

It was in the morning, when Patrick relieved Norman, that the black whales were sighted. These were more of a danger than tankers, as they tended to rub their backs on the keel of sailing boats. Our keel may have sheered-off with such boisterous contact, or the whale might flip up one side of the keel as it grazed by; either way was a shortcut to a potentially fatal capsizing.

There were countless stories of yachts that had sunk after an encounter with these beautiful elephants of the sea. It was not a malicious act; the whale was merely playing and wanted to scratch an itch.

Norman and Patrick were terribly excited by the sighting of these marine mammals.

They shouted down to my bunk, but I was too tired to respond.

Apparently, they could see one whale spouting water and diving under the sea, shadowing us. They were perturbed by his or her close proximity and its approach.

Could this overgrown fish merely want to frolic in our wake or was it itchy? This worry caused much debate on deck. I was too exhausted to partake.

It was as if they had never seen Jacques Cousteau, The Natural World or David Attenborough.

Either way I was not interested, there would be more rare whales on our trip as far as I was concerned and therefore, I need not worry about these two.

Needless to say, until this day I have never seen a whale and these two brothers of mine had no camera.

The only image I could have had was my own sight and the only concrete and lasting impression that I could have had of this creature was in my mind's eye and that could only be supplied by my initial sighting.

To this very day I curse the morning that I was too lazy to rise and missed perhaps the last chance to see the whale in three dimensions, not on a screen but in the ocean.

How I wish I had. I could have taken a look and returned to bed, but by the time I stirred, the whale had lost interest in our pathetic wake and moved off looking for tanker wakes and perhaps for their hulls which could, depending on their speed, graze as much as scratch their back, vertebrates that they were.

From that day on, I had learnt the invaluable axiom that it was better to do today what could be done rather than to put it off until tomorrow.

My laxity, lassitude and lack of action had made me miss the opportunity of seeing a whale. From then on, I was determined to do what I could in a day, to never be too tired to do something or too lazy to get a job done.

I have always benefited when I have stuck to that tenet and often suffered by ignoring it or being too tired to follow it, or too busy, or too lazy or just too willing to make an excuse not to do something.

I was tired, but my appearance on deck would have taken a minute, my effort would have been rewarded. Regret at having missed this magnificent whale may well haunt my twilight years. All is not lost. I have to find an opportunity to reclaim that which I have missed. There is always a second chance.

Even Shakespeare had said,

There is a tide in the events of men,

Which, taken at the flow, leads on to fortune.

Omitted, all the voyage of their life

Is bound in shallows and miseries.

It was these miseries that we would avoid by degrees.

I vowed that no matter what it took I would try to do immediately what could be done now and not leave things until later. If you are hungry you should eat; if you are thirsty you should drink. I learnt that to put something off is a heinous crime and it was something to be avoided at all costs.

At the time all I wanted to do was rest and this I did well into the morning.

Pangs of hunger woke me tram my sleep and I looked about me soporifically.

It was dark in the hold of the boat.

I could hear the rush of water against the hull, a soothing swish. We were travelling fast, pushed on by the prevailing west winds. I knew it was daytime before I opened my eyes because of the stifling heat and the smell of the bilges.

At night the smell of oil and stagnant water seemed less oppressive. How oil had seeped into the bilges I did not know. Our engine bolted on, and it was now lying flat in storage, clearly the two-stroke motor leaked engine oil whilst managing to trap the marine fuel.

Perhaps, it was the wood oil, but such a strong smell prevented long siestas. Even exhaustion could not overcome the heat and stench of the cabin, which was overwhelming. \

The forward hatch was open, and the cabin doors were bolted back; there should have been a through-draft, but this boat was designed for the northern hemisphere and for keeping draughts out, not for letting fresh breezes in.

Your senses were more attuned at sea. Ears pricked for the sound of another boat or of rain that signified a storm. It was a sense akin to a nursing mother's. The sense of smell was honed to the waft of stormy weather or the stench of fear. All I received was stale bilge reek, but I knew I needed nicotine. The cabin was in its usual shadow, almost like night.

By craning my head, I could see the shaft of light; it was like the light at the end of a long tunnel, a letterbox of searing sunshine that slipped though the gap in the cabin doorway.

The cabin hood was almost completely drawn back, but the sunlight only penetrated as far as the bottom of the steps, thanks both to the design of the hatch and to the shadow of the boom and sail.

My mouth felt dry, I was thirstier than anything else and voices drifted down from above, scattered with occasional laughter. I waited until my eyes had become accustomed to the light below, knowing the sunshine above would make me squint all the more so if I did not.

By dressing quickly, my clothes cold and damp, I managed not to mind the sudden chill. This enabled me to prioritise my needs.

My slumber had brought my body temperature down and it was therefore important that I get up on deck to warm my bones. My nostrils told me as much. I had already decided that coffee was on the agenda and food could follow.

I would therefore greet the day and my brothers by bringing the primus stove out into the sunlight and brewing coffee at their feet, just like the good galley slave.

A cigarette with the coffee would help reduce my hunger pangs and then I could eat the dry, hard bread and mouldy cheese that was everyone's breakfast. From there I could dream of Columbus.

I was pleased we had no rotten meat on board, no scurvy amongst the crew; there were no rotten apples in a barrel and no rats on board. The absence of rats failed to console me; after all, I knew that rats always desert a sinking ship.

The fact that we never had any in the first place convinced me that we were barely afloat and therefore had no right to be in the ocean at all.

No self-respecting rat would be seen dead on our boat. I knew from my history lessons that Mendez and Columbus had seen sharks circling around the three ships and saw it as a bad omen, a sign of a storm and a bad one. What could the sighting of a whale signify?

As I rose off my bunk, having put on my deck shoes, I was perturbed by imagining the size of a storm that needed a whale as an omen.

Would it be a hurricane or a tornado? Being a fatalist and a smoker, I decided not to share these doubts with the crew, content to have my last cigarette like all the best men who are condemned. As I walked up the cabin steps to the deck, I was relieved to notice that I was wearing my brown trousers and was therefore ready for any eventuality.

'Hey, Finn, how are you?' they chorused.

'Fine, fine, how are you?'

'Magic,' my brother, the Captain.

'Great,' my brother, the bosun parroted.

'Good, how long have I been asleep for?'

'Oh, about five hours,' Patrick volunteered, 'that whale was amazing, and we saw a shark too.'

'Oh really, was it circling?' I replied archly, I did not believe him.

'Yes, and later we saw some porpoises,' he assured me.

'Interesting,' I replied, not wanting to give too much away.

They were obviously oblivious to fifteenth century maritime folk tore. It seemed that, not only had the whale come to warn of us of the impending doom, but also, he was accompanied by the dolphins and the ultimate herald of the doom, the shark.

Within hours, I could end up a latter-day Robinson Crusoe without a Man Friday and without my brothers.

I wondered which part of the boat I would end up drifting to shore on, a bit of mast, the bow, a plank from the stern, a chunk of the port hull?

Being shipwrecked in the twentieth century was a little passé, on a par with being guillotined. It was just not done, even for effect and least of all to get attention. I, of all people, did not need that sort of attention. It seemed rather pathetic under the circumstances to worry about eating, but if I was going to be afloat for days, perhaps carried by the dolphins or eaten by the shark, then I should get my strength up. I surprised myself by what I said next.

'I'm really thirsty, would anyone like a coffee?'

'Rather,' replied my brother, the bosun.

He had been reading PG Wodehouse and it had totally gone to his head. Thankfully, he had left the tweed jacket, corduroys, blazer, and whites at home.

'Why not?' said the Captain of our souls.

I felt like saying, 'Because neither of you said 'please'.'

I held my tongue, however, as I knew we would be so much flotsam and jetsam from now on. It surprised even my cynical self that I should be so superstitious. By the time I had finished boiling the kettle,

I was convinced I was overreacting. This was notwithstanding, my previous doubts, especially those recent doubts about sailing with Geoffrey. At that time, I think I was unaware of or just ignored my doubts.

On reflection I know that my anxiety was not just straightforward apprehension about a new ship and trusting my life to a new skipper. It went deeper than that.

I could smell danger, but my inner voice became fainter and fainter as my brother gave me reasons why I should go on Geoffrey's boat and, eventually, I was so determined myself to go those wild horses or even foaming white horses would not have prevented me from boarding the boat.

I had once known Geoffrey's boat's name. I am sure it was a pretty girl's name, but my mind has blocked out any recollection.

Obviously, the name had once conjured up such positive feelings in me that I could not cope with a negative connotation being associated with it, so I have forgotten it completely.

Whatever, I had my own reasons for not going on Geoffrey's cruise into the seas of Hades, but I had allowed someone else to sway my judgement.

I had survived but I might never have been traumatised if only I had listened to my inner self, not more vocal, outside influences.

I knew then that it was not so much a case of learning from our mistakes, but that our mistakes, which we call experiences, should never be made.

There are many experiences an individual should be pleased to avoid having and mistakes one would have been happier not to have ever made.

The day went on.

Patrick went for a rest after we all had lunch. It was breakfast or brunch to me. I called it brunch because that allowed me to partake of some of the warm red wine that was being passed around.

We also had some cool lemonade stored in the bilges and this was added to the second glass to make a refreshing drink.

After losing two bottles of lemonade whilst cooling them in the sea, we had concocted an elaborate tethering and knot system that prevented the wake from pulling the bottle from its rope. This was so complicated that we only did this when we deserved a real treat.

We drank, toasting each other and secretly wishing for ice or a chilled beer.

If you look at a conventional atlas, Spain consists of three major ports: Huelva, an industrial centre at the end of a convoluted channel, which we avoided; Cadiz, a bulge on the coast; and Tarifa, northeast of the African coast and of Tangiers.

If you took at a Michelin map of the same coast, it is dotted with a marvellous array of small fishing ports, with boats that ply the Atlantic from the Gulf of Cadiz down to Cape Trafalgar and the Strait of Gibraltar.

These were the best of times. We had already had the worst of times, running aground in Faro, seeming to take forever to get to Tavira and the Spanish border, demarcated by the River Guadiana. I had got used to the boat and it had got used to me.

Equally, my brothers and I had all got used to each other.

I even joked about my storm experience, saying that we could have gone on from Portimao to Lagos, particularly as I had never seen it before. In fact, our heading would have taken us past the Cape of St Vincent and out along latitude thirty-six straight to Boston.

That situation seemed so far removed; the past time was a different country and we had done things differently there.

No matter how I tried to bury the trauma, the event still weighed heavily on my mind. In a small space, with little to do and not much to think about except the course you are taking and the trim of the sails, even minor incidents weigh heavily on your mind.

You have all the time in the world to think about past experiences and to review recent events. There is little else to do, apart from sleep and eat. Our trip was not all about work at the tiller, rest in our bunks and food on our plate.

Sometimes it was; on other occasions it wasn't.

Nothing can replace the exhilaration of sailing at speed through fair weather or foul. Sailing is all about the best of times and the worst of times, but occasionally it can be bliss.

On this leg of the journey, we were having the best of fun. Our eventual target was Gibraltar, but in the meantime, we cruised speedily along the coast. Day sailing, the most pleasant of any sort, took us down the coast from fishing village to fishing village.

The tides were kind and allowed us to come into harbour in the evening, just as the Spanish were coming out to dine. We could be tied up, showered and at the restaurant table for the quieter second sitting. A late night followed by an early start to catch the right tide became second nature.

We were on manana time already.

The bedding always needed drying out and, once dry, provided an ideal day bed for an hour-long siesta. If the wind was high, a blanket and hat would keep you warm.

After so long on the boat, we were accustomed to sleeping at a slant and many of our tacks took four or five hours to complete, quite long enough for everyone to have a snooze.

We enjoyed our breakfast with the local fishermen. They could not work out where we were from and we could not understand the jokes they were telling about us, so every- one was happy there.

We rubbed shoulders and ate tapas with brandy, on occasion surprising the locals with our alcohol consumption. Patrick, less hardened, had his brandy with thick syrupy coffee.

We had ours neat. If you have never had anchovies, sardines, and brandy first thing in the morning, it is a rare treat, better than kippers and Kenyan coffee.

Our experience of the local coffee was not so successful. It was too strong, too bitter for my tastes, needing lots of milk, but there only seemed to be yoghurt available on the dairy side.

We even tried yoghurt mixed with anchovy, which is quite tasty too if you are hungry enough.

It was chilly, too, before the sun came up and they had a habit of drinking their brews warm, rather than hot, so the brandy was merely central heating, and the fish was all we could order.

There never seemed to be any bread, but we could smell it baking when we walked in the streets afterwards.

We were adapting to the local ways, the chameleons that we were. It was always a worrying time though when we left the harbour. Would we tip the dinghy up on the way out to our mooring? But we never did.

Unsteadily, we managed to hoist the anchor, unfurl the sails and sail majestically from port.

Tying up was a dream. We just found a metal buoy to tie ourselves up, dropped the anchor for added security and slipped the dinghy over the side, easy with three people.

The tender, as we had been commanded to call the dinghy, was a cumbersome wooden hulk of a boat and it took two people to up-end it and put it into the water.

Dragging it out and flipping it over was tiresome and tricky, particularly as this was done on the tapering stem. The whole operation was made much simpler with an extra pair of hands.

This part of the adventure was so like a holiday, so close to how I imagined that it would be, that it was almost unbelievable.

Day after day of sunshine, strong winds taking us at racing speeds through the gently undulating surf- it was wonderful. That is until we reached Gibraltar, or rather tried to reach Gibraltar. The Strait is famous for its becalmed water, but not many people are aware of this. There are great pockets of sea without a wind.

Our sailing days seemed to be over. We had made good speed from Tarifa, but with neither the Spanish coast nor the African coast in sight we became becalmed. We strapped the outboard motor to the side, but it kept conking out. It spluttered and revved and then when it was put into gear it choked itself out.

Again and again, we tried, until the air was full of the smell of burnt and unburned fuel, more like a garage forecourt than the entrance to the Mediterranean.

From there we drifted slowly, a progress of almost imperceptible proportion. The jokes ran out about the time the last bit of cheese did and conversation dried up with the downing of the last beer. We took it in turns to take watch and slept on our bunks waiting for even the slightest breeze or the smallest clink of one of the metal sails hooks.

But no sound came.

We were in the doldrums and down in the dumps. Our bubble had been burst. Resigned to our fate, we tried to keep each other's spirits up, but when so little progress was being made it was difficult. Our problem was knowing our exact location.

This was a busy shipping lane and at one point only eight miles, or thirteen kilometres, separated Europe from Africa.

Through this narrow lane passed an awful lot of shipping, going in two directions. They were visible to each other, through radar and sight, but we were too small to be clearly seen, even on a screen.

If a boat hit us, the crew would most probably feel nothing, not even a jar. Steel tends to slip through wood quite easily. The next problem was the currents that could sweep us on to the shore, which we could not see, and break us on the beach or against the rocks; either would do the job well enough.

Because the Mediterranean is virtually a land-locked lake, the water is saltier due to evaporation. The lighter, less salty, colder Atlantic water flows in over the warm water and this sets up the currents that could dash us on the shore or send us into a sea lane.

The next day, I awoke to see, revealed in the mist, the coast of Spain to our port bow, and the coast of North Africa to our starboard bow. I remarked on the mist and was told that a fog was rolling in. I realised we would be powerless, blind, and invisible.

The fog made the boat damp, but it was the chill at night that I most vividly remember. As every schoolboy of a certain age will tell you, cloud cover on a warm day will keep the heat of the day for longer; a clear sky and the heat rises. Water condenses at a low temperature and that is how clouds form.

On the second night of our becalmed state, we had not seen the sun; there was no warmth to be kept in.

We were in the condensed water, and we could see nothing. Worse we could hear nothing. There was an eerie stillness. Apart from the lapping of waves against our hull and the occasional metallic clank of the steel rigging, there was silence.

I almost prayed to hear the lapping of water against a beach to give us some indication of where we were.

It was impossible to tell whether we were in the shipping lanes. We were drifting almost imperceptibly, but without being able to see our meters, or gather a bearing from stars or the sun.

We could only tell from the compass that we were pointed in a south-easterly direction.

The luxury of radar enabled this busy mouth to be navigated by the containers and tankers that poured out from Egypt, France, Greece, Israel, Italy, Russia, and Turkey on their journeys to Northern Europe, Africa, South America, the USA and Australia.

It was a miracle none of these ships had hit us.

Being crushed by a container ship carrying olives to expatriate Greeks in Australia was as likely as being turned over by a tanker.

NATO ships would still be patrolling the waters despite Britain's commitments in the Falklands, and deep-sea fishing boats would still be aiming for harbour within their specified number of days.

We alone were vulnerable.

Satellite navigation would only have been available on the largest of the super-tankers. It was difficult to accept that other shipping would see us. We prayed that the radar operators were well trained and alert.

Several ships had beached or sunk off various coasts through shoddy navigation. It was highly likely that our vessel could be overlooked.

I imagined some radar operator flicking ash on to his console as he peered over it, and by the time he had wiped away the dust, spotted us too late, a small white dot on his green screen.

His cry to the bridge watch coming too late; Waterwitch being sliced in half and at the bottom of the ocean in seconds, pulled down by the heavy metal keel and metal mast.

We made no contingency plans; we could not contemplate such.

In fact, we never wore a lifejacket, which on reflection was stupidity in the extreme, but we knew where they were. Being hit at twelve knots by several hundred tons of steel ship would most probably not make a difference to your chances of survival. The feeling of total powerlessness pervaded the boat.

Nature held our fate.

We talked little but used the time to rest. Fortunately, we were all so tired from late nights and early mornings that sleep came easily.

Thoughts of being sunk lasted only for a few moments; if it happened there was nothing, we could do about it.

At first, we had used a small hand-held foghorn which we blasted every five minutes, then every ten, then every hour; but the noise made sleep impossible and the sheer boredom of waiting for the magical moment when we could squeeze the trigger soon put paid to that.

It was decided to leave the foghorn on the bench and at any unfamiliar sound out to sea; we would give three quick blasts followed by a long one.

What we were to do after that was left to whoever was on watch at the time?

Boredom was our key worry, that, and the cold.

I remember that my damp jumpers stayed on for two days along with all my other clothing, underwear, and socks. My chest and my arms were warm.

I wore a black woolly hat that I found on board, but my legs and feet were chilled. It was by no means as bad as trench foot, but the numbness and the inability to do anything about it annoyed me beyond belief. My other socks were dirty or damp or both.

The only perilous part of our enforced stagnation on board the boat was walking along the deck to the main mast halyard. This was so you could urinate over the side.

It was no good standing on the sloping aft or on the gently inclining sides of the cockpit.

If you slipped as you undid your trousers you were finished. The halyard allowed you to lean against a metal cord while you completed the process and gave you immense stability. The deck was dew ridden and even scrambling along was a chore, slipping at every second step. To crawl would have involved getting your trousers and hands wet. After one attempt, when I almost got the seat of my pants damp too by slipping backwards, I decided to abandon such foolhardy exercise which in no way was proving beneficial, except for my adrenal glands and of course my bladder.

I hit upon the idea of using the bucket and then throwing the contents over the side and hoped that this would be the only excretion I would need to undergo. I missed a good old-fashioned flushing loo.

There were other things I missed too, like my Walkman, batteries for which I had promised myself I would buy in Gibraltar. I wished for some wind, some progress, sunshine, or moonlight or indeed anything but this blank grey canvas.

My mind wandered back to all the meals we had, and I knew we were down to the last few tins and the bread was finished. Who would we eat first, which limb? I knew it was not that bad, the fog could not possibly last more than a few days, but then I realised we had all thought this was just a morning mist.

I wondered whether there was enough gas in the foghorn canister now that we had blasted out a warning so often. I pictured myself standing up in the boat to blast a warning and no sound coming from the red funnel.

Our loudhailer would be useless.

We were a small fish in a big ocean, and I did not like it one bit.

Further, my flippers were freezing. You cannot stomp like anyone would do on a cold and frosty morning on terra firma. The noise of feet on wood would disturb the rest of the crew and put you right at the top of the menu.

Walking around is difficult in a four-foot square space with a big bench across it. The only option was to sit and wait until it was your turn to lie down, at which point the novelty of being horizontal would have you elated.

Watching the clock and compass was obligatory to ascertain any shifts in direction and when they occurred, so that when the fog lifted, we could plot a course.

But trying to see both, even in daylight, was a strain on the eyes and at night it was impossible. Having only a compass and clock as entertainment made me miss even the television, something a teenager I had never had time to do. There is no way I can describe the frustration and the mundane inactivity. The benefit of it all was that it has instilled in me an almost saint-like patience, compared to my adolescent impatience before the trip.

If ever you want to learn how to wait, forget the bus queue and sail away. The glamour had worn off completely; this was the downside of sailing and waiting for the upside was stupefying.

When we swapped watches, the relief wanted to talk, but the one on watch was glad to get up and go below, change position, lie low. Sitting for four hours on a damp bench, ears pricked for any sound, is exhausting; sitting with nothing to see or do is worse.

Each time I went below to my bunk, I had certainly had enough of living in the clouds. Anyone who says someone has their head in the clouds cannot possibly have shared a similar situation to ours.

On the other hand, if someone says that a person is foggy, then I can totally relate to that. I started my trip with thoughts of good weather and a vague understanding of climatic conditions. By now I was an expert on meteorological signs, symbols, occurrences, and the whole chaos of weather. You just can't rely on it.

One thing we could rely on was that, until we got to Gibraltar, there would be no parts for our British Seagull engine. Until then we would have to sail everywhere and to achieve that we needed wind. Believe it or not we had tried rowing once, using the paddles from the dinghy, but the design of the boat made their use cumbersome and ineffective.

None of us considered ourselves strong enough rowers to tow the boat behind the little tender.

Besides, not one of us was prepared to do that, knowing what great effort would be expended and what little progress would be achieved.

It was wind power or motorised power for us. The Seagull is a wonderful piece of equipment, solid, reliable, light, and fairly powerful, beloved of fishermen and day sailors alike. The only problem with ours was that it had been built thirty years ago and parts do wear out after such a long time. The British had been singularly inefficient at marketing the engine outside Crown Colonies and the United Kingdom.

Spanish sailors admired the design but could not recommend a designated stockist. Such specialised equipment needed proper parts. My brother, Norman, had stripped down practically every motorbike engine available in his bedroom from the age of fifteen. He was in his twenties now and had managed to put them all back together again, if not blindfold, then certainly without a manual.

We all admired him for this, and he had stripped down the Seagull, just for fun, most probably on a free afternoon in Vilamoura. Noticing the worn part, he had tried to order it in Portugal but to no avail. He had not even been able to get hold of the part when he came back to England, but he had been informed that their Gibraltar agents had one and would reserve it for him.

All well and good, but the part had not lasted, and Gibraltar was some way off in the distance somewhere in the fog.

It would have been unwise to have tried to use the engine in our position. We could have quite merrily chugged along into the path of a ship or into a rock formation, perhaps the coast even. We were bobbing and navigating blindfold.

The Michelin map proved equal to a chart for plotting courses on long tacks, but charts are maps of the ocean and therefore pick out the odd rock outcrop, a small island or peninsula.

These can be avoided to some extent, but they have to be seen. There were other dangers beside land formations, tides, and other shipping and this we discovered late one night. Norman was looking at his biro-marked map, the long lines bearing southeast and then northeast, giving the time for which, each tack was followed as we shadowed the shore.

Then, he cursed the chandler in the City of London for not having charts in stock of the mouth of the Med. However, in conversation, Patrick noted that it was strange that the previous owner had none of these charts. We all knew the story of how Waterwitch, after an illustrious racing career, had wound up sunk in Gibraltar bay.

The fact that she had sunk already had not passed us by, and we were not sure whether she would make a habit of it or not. Salvaging her had not proved much of a problem, though the whereabouts of her logbook and the reason she sank remained a mystery.

After all, her racing prowess had been proven in Scandinavia and America.

It was then Norman remembered that, when he had bought the boat, the owner had shown him a chart of Gibraltar harbour to indicate where the boat had floundered. A brief rustle of paper preceded the spreading of the curled paper across the chart table.

We had little paperwork: the log, the Michelin map, our passports, plus a pad for shopping lists and notes. We were ahead of our time in having a paperless office. By the light of the hurricane lamp, which flickered spookily, as if it was about to fail, we noticed that there were in fact three charts, which had been rolled up all this time.

I hoped that the last owner had not given away the Gibraltar chart to someone heading that way, since his days at sea were over. I moved over to get the other hurricane light, which burned brightly, hanging from the cabin roof just by the steps to the hatch.

Patrick saw me coming back with it, so he lifted the spluttering lamp off the chart table and hung it from the cabin roof.

We huddled next to each other, hunched, as if we were auditioning to play Quasimodo. Meanwhile Norman spread the relevant map on top of the pile. Patrick placed the fresh lamp on the far corner and held another, while Norman held the bottom, and a heavy brass ashtray held the fourth corner.

I lit another lantern. We had three inside and four outsides. We often kept one or two of them burning some nights; they were superfluous in this 'pea-souper' of a fog, but we had refilled them and put them back on deck before this briefing took place.

It seemed a good opportunity to fill this lamp as the paraffin was still at my feet. I was pouring the paraffin out of the five-litre plastic Jerry can into a smaller plastic bottle using our green funnel. The clear funnel was for foodstuffs and water. I closed the top of the larger container and fitted the funnel on to the hurricane lamp and was just about to pour from the litre bottle when it happened. Norman swore, for the first time in many days, and the shock unsettled all of us. It appeared that we were on a course over an exclusion zone.

'I don't believe it,' Norman exclaimed.

'What's up?' Patrick asked.

I remained silent, letting them continue their exchange.

'We could well have entered an exclusion zone,' the skipper admitted.

'What's the problem, is it a military area?'

Sort of.'

It was nor often that sheepishness crept into his voice.

'They'll realise we're lost in the fog; they wouldn't exercise in this weather."

'I doubt that the weather would stop them, but their radar would be sophisticated enough to pick us up; they have very advanced equipment.'

'So why do you still look so worried?' asked Patrick.

'I don't know how to tell you both,' replied Norman quietly.

'Come on,' urged Patrick.

Even I joined in then. 'Tell us what it is.'

'It appears we are sailing over an ammunition dump.'

'What?' I managed to stammer.

I thought I've almost been drowned; now he wants to blow me up. Where will this have crazed individual stop? Paranoia was setting in again. I had not had this type of excitement on my last trip abroad.

'That's not so bad; it will only be a few naval shells. If they haven't exploded yet they won't go off now.' Patrick assured him.

'It's a bit more complicated than that,' said Norman.

'How so?'

'This dump has mines dotted all around it.'

'You mean we're playing the game Battleships, but for real?'

'Yes.'

Sitting over an unexploded bomb, drifting towards possible collision with a mine suddenly made our peril in the sea-lanes pale into insignificance. We were moving and so might the mines; there were tides here, but the currents were stronger. Where oceans and seas meet there is normally a maelstrom of activity. We had witnessed this swirling, noticed the flat calm turning to choppy water where there was no wind. That had been before the fog descended.

It was uncomfortable and you were not sure when a tidal surge or change of current would change a mirror-like surface into one of intense activity. The waves were not large, but small and frequent, agitated wavelets. Ideal conditions, we all secretly felt, for a mine to start swinging or to break free from its rusty moorings.

The calmness on board was reflected by the calmness outside for the moment, but we could not tell when this would change.

We waited even more patiently and quietly for a breeze or a stronger current. It was almost as if we were on a lake, drifting out to an island, but with the added bonus of being blown to smithereens at any moment.

This was not the fun I had envisaged, but it enabled me to take stock. Perhaps my brother was not a pathological assassin after all, I reasoned.

He had invited me because he liked me and enjoyed my company, and it was cruel and unfair of me to think otherwise. I blushed at the thought, even though I had never verbalised it, recalling how I had uncharitably suggested that it was because he could find no one else who would go with him.

Many of his friends would have jumped at the chance, had they not been involved with girlfriends who would not let them go, or new jobs or flats they could not give up for three months, or no common sense, or if they lacked any wish to live. I had started to criticise again. I told myself off for being so unkind. I tried to focus on the positive; then I tried again.

Finally, on the third attempt, positive thoughts managed to penetrate my consciousness. All that I had been conscious of was my pain and suffering. The good points were buried deep in my psyche. It was as if only through deep meditation could I free these good points from my subconscious.

Having done this, the next spiritual step was transcendental meditation, but I was too weak to attempt this after the first struggle. Truthfully there were many good points. I was provided with a roof over my head; I did not have to sleep in the cockpit; there was a bunk, so there was no need to use the floor. I was fed, too, and watered, just like a horse, although wine and beer were a necessary and welcome bonus.

However, I was a workhorse, not a show horse, and my master used the whip a tad too often, I felt.

I couldn't understand why I was complaining. Norman's short temper was due to the responsibility that he felt towards me and towards the ship, in that order.

I had really lost the plot if I felt other- wise. He had brought me thus far safely and anyone could have bad luck and stumble over an ammunition dump in the fog. If I felt otherwise, it was down to my own low self-esteem, I realise that on reflections and that was my fault. Confidence and self-love come from within, and I was not mature enough to realise that simple axiomatic truth.

External factors should not have affected my views or feelings on that matter. In my mind, I had arrived a confident and willing crewmember and I was now suffering from a persecution complex brought on either by the experiences that I had endured or the company that I had kept.

At that stage I was not sure.

I had to pull myself together and show how much I appreciated Norman and his skills at navigation and sailing. I already admired him as a younger brother admires an older sibling, but his sailing skills were phenomenal and his pinpoint accuracy in navigation was a marvel.

I had an awful lot to be grateful for. He had asked me because with my sailing experience and love of travel he felt I would enjoy it, yet I pilloried him in my head and my attitude had often been that of a spoilt child. I wondered how he had coped with my truculent behaviour.

My lack of maturity or sensitivity was no excuse.

It was not entirely his fault that I had ended up sailing with a lunatic like Geoffrey, nor could he have known about the storm. It was just bad luck. It was reasonable to suppose that if someone had been sailing for thirteen years that they would look after their brother and if the voyage had been a smooth one, I would have been grateful for the experience.

As it was, I was alive for the time being and Norman had kept me so by his helmsmanship and his resolve. He took a drink or two when things got rough, but at our age we were quite heavy drinkers.

Three or four glasses of wine, or six bottles of beer, were not uncommon to contemporaries back home, but in the small confines of a boat, one notices things more.

In fact, we drank half as much as we would back home in England.

It was the close proximity and magnification of events, which made my brother's small slugs of spirit seem unreasonable.

My fear of what might occur and my need to keep a clear head prevented me from drinking, but it was not for me to say that a tot made my brother more or less clear-headed or effective. Alcohol affects people differently. I was two glasses of wine and off to sleep; Norman was more hardened and more practised.

Latterly I have been to supper or drinks parties and the amount Norman consumed seems paltry in comparison.

It was simply my expectations of him and the associated connotations of alcohol: if you needed alcohol to cope then you had serious problems.

Norman was not like this at all. He just wanted to have a tot, relax, and review the situation. He was always the best person at stepping back from a situation and taking a broad view. Others would be so close to the problem that they would not see the answer even if it were right under their noses. The irony of life is that sometimes the truth dawns too late and it was typically perverse that now our fate was sealed, and we were going to blow up, I had finally had the scales taken from my eyes and undergone my own conversion on the road to Damascus.

It took adversity for me to realise how foolish I had been.

I resolved to somehow show him this realisation. I had to do something to let him know that I faced my fate with no fear and that I would die rather with him and Patrick than any other comrade-in-arms.

My mind made up, I offered everyone a cup of coffee. It was the least and most that I could do. Norman's gratitude showed me that I had somehow got through; my subliminal message had reached its mark. I was heartily sick of being coffee boy and powder monkey, but as it would most probably be the last coffee that I would make, I was pleased to make it.

We all sat up on deck, in the small cockpit, smoking and looking out into the cloud of fog. The water was almost still, we could hear that much, as we could hear the ripple of the wake we made. Our vessel was like a log gliding along a lake. It was as if we were a toy yacht in a boating pond.

We could be picked out by the hand of fate at any time. Such a hope, such a dream was what I clung to. If it had not been so cold and damp, it all could have been a dream.

The atmosphere was dream-like, the feeling of suspended animation as if time had stood still.

We smoked and chatted, and I told them of the time when I had wanted to join the army and had gone on an officer training course, only to lead my troop directly into a minefield.

All of us were taking cover behind a bush and one of my cadets noticed that the sergeant-major from the base was standing up.

He enquired why this was when we were meant to be avoiding being spotted. The Sergeant replied that we had been blown up. We all chortled at this.

We would have laughed at anything, but our merriment was short-lived when we all realised almost simultaneously that we were not in a mock minefield and there was a real danger of hitting one of the spiked, submerged bombs.

'I didn't even know they dumped live rounds at sea, or left mines hanging around.'

I wanted to show Norman he bore no responsibility for the European governments' inability to clear up the mess after a war.

I should have mentioned that the mines were in fact suspended on a wire, but whether they were hanging around or suspended, it made little difference to our fate.

'I suppose it was easier to haul everything to one spot and keep it there, rather than go to the expense of exploding the mines and damaging fish stocks into the bargain.'

'So, these mines are just round mace-shaped bombs on the end of a line, held down by a weight?' Patrick asked.

None of us were munitions experts, unfortunately.

'As far as I know, yes, they are you can get a hook under them and drag them by the wire along to a place like this and then keep boats out of here.'

'What if a tanker strays into the area?' I asked.

'It's unlikely, and if it does, it is just one of those things the insurance people have to deal with. I think the shipping lanes are kept to and are well marked.'

'Okay," I readily responded, feeling reassured.

'Ships passport to port, so any ship coming in will be off the African coast and any ship heading out would take a wide berth around this area in any storm. It's too crowded and the fish stocks are fairly low around here. This is no man's land. You would get more fish in the Atlantic or the Mediterranean'.

'That sounds slightly less reassuring," I admitted.

This area is notorious for currents, so the fishing fleet avoids the area. We must be one of the only half-dozen or so boats that have strayed into this area since the war ended in 1945.'

'That's comforting,' I said sarcastically. 'All these bombs have been waiting for us.'

This was not the reconciliatory talk I wanted, so I waited a while for the conversation to change tack, not too obviously.

Patrick and he chatted on, fascinated by the location, its existence, and the relative dangers of traversing this stretch.

It was all too much for me and so I retired to my bunk and waited for the contact and obliteration, which never came.

The fog lifted on the morning of the third day. I was awoken by sounds of great excitement. Slipping on some shoes and bounding up into the cockpit revealed an incredible sight before my eyes. It was as though some giant god was sucking in his condensed breath as the fog rolled back.

Every moment more and more cloud receded, like an avalanche in reverse, revealing more of the sea and more of the sky.

It was, in fact, a sunny day, but for the fog. We must have watched for a whole hour, still becalmed as we noticed we could turn and see clearly behind us, then clearly beside us, but there was no sight of shore, certainly not in the haze that replaced the fog.

We were now visible to shipping and our demise would make a spectacular spark on the horizon, sending crews scurrying, watches wondering and binoculars searching.

There might even be a dramatic black plume of smoke for a moment before our charred vessel sank to be exhumed centuries later by marine archaeologists excavating an ancient site, or divers preparing the foundations for an underwater city.

Suffice to say we made it through on this occasion, and it was not until past midnight that we approached the outer walls of Gibraltar harbour.

It had taken us a whole day to gull wing a fifteen-mile distance.

We had been in no hurry.

The sugar had run out, but Patrick was the only one who took it, so he could suffer a few hours more. Visible to the customs, they hailed us in English.

Perhaps, a Gibraltarian patrol boat had spotted the British Ensign earlier in the day. More likely they tried English first to check we were not Spanish, perhaps a party of Spanish liberation forces. Norman dusted down his loudhailer and informed them that we had no power but for the sails.

There was the slightest of breezes that evening and after half an hour of waiting for us to sail to the pontoon, they sent out a motorised whaler to fetch us.

It was all highly embarrassing, inching our way towards our goal, the harbour wall, and only managing a millimetre a minute.

The customs men checked our boat and took pity on us, towing us all the way to the marina.

Gibraltar's modern marina is like any other, full of expensive white speedboats and white-hulled catamarans and yachts.

Frankly, our boat with its mottled blue undercoat and a speckling of grey filler was not conducive to the atmosphere and so we were tucked away in a quiet corner by the harbour master.

He might have refused us but for our military escort, a naval leading seaman and a pilot, who, up until then had naively thought that, after five years service to the crown, they had seen everything.

There was a Lipton's supermarket a hundred yards from our berth, but we would have to visit the following day.

We headed for Main Street, but all the bars were closing. Fortunately, a friend from school had been expecting us and they showed us customary Mediterranean hospitality.

The next night we ate on the boat, tomato stew and tea. We had sussed out the port.

Having stocked up with provisions and spent the day in Gibraltar, we decided to leave the next day. There was a party to go to and unless we wanted to crawl up the Rock to visit the Barbary Apes, we had seen all there was to see.

Main Street is fabulous for shopping if you have money.

The naval area is a concrete jungle of high-rise buildings as depressing as those back at home in England. It would have been possible to spend several days in the bars around Main Street, but we were travellers not tourists. We even gave the museum a miss.

Two boats stood out in the harbour, black as night contrasting with the white. They belonged to smugglers, and I wandered along the pier one day and noticed that there was a painter filling holes in the boat. I was sure that they were bullet holes.

Legend had it that these boats went out at night to collect contraband from Morocco and drop it off at various buoys along the Spanish coast.

They were by far the largest and most powerful in the dock and it was alleged that the alleged bullet holes came from naval helicopters, Wasp gunships, operating from a British frigate that had tried to make them heave to. They never did stop.

They could outrun even the helicopters, but they could not always outrun the bullets, warning shots across the bow that sometimes perforated the hull.

It seemed an exciting world, compared to the tranquillity and calm of the island. It really was a restful place. It was good to see that it had its dark underbelly of corruption like anywhere else, it made it less dream-like.

We were walking on sunshine.

We had survived again, and the sun was shining which always helps. Being desperately behind schedule did not bother us. Norman would come out with some statistics, which did not seem to add up, saying that provided we maintained nine knots we would be back on time and keep to our schedule.

We had only ever been at nine knots three times in as many weeks and that was for two or four hours, but with my need for reconciliation and my desire to trust my brother again, I said nothing.

Unfortunately, the border between Spain and Gibraltar was closed in another dispute about sovereignty. It was ironic. I took a walk past the airport to view Spain.

We had heard gossip and read whatever papers we could about the Falklands War.

Occasionally, batteries allowing, we had listened for a while to the World Service from the BBC on a transistor radio we had on board, but the reception was poor, and the hissing drove one to distraction.

To me it seemed as likely that the Gibraltarians wanted to be part of Spain as the Falkland Islanders wanted to be part of Argentina.

The islanders in both cases were happy to get on with their lives without politicians interfering and it seemed rather unfair on the Gibraltarians that they should be hemmed in, prisoners to a closed border.

It would have been wiser, I felt, to open the border and show the islanders what benefits they could enjoy by being a part of Spain. The wealthy of course could sail out on their yachts or book one of the prohibitively expensive flights out of the airport.Patrick was prepared to pay double for his flight, as he was asked. It had cost us sixty-nine pounds return to Faro and he was being asked one hundred and thirty singles. It was no surprise that Gibraltar was not a tourist magnet.

Unfortunately, all the flights were booked solid, not a seat to be had until the following week. It was decided to sail to Puerta de la Duquesa, a purpose-built marina and apartment complex not far up the Spanish coast. He had to get back and the wind alone could make him miss his flight back from Faro.

Norman fixed the Seagull engine but with a speed of four knots, there was no guarantee that we would be able to get him back to Spain, on a train and at the airport on time.Gennine, a friend from London, invited us to a party the night before we left. It was fun and we talked to everyone we could.

For the first time we could have a conversation with someone we did not know, and it was stimulating and fascinating, learning about life on the Rock, their aspirations; what they knew of the Falklands War and the border closure; why Spain felt it could hang on to one of its colonies in North Africa that had been petitioning for independence, yet was insistent that the Rock be returned to them.

If the people favoured independence, then, that was fine, but they did not. Many of the wealthy families relied on the various military establishments for their income. All three services were represented, and they provided a lucrative market, particularly for those involved in food and liquor. There was another excellent reason for staying British and that was that most of the inhabitants had government jobs, clerks, or lawyers for the Crown. If the Spanish had removed the government and transferred it to Madrid, then Gibraltar would witness mass unemployment at a stroke.

We decided to leave earlier than planned to get Patrick back on to the mainland. It was morning when we set sail in buoyant mood, with the ballast of beer bottles and wine flagons snug in the bilges. Norman had kept a net with six dumpy San Miguel bottles hung from the side of the boat overnight.

The seawater had chilled them to perfection, and he hauled them up before we metaphorically hauled anchor. Casting off after we had started the Seagull engine seemed only sensible. The two-stroke motor spluttered and belched a cloud of grey smoke on the first three attempts, but then it chugged into action with a big puff.

It vibrated the whole boat and I had forgotten what an old boneshaker she was. The sound of it popping merrily in the water, leaving a trail of oil from the abortive starts, reassured us. It was leaking; it must be working. It was a tiny slick and hardly as ecologically damaging as the bigger diesels in the dock.

The exhaust smoked slightly on the water's surface. I took the bow rope and together Patrick and I pushed the boat backwards out of its berth. He jumped on first and offered me an outstretched hand, but I leapt on to the bow and grabbed the handrail, I did not want to risk him losing his grip.

Once we were on board and drifting backwards, Norman engaged reverse and with a clank the propeller spun. He eased the throttle some more as we prepared to fend off other boats at the front. We cleared our parking space, sorry, our berth and Norman brought the boat around in an arc. The engine clanked again as he found neutral and not a moment too soon clanked again as he found forward.

Both Patrick and I had feared he would reverse into the boats on the other jetty, but as always, Norman pulled things off just in time.

To crash at this stage would have been the final straw. Somehow both Patrick and I would have found the extra money for a ticket home and Waterwitch would have returned to her spiritual home at the bottom of Gibraltar harbour, although this time in the new marina.

We motored sedately past the lines of boats, faintly ridiculous with our noisy spluttering engine. I took the tiller, or rather Norman gave it to me. An honour, I felt.

Perhaps it was because he trusted Patrick's helmsmanship less than mine. Within minutes he had untied, clipped on, and hoisted the mainsail. With a bound, he was back at the tiller with a demanding look. Smiling sweetly, I handed over control. As ordered,

I opened three bottles of beer and handed them around. I had made cheese sandwiches earlier that morning and we all wore clean clothes, laundered for us by the local dry cleaners. We had also benefited from the luxury of showering every day. We clinked bottles and drank to a superb holiday.

Actors one and all, we would forget the bad times and remember only the good, with luck.

The sun was hovering over the horizon and I hoped-for fair-weather sailing from now on. It was the end of May and June would bring better weather. There was general euphoria. We were off on another adventure. Patrick was the most euphoric, the most pleased of all. He would be off the boat within a few hours, elements willing.

No wonder he was so keen to celebrate.

Once we were clear of the marina, we headed for the harbour wall. Norman rushed forward, dived into the hatch, and brought out a bag. He unfurled the jib, attached the clips, and hauled it up. We had been talking and it was only when the sail was halfway up that we noticed it was his brand-new nylon racing-jib.

This man was in a hurry. The foresail transformed the boat. It was true that the mainsail was the same grubby, sea-stained, grey canvas it had always been, but Waterwitch was wearing her best coat, which turned her into a Technicolor dreamboat.

We would be passing the customs house with our white side showing the fully painted port hull. This, with the flowing lines of the thirty-square metre blue and yellow racing jib, would create quite an impression. We downed the three other beers.

The wind was strong enough for us to cut the motor now.

At six knots, helm steady and lashed to the sailing horse on the bench, we headed with full sail past the harbour entrance.

Our reception committee from two nights ago was still on duty, about to be relieved and we stood to attention and saluted the English Ensign that flowed above the customs house. In turn our saviours, who had brought us back in under power, saluted and then, raising their caps above their heads, waved us off.

We were Irish but we were proud to be sailing under the English flag and grateful for the warm reception we had just had.

Stories had been circulating about Spaniards putting broken glass in English tourists' beer to show their solidarity with their Argentinean cousins and to make clear their distaste of British foreign policy, forgetting that it was the Argentineans who had invaded.

We knew our presence might not be welcome, so for good measure when we hauled down the Union Jack, the courtesy flag for British Dominion waters, we hoisted not only the Spanish flag, but also the Irish tricolour.

We were fellow republicans when it suited us and loyal subjects of the Crown at any other time. We were not interested in the politics of Ireland, nor did we wish anything but peace around the world.

We were Irish from the Republic; whatever happened in Northern Ireland was beyond our control and we certainly didn't support any faction, but we were proud of our heritage, even though England had been our birthplace, our home and the source of our good health and education.

We had enough problems, however without being persecuted for flying the Red Ensign.

The gods were smiling on us. All the prayers to the various maritime saints were answered and we had a pleasant, smooth, and fairly quick cruise.

It was not far to Puerto de La Duquesa and we had made good time. After all, it was the next stop along the coast from Gibraltar; even we could not miss it.

Patrick was already packed, and we tied up at eleven o'clock.

It was an emotional farewell, not least because I would be on my own again. We shook hands and patted each other on the back, vowing we would never forget this trip and smiling as we said how much fun it had been.

As an aside to me, Patrick wished me luck with 'old crabby Ahab', and we laughed because he had not been as bad as we had portrayed him. He had helped us to survive and given us a memorable and mostly enjoyable experience. Our expectations of him were unfairly high. We wanted him to be superhuman and he was, like us, merely mortal.

Patrick and I walked up the road through the deserted and desolate apartment buildings. One Spanish cleaner swept the steps.

All the blinds were drawn.

This was a ghost town - no one was here. The time-share owners would be out in July and August. It was soulless but added to this bleakness was the feeling that this was removed from reality.

There was really nothing Spanish about it, the design perhaps, but there were no real people there. No shops, no bars, no cafes, no squares; it was a block of whitewashed landscaped concrete.

It was then I remembered the real people we had met along the way: the Mozambique camp with the smiling Africans; the friendly Portuguese that one found only outside Vilamoura, in the nearby town, in Olhao and Portimao; the warm smiles and friendly welcome of the fishermen and cafe owners in Spain.

That had been real, and I realised how much I had taken for granted, yet again.

I had been fortunate indeed to have seen the real Portugal, the real Spain, and not be limited by an apartment where the maid and the fittings are the only authentic Spanish items in the whole place.

The buildings looked as if they had more snagging to undergo, they were so recently built, and the driveway into the complex had not even been started. It was a dust track that led us up to the road, so new was this development, and it explained why these apartments had not been let out. Even a complex like this needs life, laughter, voices, the giggles or screams of people having fun in the sun. Patrick was planning to hitch hike to the nearest town, bus it to the nearest train station and take a train to Tavira and on to Faro.

From there a taxi would take him to the airport. It was ambitious and after an hour in the sweltering beat, he decided to phone for a cab. Norman came up the hill and he decided the best option was to rent a car. He would drive Patrick to the border. He knew exactly where the ferry terminal was and on the other side of the river was a train station that would bring Patrick directly to Faro. It was settled.

Fortunately, we could rely on the marina master to keep an eye on the boat. There was one office in the complex, which dealt with services, and, by a stroke of great good fortune, it was also the offices of the car rental agent for the area. He picked us out a sporty Fiesta. Patrick's maturity allowed him to think that it was a safe option, but when it was revealed that the only person able to drive (due to holding an international licence) was Norman, the agent's broad smile weakened.

It was too late for him to change his mind. We put pressure on him; saying that we really wanted a white car, knowing all he had was the blue sports version. Being apologetic at once, he forgot his reservations and handed over the keys. Patrick paid him off with his travel funds and we promised to have the car back by the same time the following morning.

Patrick, being, by nature of cautious disposition, offered to sit in the back. I fastened my seatbelt, said a prayer, and pretended that it was the law to wear one's seatbelt even in a relaxed country like Spain. Norman had left Britain before the wearing of seat belts had become compulsory and gave me a derogatory look, as if to say, don't you trust me?

Norman used to ride motorbikes and drive cars on the edge. To him a car of any size was a sports model, and basically a bike on four wheels. If it had been physically possible to do a 'wheelie' with a car or to lean into the corners, then he would have done so. Clutching his bag for protection,

Patrick smiled weakly at me as I turned my head to see if there were seatbelts in the back. There were not. I think Norman saw his timid smile of resignation in the rear-view mirror, because I saw him smile too after glancing up, before driving off.

He eased out on to the tarmac off the dust track, just to be out of sight of the car rental office. Then he smiled again as he checked his wing mirrors for any following traffic.

A quick glance showed me that the road ahead and behind was clear, as clear as a runway and it might as well have been.

Norman stamped his foot hard on the accelerator and the rev counter and speedometer flashed up along the dial. We moved with a sudden lurch of power thrown back into our seats by the G-force of take-off, I couldn't see how fast we were going, but the engine strained and the white arm of the rev counter was almost on red.

He depressed the clutch and slipped into second, stamping his foot hard down again.

Pressed back in our seats for the second time, we waited for third, but Norman went straight into fourth, floored the pedal and changed up into fifth. I didn't even know we had fifth gear and had only been in one car before that had a five-speed gearbox. I leant over nonchalantly to check the cigar lighter worked.

At least, I pretended to; in fact, I was leaning over to get a good look at the speedometer. We were doing ninety already. Ahead the road shimmered.

I shivered and Patrick looked white.

I noticed that his smile was now even slighter when I turned again to ostensibly offer him a cigarette, but also to check on him. He no longer clutched the bag, but clutched it to his chest, as if he were a parachutist whose main parachute had gone, and this was his reserve.

He would not let anyone get it or let it go.

'I'm in no rush,' he murmured weakly.

'Nor am I,' Norman replied, eyes flashing.

'Good, I'm glad I'm wearing my brown trousers today.'

'How do you feel, Finn, about this speed?' he asked me, involving the adjudicator again.

This time it was my turn.

'I feel fine about it,' I said, not wishing to upset the driver, knowing full well that he would only press the car harder if pushed.

'I'm just a nervous passenger, that's all,' Patrick replied rather sheepishly, perhaps deciding, as I had, that it was not a point worth pursuing.

'You're more than welcome to drive,' Norman suggested sweetly.

'No, no, you're doing fine, a great job, I really appreciate the lift, I'll just take in the view.'

A straight road at speed is never too much of a problem, as long as your tyres don't blow and you do not meet any traffic coming the other way, especially if it is a farm truck being overtaken by an underpowered Seat.

We experienced that once and were relieved that the rollercoaster that we were in also had brakes that worked proficiently. For the majority of the time the road was clear. Nothing could catch us from behind except a motorcycle cop and even he would have had difficulty.

Ahead we passed few cars as it was a market day and all the traffic had travelled to the local town way before we had left our boat. Those not at market were not using the roads, thankfully. Speed kills, but you get used to driving fast and Norman was a competent and experienced driver.

He was familiar with the Fiesta, and he had driven a wide range of different cars. It was not he that we were afraid of, but other traffic or a tractor pulling out from a junction without seeing us.

Regardless, he sped on.

Naturally, he moderated his speed in the villages and towns that the road cut through, but once outside the city limits, if the road was straight enough, then he would floor the accelerator pedals.

Braking was less the application of the brake pedal, more moving through fourth, third and second, using the engine's braking speed rather than its disc brakes.

If we had stayed on the flat that day, we would have been fine, scared, but fine.

However, as ever, plains gave way to hills. Thankfully, they did not give way to mountains.

Norman was really enjoying himself.

He had driven for two hours flat out, and I felt that I needed some refreshment, preferably alcoholic, so that I could obliterate the whole experience.

Even a coffee and some food would have brought some comfort. I have always been a comfort-eater; if depressed I can eat ravenously.

When things go well, food is not even on the agenda until the acids burn a hole in my stomach, at which stage a piece of toast will suffice. There may well be a case for arguing that so many people enjoy food for this reason and that obesity is now a problem with so many societies because of comfort-eating.

One can't help but wonder if some of the budget of an over-large family went to the starving around the globe, perhaps the feel- good factor would make people eat less; at least then they would be feeding people and feel that they were making a difference in this world.

On a personal level, control was being wrested from me. Norman refused to stop.

He didn't need coffee, he asserted, and he wanted to 'break the back of the journey'.

It was quite obvious from our protestations that we did not want our backs broken into the bargain. With almost demonic resolve, Norman pressed the accelerator. Patrick wanted to get his flight if he could - any revolt from that corner may have resulted in him walking to the next town.

Arguing was not on my agenda either. He could drive like a maniac for all I cared; I just wanted him to be nice for the rest of the trip. This solidarity did nothing to mollify Patrick, but it did keep him quiet. All we needed was to have him whimpering in the back like a frightened puppy. The fun had just begun, although we did not know it. Only one person in the car was determined to break for the border and he was driving.

Patrick just wanted to make it home in one piece and I was beginning to wonder whether my traumatic experiences in the storm were really that bad after all.

The road, visible in the distance, rose into the foothills of south-western Spain. It was an area of outstanding beauty not known by many visitors to Spain since they favoured the sand and sea in the southeast.

We headed for Seville.

Gibraltar had been in view from the start of our journey, a big black rock visible out of Norman's window, but we soon left it behind. I could not work out why we had to go to Seville before reaching Tavira, but my brother's Michelin map showed me there were few coast roads between our berth and the border.

Just before rising into the foothills, the road twisted along the coast, hugging a rock outcrop for a few miles. There was a radio that failed to pick up anything, least of all the BFBS broadcast from Gibraltar. The silence was punctuated by odd comments made every few miles or so.

'That was incredible, seeing those whales,' Patrick had ventured early on. The canvas cover of his bag was squeezed out of shape.

'Yeah,' Norman agreed; he had seen more than twice his fair share of marine mammals. The comment, any comment, seemed to make him drive faster. The accelerator moved nearer the floor.

I noticed this and therefore remained silent.

Another ten miles along the road, Patrick's white knuckles had become cramped and so his hands lay over the bag, as though keeping it in place.

Patrick tried another tack. 'Thank you for having me along.'

The only trouble was he sounded like he was praying and had stopped praying out loud halfway through.

This is how the prayer came across: 'Hail Mary, thank you for being so gracious, but I need you to help me some more; dear Saint Christopher, thank you for keeping me safe, but now the wolves are closing in around my campfire, please, look after me, now more than ever.' Patrick seemed to be saying, 'Thank you for having me, but can I get home in one piece.'

It might as well have been a plea for mercy from a Morisco to a particularly nasty Spanish Inquisitor. Norman's left leg muscle twitched, and his left foot stepped that little bit more on the pedal.

When we reached the twisty mountain road that led into the hills, Patrick threw all caution to the wind in an effort to distract Norman from driving and therefore force him to lower his speed. The black tarmac twisted like a snake along the line of the steep rocks and became an endurance course for driver and car.

Like the Monte Carlo Rally, there were plenty of opportunities for the driver's skills to be revealed through the chicanes.

Patrick and I were hurled about in our seats as Norman put the tiny car through its paces. If we did crash, there would be little protection for any of us. Our driver thrived on danger. Never once did he apply the brakes. Where the more faint-hearted would have stamped on theirs, my brother just span the wheel and slipped into second.

'These coastal roads are amazing,' Patrick tried one more time. 'It's just like southern California.'

You could almost hear him thinking that the speed limit over there was fifty-five. Norman just grunted, whacked the gear lever into third and grimaced. This was tricky work, he wanted to put body and soul into winding along the coast and reaching the summit in the hills.

He had a look of grim determination rooted to his face; his arms at ten to two, though bent, were flexed, showing that his hands had a tight grip around the small steering wheel.

His right hand darted out at the beginning and end of each corner, first to shift into second to brake into the bend, and then to change up into third for a fraction of a second, before jabbing the gear lever into second again as we approached the next bend. Driving on gears is a noisy and strenuous method of driving, particularly if you do not know the road ahead. It takes great skill, which our driver possessed.

On several occasions, as we wound our way up into the hills, Norman misjudged the depth of a corner or his own speed, and we saw shale skidding up from the side of the tarmac. Going up the hill was not so bad, because I was on the side closest to the hill and so I could not see the edge; but as we drove down the other side the road was exposed.

Three times we left the road as it twisted toward sea level, and I had a great view outside my window as we neared the edge. Only a miracle kept us from being hurled from the hill and smashed on to the plains below.

For my part I had tried every tactic to get Norman to slow down - offering cigarettes, coffee, sweets, saying that I needed to go to the loo, all of which landed on deaf ears. Norman needed to concentrate and that's what he would do. His replies were often grunted, but I understood that they were in the negative.

Eventually even I realised that nothing would distract him, and nothing would encourage him to go any slower. The absorption in his task was admirable. I cannot say we were in particular danger all the time.

Just like on the boat, the potential danger was more of a worry than the actual threat. Apart from the many times we almost lost the road, plus the three times when the back wheels skidded and slewed the rear end out, we were never in great peril.

The fact that the Fiesta was front-wheel drive saved us on several occasions, the back wheels having lost all traction and spun off the tarmac. We were dragged back on to the road by the power in the front wheels.

Patrick and I were grateful that the mountains were not higher than they were. After half an hour of being thrown about in a small car, we were heartily fed up.

If he had driven fast, we would not have minded; but he was driving recklessly. Patrick had moved his bag to give himself something to be thrown against rather than the side of the car.

We had smoked on the plains, but here we just took in the cool mountain air.

Lack of nicotine jangled the nerves of the passengers. It would have been a serious danger even to attempt to light a cigarette and smoking it would have been impossible. I was strapped in by my seat belt and still I felt like my bottom was sliding all over the place. Mutinous rumblings started to issue forth from the pair of us.

He had gone just too far.

This time we made a concerted effort against him. We were no longer the Three Musketeers.

We persuaded Norman to stop for a coffee at the bottom of the hill. We drank it hot and sweet for our nerves and I found room in my stomach for several toasted sandwiches.

The curling mountain road had almost finished me off. I did not want this type of danger. It is all right to see it in an adventure film, but to experience it is quite another matter, just as seeing a storm in a film can never compare in any shape or form with the real event.

Finally, I realised that my brother was not trying to kill me.

He was trying to send me mad, so he could disinherit me. Once insane, he could help himself to my riches, a competent portable stereo cassette player and three lamb's wool jumpers.

It became clear now that it was these he wanted, and his greatest wish was to drive me around the bend by driving me around the bends.

At first, I thought Patrick was in on the whole caper, but his pale complexion and worried look convinced me that Norman was working alone. Perhaps he wished to drive both Patrick and I mad. He might not stop there.

The only other event on the journey to the border that my psyche has enabled me to remember was crossing over the steel bridge in Seville and cutting up the lorry drivers as we drove along.

Norman drove in a continental fashion, the type of aggressive or assertive style that is encouraged in Latin countries and frowned upon in the UK. In truth he drove brilliantly, managing to scoot through Seville, a busy and choked city.

We were able to get from one side of the city to the next and to the border in record time. It was only then that he wanted something to eat and drink. For four hours he had put his all into getting us to the border. As we waved Patrick farewell, I admired Norman's resolve and tenacity.

Chapter Eighteen – Just the Two of Us

The journey back took five hours, not four, and Norman even allowed me to drive on the way back. I was now convinced our fraternal friendship was on a different plain. For the first time in our lives, we were treating one another as equals, both entitled to the same amount of respect.

The suffering of the first month had been worth it in order to find ourselves at this state.

Patrick and I had got on well, in fact better than before, and I think the same could be said for Norman and Patrick. The important part was that my brother and I, traditional rivals, were now seeing each other as mates. It was brilliant.

I am not sure what sparked it off.

Perhaps, it was seeing Patrick depart that convinced Norman that he did not really have that bad a crew member on board. You have to remember that I had already had four weeks experience beforehand in Greece, dinghy sailing from the age of sixteen and experience in Portugal with Norman.

Patrick had taken the car ferry from England to France, and he had been on the ferry from Fishguard to Rosslare. He also knew the front end of the boat was the bow, the back the stern and that the sides were port and starboard, but he was not sure which was which.

I could not fail to shine. Patrick had made even me look good. There was also the added bonus that there was more room on board. Patrick was sorely missed, for he gave us an extra rest between watches. But he would have been missed more on a larger boat where he didn't get in the way so much. That was the problem with having three on board. The boat only really required a two-man crew and only one person to pull in the mainsail, which could be done from the helm since the sailing horse was attached to the bench seat in front of the helm.

In fact, for those as experienced at sailing as Norman, it was quite possible to sail her single-handed over great distances. The third member of the crew therefore was often of no use. If the third could make coffee and go to their bunk and take over watches in the night then that was fine, but they also need to breathe the briny air and take in the sun.

The cockpit, when sailing, had become crowded with three sat there and tacking became even more of a problem. Generally, you had your own head to look out for, ducking as the boom came around, warning of the boom coming, to give your shipmate a chance to duck as you pushed the tiller either away or towards you, and crossing over to the opposite side, taking up the slack on the jib rope before you tightened up the mast on the sail horse, by pulling in the boom cables. The two of you could then sit on the bench and look ahead to your course.

With three people on board, the whole difficult dance became interrupted by another object to traverse around. No matter where they were, they would be in the way, if they were on the deck or on the cabin roof, sailing necessitates movement.

Only when the superfluous member of the crew was in the cabin making coffee or asleep could they be considered well and truly out of the way. Unfortunately, one cannot be sent to bed or to make coffee every time the boat has to perform a tack. There was room for three down below, but for three small people who were prepared to crouch down all the time.

The main cabin was the true sleeping area. The benches that doubled as beds, with their curved seats that followed the round of the bow and always made sleeping difficult, were a temporary and ad hoc extra accommodation, I am sure that when she was racing there were three on board, but one was at the chart table plotting courses and smoking a pipe.

We were not racing and were not used to spending extended periods down below. To sleep there was fine, but once awake you wanted to be up and in the sunshine. Waterwitch was ideally suited for the cold weather of England and Scandinavia, in which areas we all would have wanted to huddle in the cabin below, but on this holiday, we wanted sunshine and three people in the cockpit with the boom, its ropes, the mainsail and the jib rope made for too much of a crowd. I am sure that Norman was glad to have his crew back to a manageable size.

Watching Patrick and his schoolboy errors had boosted my ego. I was a damn fine crewmember, no matter what others thought. Norman was very fortunate to have me, and it was he, not I, who should be grateful. So far on this trip it had been I who had felt grateful and beholden to Norman, which allowed him to walk all over me. That was in the past though. Now I looked forward to a period of mutual respect.

That evening we parked the car by the offices and returned to the boat, unlocked the small padlock that kept the hatch closed and wearily sat down in the gloom of two hurricane lamps. No matter what weather we had outside, as soon as you went below it was winter and this was your cosy refuge, a small, dim lit place like a cave, a Hobbit hole if you like.

Most families would have found the cave too cosy, too small, but we liked it once we were sat down. The chart table doubled as a dining table in harbour, so it was left set up for either purpose, although it could be folded neatly away when we were at sea. I spread the clean tablecloth across the top.

It was surprising how long the bread stayed fresh if it was kept in a supermarket plastic bag; although we had bought it almost two days ago in Gibraltar, it was still soft and pliable even if the texture had got a little heavier. We had a selection of cold meats and cheeses, which I spread about the cloth, butter was still a luxury and the soft cheeses that we had bought would have to serve as substitutes.

For the first time in ages, we had fruit on board: apples and oranges.

Norman got hold of a couple of reasonably clean glasses, we did all our dish washing in a green bucket with cold fresh water and plenty of detergent. The washed articles would be allowed to drain. Occasionally we wiped them dry with the one dish cloth on board but often that was so damp, or dirty, that it hardly seemed worth the bother.

Norman prised open the plastic lid from the wine bottle. He had managed to find an old bottle of Portuguese wine, and, in our time-honoured tradition, he diluted it with some lemonade. The glasses were not tall, but they took more than most restaurants' wine glasses. The lemonade was added to take away the rough taste of the vinho. It was a symbolic celebration. We were back on our own again just as we had been when I first arrived.

The meal and the drink were so similar to my first one on board. For the first time, since before Patrick's arrival, my brother and I chatted.

We talked about the voyage so far, who was coming out to Ibiza to meet us, how long they would be staying and what they were doing in London at the time.

My brother had always been very kind, allowing me to come along with him when he went for a drink in town, encouraging his friends to meet me. Most of them appeared to be women, which was pleasant for me. They were that much older and knew so much more than I did and talked about art and literature.

He had always looked after me.

He had always been good to me.

I could not believe that I had thought anything but good of him. Time after time he had invited me out to drinks and to parties and now, he had asked me to help sail his boat.

For the first month I had acted like a truculent, spoilt child. Every movement that he had made had carried with it a negative connotation.

It was unfair that I should have perceived him as overbearing and it was unfair that I had teased him with the connivance of my brother Patrick, calling him Ahab.

He had feelings too and he was in fact much more sensitive a person than either Patrick or I.

As Patrick's plane headed out across the Portuguese coast, heading northeast towards England, I was glad that the premier crew were back in action. It was just the two of us, the old tars. The tourist had been and gone.

We had shown him a good time and he had gone home happy, even if he had been shaken a little by the journey in the rental car.

He had wanted to be in time for his flight and Norman had guaranteed that he made it. Thankfully, Norman's driving, on the way back, was a lot slower and calmer. His mission had been accomplished and he could relax.

He even had five or six cigarettes on the way back. He had denied himself this luxury for the whole day while he focused on seeing Patrick safely to his plane. When we had driven back, the sky had been a dark blue and clear of clouds.

I knew tomorrow would be a gorgeous day. It had been a warm windless night and we drove along the road with our windows open and occasionally our arms hanging over the door, even more seldom a handheld a cigarette in the gentle breeze.

As we drank and talked that night we reminisced about the good old days. We had been at school together since I was seven and he was nine.

He had moved up a school and left me behind but made sure that when I did follow him through the next school, my way had been paved by him.

My brother had given me my first driving lesson and my first go on a motorbike. The fact that I crashed it was not his fault. We were riding it in a forest.

It was a monster of a Triumph 650, six hundred and fifty cubic centimetres of raw untamed power. My body shook due to the juddering vibrations of the bike underneath me. I was only fifteen at the time and the sheer size and thumping sound that carne from the bike scared me.

Norman had been riding it for half an hour already, so it was warmed up. I brought the revs up and the noise felt deafening. I wore no crash helmet,

'No need in this glade,' it was argued.

I was never sure how he could afford the bike but not a crash helmet. Easing the clutch out, already in first gear, my hand must have slipped, and the clutch opened.

The high revs trans- mitted the power straight to the gearbox and from there straight to the chain; the back wheel spun on the mud and then the back end of the bike swung out.

Within a second, the bike had churned up an arc of brown mud. The bike collapsed underneath me, wrenched away by the spinning wheel.

At first, I was still upright, then I was on the ground watching the bulk of the bike spin away from me. That was when I went into shock.

I wandered around dazed.

The bike lay on its side, the rear drive wheel still spinning, the engine still roaring.

My brother's prompt action was to throw me on to the ground and tell me to stay there while he went to check the bike and switch it off, He sat beside me as I got my breath back and regained some semblance of composure.

Lying there I remembered how everything had gone into slow motion, as the bike slipped from between my legs and wrested itself from my grip. I fell, but immediately got up, a purely instinctive reaction, because the best place for me was the ground. I just watched for much of the rest of the afternoon as my brother and his friend scrambled along a hardly used path. Later that day, I went on the bike again.

Then, and on subsequent weekends, I took things easy and treated the bike with respect, and, in turn, had no more accidents.

As we drove over the Sierra Morena and the foothills of the Sierra Nevada, there were times when the scene outside my window or in front of the windscreen also went into slow motion, but each time a shifting of gears or a jab at the accelerator provided our escape.

It was a long way down and that car would have been broken in two if we had left the road; but in a way, as always, I trusted my brother and as ever in these truly dangerous situations, he always came up trumps.

I would not however, subsequently, put myself deliberately into any dangerous situation with him, just to show how reliable he was. But at the time, luck was on our side, and he always came up trumps.

Chapter Nineteen - From Estepona to Malaga

Rising early, we trudged up to the office, put the documents and keys through the letterbox and checked the car over one last time. She was dusty and there were marks on the dust where stones had been thrown up, but she was not dented, and the ashtray had been emptied. She had survived, despite being driven close to the edge in more ways than one.

We were anxious to get going. After paying our mooring fees for the night, it was a question of preparing Waterwitch for sea. Everything was stowed, including the chart table; the lag was folded under the tabletop, and it was swung on its hinge to lie flush with the wall that divided the master cabin from the main cabin.

We rolled up our mattresses and bedding.

There was no telling what the weather would be like, but already the day had started with a dismal, grey, heavy stratus filling the sky.

It did not bode well.

The racing jib was stowed in the forward hatch, slightly ahead of the end of the main bunk, my brother's double bed. Mine was not only a single, but it was also a small single, two feet across at its widest, and then curving upwards towards the deck with the rest of the belly of the boat.

The flaps, the two-foot-wide boards that I have mentioned, were often the only prevention from falling out of bed and often when the boat was heeled over, I slept in the 'v' that the bed and board made.

It was an unsettling experience to wake with a sensation of falling to find yourself supported just by a two-foot plank, two small bolts and two small hinges.

The angle of the boat led to your weight being distributed unevenly, between solid bunk and fragile plank, the plank getting the majority. Then it was impossible to move - to shift could well break the plank.

On several occasions I had called Patrick down to help me.

On other occasions I had reached out for some purchase. If I was in a good position, I might be able to free my arm and grab hold of part of the bunk, one of the wooden slats that criss-crossed along the frame, a lattice of strips of wood that would be revealed once the mattress slid from on top of them.

This mattress was an inch of thin foam covered with cloth; my brother's was two or three inches thick with a canvas cover.

The mattress moved with you and therefore made any solid movement difficult - it was a slippery mat underneath you. Several times I had to lie still in that 'v' groove because my arms were not in a position to reach up and grab any part of the bunk.

I drifted off back to sleep in that position and awoke later to find that we were on a different tack, and I had rolled with my mat mattress almost completely up the wall of the cabin, my mouth inches from the underside of the deck as we were keeled over so much.

Next to my ear I could hear the water running, not underneath me as usual, or beside me as often was the case, but right next to and all around me. I would have been submerged in the water, but for the wooden skin all around me.

During the day, my bench bed became a storage area for stowing spare sheets, anchors, ropes, coats, and anything else that we might need. The other bench was left purely for navigation with all the instruments that might be needed to plot a course -and the marvellous Michelin map.

Norman was busy in the bow swapping the racing jib for the cruising rig. I saw him put his hand on the storm jib, but he hesitated. He rolled both bags out on to his bunk, but it was the standard cruising jib that he chose. The storm jib might be tempting fate just too much.

My new outlook on life coloured all the tasks that I did that day. We had showered in the dock showers. The water was not that warm, running as it did from a solar-powered heat exchanger, but it was warm which encouragingly meant that they had already had better weather here in the Med than we had had in the Atlantic.

My razor was too blunt and my stubble too thick for shaving to be a possibility, but I brushed my teeth so well that they shined.

The beard would stay, and I would flash a smile instead of a sword, a modern-day buccaneer. I say my stubble was too thick, but the whole effect was rather pathetic.

After a month, I had little blond hairs that made my beard look like a false one, as if I had not shaven for a day or two. Annoyingly there were gaps in the beard. It was not full fuzz, more a faux fuzz.

Furthermore, different parts of the beard grew at different times and therefore needed trimming every so often. I had seen Norman do this on still nights or when we were becalmed. It looked both awkward and dangerous.

I knew I could not shave every day, that would be a task impossible to keep up, but my beard itched often, and it felt rough. The sun had bleached my hair, my eyebrows, and my beard, but it still made me feel grubby.

Once the boat was readied, my brother did one last inspection. Going to the front, he checked the forestays that supported the foresail. He inspected the shrouds and the mast, the former by physically pulling on them, the latter visibly by looking to the crow's nest.

Returning to the deck, he checked the rudder was free by moving the helm from left to right, port to starboard that is.

The sailing horse with its pulleys and ropes was attached to the front of the bench and he checked the screws that secured it to the wooden plank we liked to call our navigation bench, or our bridge. Then he checked the huge wooden pulley wheels. They moved freely. We were ready to go from a sailing point of view.

Lastly, he pulled out the engine from under the aft housing and strapped the British Seagull on to the boat. Two deadeyes, set up in a vertical fashion, accepted the two prongs that protruded from the nearside of the engine.

I had lifted the engine once, finding it to be too heavy, its long metal tube being made of thick steel. This made it awkward to mount, often taking two or three attempts.

You had to struggle with the heavy black engine cowling at the top, covering the two-stroke motor; then with the thick steel pole that covered the drive shaft and housed the exhaust; then there were the three nine-inch propeller blades, again made of heavy steel.

You had to haul this monstrosity over the side, and then, leaning over yourself, you had to line up the two deadeyes with the two prongs, the engine becoming heavier and more difficult to handle all the time.

I was relieved and pleased when my brother managed to attach the engine on the second attempt. I had often taken five or six goes and only ended up exhausted and frustrated.

I thought the engine was scarcely worth bothering with. In truth, I was amazed at how so small a unit could push three tons of boat through the water at such speed and so effortlessly.

Waterwitch was a slim lady. She glided everywhere she went - even the smallest of breezes would move her. She would sail even on the tail wind from a gossamer wing.

Norman had spent money on fixing her and was never one to shell out in vain. He would get the usage he wanted from the engine and make up for her previous inactivity.

I cast off at the back, as he breathed life into the motor by pressing buttons, pulling chokes, and moving levers to open up both oil and petrol valves. He was an expert on the mixing of oil and petrol from his motorbike days.

He pressed the starter motor and the engine popped, rather than purred, into life and as it chugged, he gave me the signal to cast off at the front.

Dutifully, the order was complied with. The rope was untied and a push from the shore for good measure moved the boat out of the moorings. A quick leap with my legs and I was on board, my hands still holding on to the bow rail.

This port was deserted, save for one small boat tucked into the corner of the marina. I sauntered back to the aft of the boat, to fend off at the back, or to take the helm. Waiting to be given further instructions,

I looked across at my brother. Norman smiled at me, clanked the motor into forward and drove around in a wide arc to the harbour entrance. This was a man-made dock and a small one at that. Our next stop was Estepona, which we hoped to reach by nightfall.

That day turned out to be a glorious day's sailing, tacking to the southeast as ever, the wind came over our port beam, lifting the outboard motor out of the water.

Waterwitch reached ten knots at one stage, but generally she cruised at between eight or nine knots, flat out as far as I was concerned.

Norman, of course, said that he had often been up to twelve knots in her and that fifteen knots was the fastest speed that he had ever managed to get her to go. I felt positive that he exaggerated, but I was not in a position to refute his claim.

The wind was warm and strong.

I imagined that he must have been in quite a storm to get her to go faster than ten knots and even then, it would be uncomfortable. Her rear section was only ever two feet above the water line when the boat was on an even keel.

There was a length of deck and then the cockpit which had a lip around to prevent water coming in over the side, but if the wind was high, so would the waves be, and as we sailed along that day at ten knots, water was lapping over the deck and splashing into the hold.

The bilge pump was located on the outside cabin wall and in such choppy waters, or when sailing at speeds, the bilges would flood. Therefore, we took it in turns every quarter of an hour to pump out the bilges.

It was a mechanical and rhythmical task. The resistance increased as water came though the pipe and then decreased once the bilges were clear and you were left pumping air. The pump was a galvanised rubber sack, shaped like a disc, pinned to the wall. A steel rod coming from the centre with a rubber handle that pointed heavenward.

By grasping the rubber handle you pulled the rod away from the disc to suck up the water. Returning the rod to the vertical expelled the water out of the side of the hull, below the waterline. Like rowing an ancient galleon, a gentle methodical rhythm was maintained so that you could last the seven to ten minutes it took to clear the bilges.

If you have ever handled a beer pump, you have some idea of what the process involved. I often changed hands halfway through because the constant pumping left me with cramps in my hands and arms.

You could change your grip but that sacrificed your pumping power, so it was best to be constant and get the job done properly, rather than lengthen the process by changing rhythm, grip, or speed. Already, within the space of a month, our biceps were bulging.

We tacked northeast and the wind kept us on course. It was not until late afternoon, twenty miles from our destination, as we shadowed the coast that led to the harbour at Estepona that the wind let us down.

No matter how often we tacked, it was difficult to make progress.

Five miles out to sea and seven miles from our safe haven, at six o'clock in the evening, Norman restarted the engine. It growled into life and took us towards some fishing buoys. The plan was to motor to a set point from which we could set a tack, which would bring us into Estepona harbour under sail.

At the entrance we would start the engine and drop the sails. Halfway to the starting position the engine spluttered and died, never to work again.

We never found out what it was that caused the engine to fail, but the wind was rising, and we had to make a heading for shore.

Neither of us fancied a night out at sea.

The stratus blanket that we had seen at the start of the day was still with us and there was no means of telling whether overnight a storm would brew or whether the sun would come out. We had got fairly cold and damp out to sea, with the spray and the cool wind. We both wanted something hot to eat.

We gybed and headed for the shore.

The ropes flapped in the wind. As evening fell, it felt as if the wind was becoming icy. We were wearing our storm clothes, but our hands and feet were cold. The boat actually hit twelve knots, which elated us both, but it was only for a three-minute run.

We could not take up a berth in the harbour itself. Sailing in was treacherous and the wind had risen so much that we felt there was a gale about to start. Instead, we headed for the beach to the north of the town, where we hove to and brought down the sails.

We had our main anchor out and for safety's sake we had rigged up the aft anchor for good measure.

The time spent on land, driving around, had reminded us how much we missed terra firma, so we were glad when we secured the boat, and my brother rowed our tiny fender on to the beach. I had with me a towel and I wore my street shoes around my belt, tied by their laces.

My jeans were rolled up and I stepped out of the cold wind and into the warm water as we approached the shore. I waded along pulling the tender by its fender until it was beached. My brother scrambled out and we hauled the boat right on to the shore, tied the fender to a shower post and headed for the bright lights of town.

Once off the beach I dried my feet and slipped on my shoes. I ran a comb through my hair and loosened my jacket.

We were both ready to eat and drink and the one thing we craved most was a packet of cigarettes. All day long we had managed without one single smoke. We were anxious now to make up for lost time.

It must have been nine o'clock when we found a restaurant that had a free table. It was Friday night, 4th June, no school tomorrow. Therefore, the young, accompanied by the young at heart, were crowding the restaurants of the main harbour square.

We started with tapas, vino and 'Ducados' cigarettes. Black inky squid, green hard olives, red wine on our tongues, black tobacco shrouding us and filling our lungs, luxury on a bar stool.

The fluorescent lights kept night at bay, and we scarcely remembered that we had a boat in a cold bay waiting for our return.

If I had had enough money perhaps, I would have paid for a hotel room and had a proper soak in a proper bath, ordered razors and had a shave, slept in clean sheets on a firm mattress.

However, I knew that would have defeated the whole object of the exercise. From now on to find refuge on shore would only be an emergency measure, a last resort when all our food had gone or there was no water.

We would stock up with enough provisions for five days and sail out to sea for three days minimum. We could smoke once ashore but for the three days or more at sea, no tobacco products of any sort, pipe, cigar, or cigarette were allowed on board.

This we decided over a large glass of port and some local cheese, as we looked into our small saucer ashtray, which we had managed to fill again. I attempted to count the white butts that lay crushed on the white china, but I did not care, and I could hardly count.

Before I knew it, I had agreed to all these conditions of sail, yet it was not my idea. (I know it should be conditions of sale, by the way).

My brother had made all these suggestions. The wine and port eased my assent, but I had no real intention or compunction of following this through. My brother had my verbal agreement though. I could not go back on that.

How would I survive at sea without cigarettes? How would I cope with being away from shore for two or three nights? This was no longer day sailing, it was touring.

Our touring holiday started with breakfast at a dockside bar with fresh anchovies, fried calamares and a tot of brandy. Already, the sun had risen, and it promised to be a fine day. At seven o'clock we had rowed back to land, the clear blue sky above, a cool blue sea all around.

The tide was low, so we beached the boat by rowing it up on a wave. I jumped out as the wave receded and raced the incoming wave up the beach. Needless to say, I won.

On the next wave, Norman moved forward to the front of the boat and as that returned down the beach, he leapt out and helped me to tow the boat as far up the beach as we could.

This time we took the fender rope and anchor chain and wrapped it around one of the shower poles. I tied a reef knot with the anchor chain and Norman tied a bowline with the fender rope.

Feeling rather stupefied, I followed Norman back to the boat. Over breakfast we had discussed our journey, a two-day tack out to sea followed by a day and half on another tack to bring us into the area of Malaga. I had been to that part of Spain only the year before and I was anxious to show my brother the opulence and wealth of the Malaga triangle, Marbella, Puerto Banus, and the Ronda.

These were areas favoured by Europe's wealthy.

It had been an eye-opener watching the yachting set preparing for an evening in Puerto Banus, their boats reversed into their berths, so that those visiting the marina could see their luxurious cabins and they could pose with ship-to-shore radio telephones, having cocktails in full view of all others.

The boats if not the people were beautiful, floating gin palaces, but brilliantly engineered and crafted. The wood and steel brought to life by marine architect and marine carpenters were fabulous.

The owners wanted to be seen, but they too shared an appreciation of the craftsmanship that their money had enabled them to buy.

I wondered how easy it would be to apply to be a crewmember on one of these motor yachts and what the penalty might be for jumping ship. I had outlined to my brother a little of what he might expect when we reached Marbella, but I did not want to spoil the surprise he might have when we arrived. Fortunate enough to have spent a few months on the Costa in 1980, I was pretty much current on the lay of the land. What could have changed in two years?

Meanwhile, life on board took on a new dimension.

We were no longer day-trippers, but real adventurers.

Even the Venetian fleet at the height of its glory stayed in harbour overnight. They in turn had used the same ports that the Romans had. It was not until into the seventeenth century that sailing at night could be considered a viable risk or a necessary expedient.

We were sailing at night, while most other so-called mariners were tucked up in their beds in harbour or mending their fishing boats.

Sailing at night is always an exciting prospect.

You did not know whom you might meet, smugglers, night fishermen or tankers. You never knew what you might hit either.

We had no charts of this part of the sea and that was why it was considered prudent to leave the coast and its dangerous outcrops and shallows, the currents that could dash you on to the rocks, or the odd undersea protuberances that could rip your hull open like a knife through butter.

I had batteries for my 'Walkman', so I could listen to that.

Maybe I should have kept my ears open for other shipping or for calls of danger, but we were far out to sea, with all three hurricane lanterns burning, one hoisted on the mast to light up our pathetically small green and red navigation lights.

Once the sun dropped and the midnight blue curtain of night fell all around us, we felt a certain peace.

There was the wash of water against our hull, the hiss of our wake, the odd strain of rope or creak of wood or thump of canvas, but apart from that all was stillness and peace.

Many times I sat, once my tape had ended, with my headphones around my neck listening to the night - the sound of the wind against our sails or the feel of it against my head or face, ruffling my hair; the noise of the mahogany hull forging its way through the yielding water, on and on, the spray swishing as the bow cut through; the murmur of waves hitting the hull with a dull thwack; the sound of waves as they lapped on the wood hull; the fizz of foam as it ran off tops of waves or off the top and sides of our wake.

From the rigging, the steel wire and aluminium mast shaking in the wind echoed the sound of a straining keel which you could hear deep in the bowels of the boat, mixed with the gurgling of water as the hull cleaved out its space in the ever-flowing water.

The slop of bilge water in the wooden bilges, below the floorboards, harmonised with the creak of the wooden planks as they expanded and contracted, either due to a change in temperature, our speed, or the sea conditions.

There were smells too from the pit of dirty, oily, bilge water, damp wood, dank musty clothes, briny water and damp wind, warm air, and hot wind.

Suddenly all my senses were more attuned; I was aware of the smells and sights around me. There was no longer a need for caffeine and a filter cigarette. These smells paled into insignificance against the new smells of adventure.

The sight of the embers of a glowing cigarette in the night could not compare with the sight of a full sail, a dark blue sky or the stars and the moon. It seemed the moon was rising earlier and earlier that year and I was sure I saw it had risen at four o'clock one afternoon.

This was back-to-nature stuff and back-to-reality sailing. We both became practised at holding on to the shrouds that led from the mainsail and carrying out our ablutions, there.

For extra privacy, the bar of the bow rail could be sat upon, but I tried it once and ended up with a photograph being taken as I was in the middle of my job. It was safer to sit over the side, thighs resting on the steel-wire handrail, hanging on to the mainsail shrouds.

That way you could check that the person at the tiller was still there, all the time, and not slipping down below to fetch his camera.

If that was the case, you had a chance to redress before the photographer returned. If it was rough outside, then the use of the bucket in the cabin down below was adequate.

It was not ideal.

Once finished, the idea was to throw the bucket over the side once its base was filled, the seawater would wash out the offending articles and clean the bucket. I tried this on one occasion when we were doing seven knots.

The first part of the operation went smoothly, but when I came to raise the bucket out of the water, I met with considerable resistance. I tried to prevent the sea running off with my bucket, which was full of seawater.

Determined to retrieve the bucket, I pulled hard on the rope, which only resulted in the handle being dislodged from the rest of the bucket.

It was a hollow triumph, hauling in a handle on the end of a piece of rope as our own black plastic bucket hurtled towards the seabed. I felt like shouting 'man overboard!'

However, as my brother had the helm and was standing directly beside me, the comment seemed superfluous.

He gave me an understanding look, as if to say it could happen to anyone. He reassuringly told me that he had lost a bucket like that under similar circumstances back in April.

I was relieved, glad also to recall that we had several buckets still left including one for storing nuts and bolts, which would become our new heads. I had already picked out a suitable container for the loose pieces of equipment.

One green bucket for the plates and dishes; designed for washing up; one for cleaning clothes in; and one for transferring water. They all had a letter or words on them to save mishap. The heads had a letter, 'H'; the washing up had the letters, 'WU'. With luck there was no way we could get anything confused and use the wrong bucket, perish the thought.

We had a green Jerry can that took fuel for the engine. During our first evening afloat on our tour, Norman had the engine in bits, examining another part that had snapped. This engine had not been well-maintained.

It was no wonder that another part had given out. Gibraltar should have been an excuse for a full overhaul or service to be carried out.

The engine was a victim of its own self- perpetuating myth; the engine was reliable and hardly ever went wrong. This meant that the whole thing could be neglected and although a part might be replaced every ten years, the likelihood of two parts wearing out together was slim.

I still maintain that if the engine had been well-looked after in its forty-five-year life then it would have lasted the trip. As it was, it could not last after decades of such constant abuse and neglect.

There were other Jerry cans, all-plastic, two clear ones, for fresh water and a third twenty-five litre oil container. That was the ballast and supplies. Added to that we had bread in a tin bread bin, cheese in a wooden drawer and booze of different types lying in the bilges wrapped in plastic bags.

We had few creature comforts, scant stores, basic sanitation, but we were sailing rough and sleeping rough - we could handle it.

The best time was bath-time. Even bearded sailors like us had to keep clean. I had never done this before, but after a while it seems the most wonderful experience. The first step is to rid yourself of a fear of sharks. It is true that sharks frequent the waters we were sailing in, but they are generally basking sharks, which cannot eat you.

At least that was what I was told by my brother.

It is difficult to plunge into the sea thirty, forty or fifty miles off the coast when you have read the book and seen the film Jaws. Peter Benchley's classic.

Mr. Benchley describes how sharks stalk humans and how they can pick up the thrashing of a foot over long distances.

There have been few sightings of great white sharks off the Spanish coast, but there have been some and people disappear off this coast as much as any other without explanation.

Who was to say that these disappearances were not linked to a killer shark in the vicinity? I could not allow myself to be frightened by the situation.

I baulked at the irony.

I had survived all that the sea and wind had been able to throw at me and now I was going to be gnawed to death by a basking shark or have one of my limbs severed from my body by some marine animal.

There are no first-aid boxes this far out to sea. Besides, ours contained a few plasters and an airline miniature bottle of brandy and one of blended whisky. There was not a coastguard chopper in sight, but neither to my immense relief was there a shark's black fin to be seen. Such sights are a bad omen to sailors, and a severe warning to bathers.

Norman made sure all the sails were furled and tied. We had picked this time of day because it seemed warmest.

The sun was at its height and a midday bathe seemed sensible before lunch. We had taken down both sails. I had folded up the jib and stowed it in its bag, bundling the whole though the hatch and into the forward hold which was, in effect, the forward cabin, too.

Fortunately, my brother had folded up his bedding and the bag bounced on the foam canvas-covered mattress. It was a warm day, and the bag was dry. The sunlight provided a warm bar of light to the inside of the cabin, which I shut off by closing the hatch.

It was fascinating to watch as my brother attached the sea anchor to a piece of rope and the piece of rope to part of the anchor housing.

By looping it through one of the dead- eyes and making a bowline knot in two ropes, my brother had rigged up the sea anchor, which was in effect a large canvas bag which was to stop us from drifting too far and too fast.

It looked like a partly closed sack, almost like a deflated but magnified sling shot.

Spinning the canvas bag like a lasso, he hurled it out into the water. It landed with a plop and duly sank. He hauled in the rope a bit and fastened it around the anchor guides on the bow. It bobbed in the distance, a distended and inflated sack, more like a jellyfish than an anchor.

My brother went below, and I heard a knocking on the forward hatch. Opening the lid, I was handed the special sea soap and the seawater shampoo through the gap. I was ordered to get ready for our bath. I hung up two towels on the wire handrail. We even had plastic clothes pegs on board for hanging out the washing.

I had stripped to my boxer shorts when Norman came up from below stark naked. With a leap he bounded on to the bench seat, hopped with one foot on to the deck and plunged feet first into the briny water.

There was no way that I would do the same.

We had rigged up a rope ladder, which was tied to the handrail. I had also managed to find a pair of goggles, so I threw the shampoo and soap to my brother. The bottle of shampoo he fielded and let it float in the water.

He was already making lather with the soap. I slipped off my shorts and pulled on my diving mask. With these goggles I could see underwater and therefore recognise any threat before it came to us. I slid down the rope steps.

Each rung of the ladder brought me closer to the cold sea. I braced myself as the chill swept over my feet. It was not choppy, but the waves were enough to wash over my ankles when I least expected it. I shivered and shuddered. I would die of hypothermia in these deep waters. They must be as cold as winter waters in the North Sea, I thought.

My brother, meanwhile, was merrily splashing around, attracting every shark in the vicinity with his impersonation of a marine animal in its death throes.

There he bobbed, lifting one leg out of the water to wash it, nonchalant and not a bit perturbed by the omnipresent and unobserved threat that could be heading our way at this very moment.

It was not in my nature to ignore any threat. I could not share my brother's devil-may-care attitude. I could not be oblivious to the danger under the water.

Every splash, every ripple registered as a danger signal. I would not be victim to a shark attack. I dipped my head under the water and saw a disgusting sight - the barnacled bottom of Waterwitch. She must have blushed at the dirty and clogged state she was in.

For the first time I saw the keel - an inverted fin, six feet deep and three or four feet along.

It looked so narrow and weak and sleek that I wondered how that, and the two anchors had stopped the boat from toppling when it ran aground in the mouth of Olhao harbour.

The memory of that night and the reminder of how far the water level had gone down and how much of the keel had been exposed made me wonder how I had survived without the boat tipping over.

I don't think I would have survived such a fall, being thrown against the cabin wall with such force. I had never really fully under- stood the impact of what might have happened had the boat collapsed on its keel, if one of the anchor ropes had snapped, or if the mast holding the anchor ropes had fractured.

I was just feeling great gratitude for my continued survival when I saw it.

I froze.

I had been treading water fiercely, but I slowed that down.

It was lying off the port bow, a horrid, white, billowing monster. At first, I thought it was a jellyfish, but it was too big for that. Then I thought it was a Portuguese Man of War, all threatening, stinging, filmy flesh. Instead, it was the canvas of the sea anchor.

I had by now had enough of keeping a lookout. It was chilly in the water. I did not want to keep patrolling its depths. I wanted to be on board, dry and eating lunch.

Throwing the goggles on to the deck, I clapped my hands and asked my brother if he would mind kindly passing the shampoo. Then I washed my hair and beard, ears, and nostrils as I trod water. I rinsed my hair and face by bobbing under the water.

My brother had finished his wash and swam past me to drop off the sea soap and collect the plastic bottle of sea shampoo.

He even offered to get lunch underway, a real treat. Generally, it was agreed that I got breakfast and lunch and my brother prepared the evening meal with any vegetables and a selection of canned foods, which we held in our bulging food store.

If we breakfasted on shore or we dined on land, then we were saved the chore.

Washing in the sea is difficult, especially when you have to keep an eye on your only refuge, watching as the boat bobs further and further way from you. After a while, the water seems to become warmer, more bearable.

As you wash yourself the salty waves lap over your ears and head. It was easy enough to do the feet and arms, particularly the extremities. Other parts of the body were not so easy. It was difficult enough staying afloat with both hands around a soap bar, but the contortions needed to reach any part of the torso involved you rolling forwards or on to your back.

The under-arms and the groin, or nether regions, were best washed on the rope ladder, as you climbed back up, then you could plunge back in the water one last time to rinse off the soap.

Such was life at sea.

Your bath was miles of sea on every side until it disappeared into the horizon. Your water came from a plastic Jerry can, your food from a tin can and other refreshment from glass bottles. With a hot sun and warm breeze, it was fairly civilised. It was less pleasant with a storm brewing.

Chapter Twenty - Two's Company

Having packed off Patrick, our sailing was smooth, and the sun shone. It was decided that he had been a Jonah, putting the mockers on the engine and responsible for our misty approach to Gibraltar. It was much pleasanter with two on board, less people getting in each other's way and more team spirit.

Making a cup of coffee was no longer just a task performed while the other two sailed, almost as something constructive to do. Now it was a veritable challenge and to offer to boil the kettle and make a brew of any kind was considered almost heroic.

For good measure, the suggestion would have to come when there was a full sail and a choppy sea, when the helmsman would have to fight the tiller as the currents tried to wrench the rudder from his grasp.

That way you could both admire each other's work, the helmsman for keeping on course and following the same bearing as when you left, which was difficult enough in calm seas, the brew-master for keeping both the pot and primus stove upright on the slopping cabin floor. The skill was to light the stove, bring the full pan of water over and on to the metal frame, holding both without spilling the water or scalding your hand with the boiling liquid.

Turning off the stove, you could not just let it fall, because the ring was still hot and would burn the deck wood. So, gripping the Calor cylinder between your ankles, you poured the pan with one hand into two cups already filled with granules of instant coffee and dried milk.

Once the pan was poured it could go into the sink. The Calor gas cylinder could be hung up on an old hook in the galley, which was, in effect, the square foot space by the hatch that we never used.

It housed a tiny sink of copper and a small paraffin stove, which was clogged and apparently hugely dangerous. We never used it because we felt that Waterwitch did not deserve to be turned into a 'fire ship' at this late stage in her life.

Whilst clearing up after you, it was necessary to keep hold of the cups to stop them spilling. More so, it was advisable to swing slightly with both the sway of the boat and the drift of your unsteady sea legs.

Then, you set your sight on the daylight outside, or at night the lantern that cast shadows on our faces or feet, just like a miner setting his sights on the shaft entrance. It was not easy negotiating the four wooden steps, often wet, across the slippery deck to the bench and the outstretched hand. I had become skilled at running this gauntlet and managed never to spill a drop.

It was important to wait for the coffee to cool.

On more than one occasion I was so cold I thought I deserved a swig of hot fluid, but a sudden dip by the boat meant a tip to my arm and I scalded my tongue on a gulp of boiling coffee when all I had wanted was a taste.

Not content with circumnavigating the coast of Spain, we had to invent sport to enliven our dangerous occupation. My brother's idea of sport was seeing how far he could tilt the boat in high winds.

He adored danger.

It was his drug. In calm weather, with little wind, he amused himself by taking photographs of me in undignified or embarrassing poses: going to the loo over the side or snoring open-mouthed with dribble coming out of the side of my mouth.

I failed to see how either of these activities could amuse.

My idea of fun was going to the bow and sitting on the deck, my arms folded, resting on the bow rail, with my feet dangling over the side. It would have to be sunny for this escapade. I would just wear shorts and a polo shirt and if it were not too rough, I would rest my chin on my folded arms.

It was akin to being on a bucking bronco, as Waterwitch ploughed through the waves, rising slightly on the swell as she cut through the wave, dipping slightly as she came off the crest and bowed into the dip of the next wave.

Then, she would rise again as smoothly and resolutely as an Arab mare cantering on sand.

The wind in my hair, the blue stretch of dark undulating water with its white foam, the pale blue sky above and, if I had my sunglasses on or if I dared, I would look at the sun that we seemed constantly to be running towards, two days on our port bow and ahead, one or two days on the starboard bow, still burning brightly and guiding our way.

At night the North Star came out first, followed by the others. Even before the sun had set though, the swelling moon was at our backs, a white cloudy circle in the afternoon. It was a fiery ball, a reflection of the disappearing sun at dusk and then at night a swollen disc of silver, brilliant in the cloudless skies.

It was incredible.

We had not seen a cloud, day, or night for days. As usual our plans had changed, and we were spending the fifth day at sea. We had bathed every second day; we had plenty of provisions, although we had finished the bread; we had ample fruit. The most difficult thing was doing without cigarettes, especially at mealtimes, just before with my aperitif, or just after with my coffee. In fact, taking coffee without tobacco was not the same.

Often a cigarette would leave your mouth feeling dry, which could be counterbalanced by the coffee; you could feel as if you had too much liquid if you stuck to just coffee and the cigarette would dry your tongue for you, getting rid of the coffee taste. It was purely habit, but a routine we both found hard to break. Norman would chew on a matchstick or on a toothpick - an evil glint would come into his eye, and he'd talk about danger and the thrill it gave him.

We talked a lot on that trip and opened up to each other. We were not the enemies that had sailed around the Cape of Trafalgar.

Our ship was a co-operative ship, a two-man communist collective. Gone were the days of the downtrodden peasant; gone was the overbearing tyrant of a capitalist, although it should be noted that the deeds of the boat still remained in my brother's name and he did not share out his money, but I also kept my traveller's cheques in a safe place.

It was more an atmosphere, a feeling.

I was no longer mere crew to be ordered around, a brother to be abused. Some vestiges of respect had been returned to me and I responded to this. I think Norman finally realised that perhaps, even for a big brother, he had been a little overbearing.

As we sailed towards Puerto Banus, we discussed most things. It was just like on the boat before we set sail and before we ran aground.

'So, going back to what you said about danger being a drug; I don't really see it myself,' I urged like a particularly brilliant interviewer, trying to discover the nub of a problem.

We had been over some old ground, talked of the dangers we had experienced as children, Norman's accident, and our close scrapes on board Waterwitch and other vessels.

'It's the adrenaline,' said my brother, steering a steady course. Puerto Banus was not yet visible in the haze, but we knew it was there. It was three and we would definitely be moored by four o'clock. That's what my brother said, and I sincerely hoped that he would be proved right for a change.

'I can understand that, but is it necessary to put your adrenal gland under so much strain? Can't you reserve it for a time when you are in real danger?'

'There is so little real danger in this world, you have to create it, create your own buzz, live on the edge.'

My brother sounded like some faded hippie with his jargon, an 'adrenaline junkie', but it did not annoy me as much as it would annoy some people. I found his attitude difficult to accept, deliberately putting himself in a dangerous situation in order to savour the sensation.

It made little sense to me then. If I wanted to flirt with danger, I could smoke twenty cigarettes, which would bring me a step closer to cancer, heart disease, emphysema, and all manner of ghastly diseases.

'I don't think you should be putting yourself constantly in such difficult situations. One day your luck might run out.'

'What's luck got to do with it? You're sounding like some superstitious old woman. The fact that you are close to going over the edge, actually succeeding in using up all your luck, makes the experience all the more exciting.'

'I can't see dicing with death as a means to an end. Maybe after your accident you feel different and you want to savour every moment, but I can savour every moment of my life without living on a razor's edge all the time," I argued.

I was the devil's advocate, get the interviewee to let down their guard or justify their stance, I should have been an international reporter for 'The Times'.

'Don't you see that the buzz comes from the fear you experience? It's exciting to be frightened. Go to any fun fare, look at the people on a ghost train; go to see any horror movie show, look at the audience. We love being scared and I like scaring myself.'

'I suppose you're right,' I admitted, trying to sound encouraging.

'If you're going to do something, do it well. Like driving the car, I put the fear of God into you both, but my adrenaline was pumping twice as fast. I was responsible. It was my reactions that would keep us on the road or hurl us down the hill or over the cliff edge. Sailing allows you to be frightened all the time.'

'I can't say you reacted well when we went for that buoy, you were obviously not enjoying being frightened then,' I countered playfully, waiting for a reaction.

'It was not fear, but frustration. I was hoping to catch up with a friend there who said he had some charts for the whole coast I could buy off him. That change in course ruined our chances of catching up with him, that and running aground in Faro just finished me off We were never in any danger, not until we hit the sand bank off Olhao,' he explained.

'So, running aground in the swamps around Faro was merely frustrating. The tide pulling us out was the straw that broke the camel's back and the only time there was any real danger, you left me alone in the boat to face it on my own. Charming.'

'It was not that real a danger. The worst that could have happened is that the keel could have snapped, and the boat would have heeled over. . .'

'Possibly smashing me inside it as your friend pointed out when he came to check on me,' I interrupted archly.

'You survived, didn't you?' he declared, reasonably. I had.

'Yeah, but I've really enjoyed the Spanish part of our trip, there's been less danger. It's out there, I know, but we should let it find us rather than pursue it. I would just love a quiet life, wouldn't you?' I urged.

'For the moment,' he acquiesced, 'but I miss the buzz of real danger. There was once a storm, about as bad as the one you were in, but this one was off the Canaries. It was raining so hard, the weather was so bad, that we turned off the engine and battened down the hatches. Lying on our bunks, we waited to hit something or to be rolled over by a wave and sunk. For three days we stayed cooped up in our cabins. It was a big boat, and you could stand up below deck. On the third day, just like Noah's Ark, the sun was shining, and the sea was much calmer,' he continued, he had a blissful expression on his face as he described that living hell.

'I won't go into my story again, but you were out to sea in the Atlantic, miles from the Canaries,' I explained, 'the likelihood of you hitting an island or the coast, or even any shipping, was minute. We saw ten to fifteen freighters that day and perhaps half were tankers. Each one seemed to be heading towards us, one tanker was fearsomely close, it almost ran us over.'

'We cannot compete on storms,' he admitted, 'You've had your sailing baptism and you got very wet indeed, but I'm glad you got the experience, I wouldn't want to be sailing with anyone more than I would want you as part of my crew. Patrick was a little bit wet behind the ears for my liking.'

'I hope he made his flight in time.'

'If he didn't, tough! It was not for lack of trying on our behalf. We got him to Tavira quicker than it took us to sail from Tarifa to Gibraltar.'

'It was ironic, seeing all the places we had just sailed past.'

'Well, we're making progress now. I reckon we'll be in Ibiza within four or five days.'

I had heard this from my brother the day before last and even my sense of scale would allow me to suppose that it had taken us a month to go less than half the distance we intended to go, so it was unlikely, even sailing at night, that we could possibly end up on time in the Balearic Islands. We planned to visit Valencia, too.

I was willing, although it would have been quicker to sail from Denia to Ibiza.

We often discussed destinations that were far off. It gave us a goal to aim for, although all too often it was an unobtainable goal, the one the best psychologists recommended you avoid. If we had just stuck to the realistic, the tenable, then we would have been better off.

We chatted on while I made a huge effort to make coffee as we took up a fast tack towards the coast and the boat began to lean over alarmingly. I had already briefed my brother about conditions in Malaga and described the marina.

'Do they have a smaller yacht haven next to the main marina?' he asked.

'I would imagine so, I never actually saw another dock,' I answered distractedly, the busy boiling the water, it was not the time to talk.

'I think we'll head straight for there,' he decided.

'No, I thought you liked to live dangerously? We should go into the main marina and have a good look at the gin palaces they call yachts. We'll show them what yachts look like,' I declared.

'I can't afford the mooring fees there; that's for sure,' he joked.

'You don't have to. Some millionaires will let us moor beside their boat, just for curiosity's sake.'

'I doubt that.'

'Either way we get to see the marina from the water,' I added optimistically; I had finished the brewing ritual and clanged about with the metal saucepan, before hanging up the Calor gas bottle.

'Getting into moorings without an engine is impossible,' I cried as I poked my head up from the hatch.

'This way we pretend to be lost. They are horrified that we are circling near boats worth between a quarter and three- quarters of a million and they despatch a little speedboat or dinghy with an outboard to collect us and tow us right into the yacht haven and right up to our moorings with little effort expended by us,' he explained.

'They might just arrest us,' I complained.

'For getting lost. I think not. We're not in South America.'

'Let's give it a go,' I asserted.

I would never have convinced him, had he not wanted to go himself I think the thought of circling around the marina with such expensive and precious shipping appealed to him.

It was the type of danger he could easily deal with. Would he let the boat drift too close to the yachts and send their skipper or skeleton crew into paroxysms of panic? That would be enjoyable, the thought of turning an ordered and quiet pool into a scene of pandemonium. It was too good an opportunity to miss.

The marina at Marbella consists of a natural bay, north of the beach houses, which lead down to a perfect white sand beach. At one stage, Puerto Banus may have been a fishing village and the beach to its south may well have been shale and unexciting.

That old port was pale and not very interesting.

Puerto Banus was bright and inviting. It was simplicity itself, a rectangle whose sides consisted of bungalow shops and cafes on the north and west sides, a harbour wall to east and south sides, which hemmed in the sea.

In between these four sides was a marina of sweet simplicity. It was over twenty feet deep, and its dimensions allowed for any of the ocean-going cruisers to moor against any of the four walls.

These large vessels could be accommodated comfortably. The prime spot was in the top left-hand corner, the northwest of the harbour. It was a perfect rectangle, the northwest being the upper right angle on the left, where the hypotenuse meets the west width and the north length.

Here was Sinatra's bar and this old-fashioned piano bar with its expensive, but strong, cocktails was a must-see for any itinerary of the south coast.

Like Harry's bar in Venice, it had a long list of celebrities who had visited. If you were in Who's Who or on the Rich List, you most probably had been to Sinatra's first or soon after.

The International Set seemed to be saying that Cannes was crowded and full of film people. It had lost its grandeur and was looking faded. Nice was too accessible and too unpredictable.

Here in the southeast of Spain, you could have the weather of the Spanish Costas and the lifestyle of an Onassis.

Things were cheaper, service was friendly, fresh fish was just as tasty and Cava was so delicious and comparatively cheap that it did not matter that it was not champagne. It fizzed and bubbled, was made the same way and it tasted fabulous with the Andalusian fare. The Valencian whites were as good as vin de pays from Bordeaux and the Rioja equal to many of the Bordeaux wines.

Spain was France, but with warmth.

It was more relaxing and laid back, the manana syndrome. It was far less pretentious.

Not that you could get more pretentious than reversing your stern into harbour so that strangers could see your salon, watch you eat on deck and hear your steward pop the cork, but it was comparable, wasn't it?

In Spain you could afford a friendly captain and a friendly steward. In France you could afford either a surly captain who wanted to visit the locations he had not seen, or a surly steward who could not wait to drink your cognac after you had gone to your berth.

This was the picture I gleaned from conversations, both when I was visiting the area last year, and from subsequent discussions on this, my second trip. There was really no competition.

There were no hawkers in Marbella and the Puerto.

It was tranquillity itself: a soporific, sedate part of the world where time meant nothing. There was no such thing as the last table at ten at the Railway Hotel. You were encouraged to stay up late, rise early do your work and sleep off your tiredness in the oppressive heat of the afternoon.

Even on board we took this advice, and on many occasions, I slept on the deck in the shade of the sail from two until four, or if I had foolishly had one beer too many and my head throbbed from dehydration, I would crawl down into the cabin and rest for a few hours.

Whether at sea or on land, it was difficult to ignore the sense of the siesta, the sublime nature of the Spanish way of life, which even to this day makes a tempting scenario for many on a weekend afternoon.

The harbour wall was marked by two whitewashed cement huts on either side, one at the bottom left-hand corner of the rectangle, directly south of Sinatra's bar.

This line was used by many to view the wealthy at play. The other smaller hut, along the south wall, marked the mouth of the marina. On our fast tack we sailed in past the gap in the rectangle, the tiny hole in the bottom left-hand corner. Before anyone could raise the alarm, we were through and skimming past the bows of the luxury boats.

The harbour master had seen us coming, expecting us to tack off at the last minute or some nautical yards before. Instead, we kept on going. It must have been when we passed his office, our painted white side towards him, that he felt this was some publicity stunt designed to promote traditional sailing.

It was at this point he saw our grubby mainsail and our grubby jib. It was possible that perhaps even then he might have lent us a rich man's berth for the night, so daring was our entrance, so perfectly trimmed were our sails, but it was not to be. Someone had complained.

They had obviously seen our darker side, the side with primer and blue paint and wood filler. It was also certain that they disapproved of our canvas. White was this year's colour, not beige. We could have got away with beige, but with a splattering of rust and white, that was too much.

There was never a greater contrast.

This marina was meant to be one of contrast- the white of the bungalows, restaurants and shops highlighted against the beige and green Andalusian hills rising to Ronda or Mijas, Alahurin El Grande or Coin, or against the pale blue sky.

The white hulls of the most expensive private boats in the world highlighted against the blue water of the marina. It was white and shining fibreglass and steel city, topped by steel masts or white radar cowlings, all floating on the mirrored blue lake. It was luxury personified; the sort of thing executive brochures were made of the sort of scene lottery winners dreamed of.

Considering these boats cost more than some houses in the nicer areas of town, you got very little space for your dollar or pound, but it did you give you the flexibility of mobility.

Waterwitch had been bought for £2,500, so she shared very little in common with the competition.

She was one per cent of the budget of one of those craft. We knew because we later found out that if your ship was not worth thousands, it was difficult to imagine that you could afford the mooring fees.

Wisely, the owners of the marina wanted travelling yachts moored south of the main Puerto, so as to encourage and enforce the feeling of exclusivity and luxury. It worked for my brother, and it worked for me.

Although we had been spotted, it took the authorities a while to react. It was part of their laid-back nature, so we felt at the time. There were two spaces, one three berths away from Sinatra's bar on the western side and one on the south side, between two enormous white cruisers.

Waterwitch was dwarfed, but my brother insisted on completing a series of impressive tacks and Waterwitch danced around the dock.

We, basically, sailed in a figure-of-eight, tacking, when necessary, the figure getting neither larger nor smaller. I was instructed to put out the fenders, our two plastic, buoy- shaped protectors with their three-foot circumference. These would have done little or nothing to protect our boat from the onslaught of the heavier and less yielding materials that made up the other boats.

Our seeming reluctance to leave off from the impressive, yet awkward, figure-of-eight performance, galvanised the port authority. It must have been the twelfth time we had tacked north, looped around, tacked south, looped around, and tacked north, repeating this process in perpetual motion.

My brother pretended he was dizzy. Soon enough a dory speedboat, its white fibre-glass hull glinting in the silvery, blue water, sped towards us.

The outboard engine sounded Japanese, but I hoped it was a Mercury or a Johnson. Waterwitch was light, but we would need to be pulled by a big and powerful American engine to get us to the yacht haven, tied up and spruced up for cocktails during happy hour in Sinatra's bar at six.

'Buenos tardes,' shouted the harbour master.

'Good evening, Senor,' replied my brother, both their voices echoing in the yacht pool. 'Do you speak English?' It was an excellent gambit by my brother.

He was playing the British buffoon, having lost his bearings.

'Yes, I speak English,' the white-uniformed dark-haired man confirmed.

There was a smile in his voice as if to say: 'I have come across people like you in a similar situation before'.

It was reassuring and relaxed, wonderful as far as we were concerned. Nothing was too much of a problem. There was no such thing as an unmitigated disaster.

Sometimes life took you in the wrong direction. Sometimes you steered the wrong course, took the wrong tack. It mattered little. The main thing was where we went from here. It was a Mediterranean attitude, but a Taoist mentality too.

We knew we were in safe hands. We had worried the crews and the few owners with our bullring display.

Our fun was had; it was time to be towed out to sea, along to the other harbour. Just as our boat was attached to the dory craft, a helicopter swooped out of the sky, landing on the southern harbour wall, the sea wall. The rotors spun for a few minutes after the engine died.

A Mercedes Benz saloon, black and big eased itself along the north-east corner of the harbour, drove along the east wall to the south-east corner, turned and drove along to the helicopter. A grey-haired man in a dark grey suit jumped out and was followed by another younger man, again in a dark suit.

The younger opened the back door of the Mercedes and the older gentleman stepped into the seat. The car drove six berths along the sea wall and stopped. Dressed in white, a steward leapt to the far door and opened it for the grey-haired man. Stepping gingerly on board without a backward glance, it was obvious he was the owner.

The Mercedes reversed back along the sea wall to the southeast corner and there it managed to back right against the stone wall, swing around in an arc and drive off back towards the row of restaurants and shops at the north side of the marina.

That was arriving in style.

We had tried our best, but our pathetic figure-of-eight, although performed with panache, seemed suddenly eclipsed by such a momentous arrival. It must be tough having legs and not having to use them often, I thought ruefully to myself. Being chauffeur-driven less than twenty yards was opulence indeed.

We could not compete with that. The dory dragged us out to sea again. As my brother pulled down the sails, I took the tiller and when the harbour master's pilot moved the outboard motor's handle to port, I followed with my helm.

When he straightened his handle, I did likewise. In this way we managed to keep within the boat's wake and to be tied up, brushed up and sat up at Sinatra's bar drinking a half-price beer by six fifteen.

It was strange to arrive somewhere before evening had come and we moved outside to watch the sun set in the west, easing back into the comfortable curved cane chairs that lined the pavement. The alcohol loosened our tensions further, a warm westerly breeze making us feel comfortable in our white shorts and shirts.

We looked smart. It was par for the course. It did not matter who we were, we were tanned and young and we could afford the price of a beer. The piano player teased the ivories. The sound of The Girl from Ipanema wafted out across the bar over our heads and out into the echoing void that was the harbour.

It was synthetic and false but grandly so. It was a wealth that was not as uptight or a serious as the wealth further north. That was top buttons done up even without a tie; this was top buttons undone, the more the merrier, even with a tie. It was so relaxed that you felt you could do something outrageous and get away with it.

Instead, we bought pancakes from the second row of shops on the northern side of the harbour and ate them ravenously as we stumbled back to our moorings, tired but happy.

The luxury marina takes advantage of the old solid-stone harbour walls.

If it was not a fishing base, then it might well have been a military harbour at one time.

It was regimentally planned and ordered in its set-up. The marina on the other hand was much more in keeping with other yacht havens around the world. A steel-topped pontoon led into the sea and another pontoon spawned a bewildering number of smaller pontoons, with a gap between each of them to accommodate your standard yacht, maximum fifty foot long, and a small space reserved for the one-hundred-plus-footers.

Whereas the harbour wall in Puerto Banus had dwarfed us, and it had been a real worry that our ropes were not long enough to reach the towpath, here we were on a level. We could actually step down into the boat.

It was expensive to stay there, the mooring fees were dear, but we had saved on the last four nights. We would be sailing away from shore for the next two or three days and possibly the same number of nights, probably more.

Despite it being double the cost of any other mooring on the Spanish coast, it was worth it for just one night to see how the other half lived and to say that you had moored your boat in Puerto Banus. More especially, to have the memory of our half-finished majestic thirty square metre boat running rings around her bulkier sisters.

It was like seeing Cinderella at the ball surrounded by her ugly sisters. An elegant, slim, and trim racing yacht, a real class act, surrounded by over-priced sluggish ships, more suited to military parades than to sailing.

Waterwitch was the real thing and those giants paled into insignificance, claiming absurdly to be yachts when in fact the real holder of that title was made to feel small by the brutish caricatures.

We slept well.

We were tired as our voyage had involved night sailing and it was surprisingly debilitating sleeping for six hours and having a watch for six hours. My brother suggested that for the next leg of the journey, we experiment with four-hour watches. I was agreeable to anything.

The beer at Sinatra's coupled with the beer we had just finished stupefied me into agreement. It was then I realised how little I could drink without feeling tipsy and this alone had made my brother's tipples seem excessive.

I think he drank heavily to make me agreeable, too.

It bothered me little. We had not been able to find a licensed tobacconist in the rarefied confines of the marina, but we managed to negotiate to buy a packet of 'Ducados' off one of the waiters in one of the bars.

Greedily, I drew on the weed, watching the end burn in a glow of embers. This was luxury. This was living, smoking after three days. The black tobacco smoked, wisps of curling clouds spiralling from the glowing end, then the draw deep into the lungs, the hit of nicotine, the rush as it went straight to your brain; the light-headedness, the euphoria, who could want for anything more?

There was nothing in life that I could adore more than that cigarette.

Deprivation only heightened the charge, increased the nicotine rush that sent my head spinning. I almost dropped the newly opened bottle of San Miguel that my brother offered me, so great was my pleasure and so badly did it affect my concentration.

I felt like a drug addict in an opium den. It was as dark as one in our cabin. That was for sure. We were addicts finally getting their fix. I looked in the shadows, but saw no demons, merely wisps of smoke like dragon's tails curling around and about in the shadows.

 It was surely sublime.

In a drug-crazed frenzy I drew on the filter again and again until the end glowed like an incandescent lipstick and before my eyes I saw the two inches of red-hot black burning tobacco, the hatch sucking up the smoke out of the boat, my lungs aching from the terrible constriction that the smoke in my lungs brought with it. The Irish have very poor lungs. It is hereditary. They should never smoke.

After discussing watches, my brother moved on to our progress along the coast, he had a plan that he had sketched out on a sheet of the logbook, which he now tossed on to my bed.

Our logbook was a cheap, unlined sketchpad. The brand name was Castelo, and it had a castle on the front, that being its only solid feature. The first few pages were sketches. There was one, untitled, of a farmhouse and a palm tree.

By its whitewashed walls and its curved, terracotta tiles I suspected that it was somewhere in the Canaries, where my brother had been for the last few years.

The next page was again a coloured pencil sketch, but it had a title and date: 'The church, Quarteira, May 1982'.

I assumed it was done before I came out. Then the lists started - lamp glass for our paraffin lanterns, hose bilge pipe, string, pulley block. I saw the intensive and extensive lists that each day had stopped my brother from doing two or three hours of painting.

I grew annoyed, but this is not what my brother wanted me to see. However, one item caught my eye. Six batteries were on the list, a set of triple 'A', 1.5 volt, which were vital for the Walkman.

Above this was another list. 'Seagull 5 HP' was written in capitals and underneath it was the following: bevel gear, shaft impeller, gaskets, oil, split pins, spark plugs. I am not a mechanic but even I could surmise from this list, neatly scribbled out, I should add, that there was something pretty seriously wrong with our engine if it needed all these parts.

There was little else to the engine apart from the items on the list, except the bolts that fixed the motor to the hull. I was no longer thinking of him as my brother. It was now 'the Captain' again. Perhaps, after seeing the log, it would remain so.

The next page revealed how we had propped Waterwitch up when we ran aground - obviously a sketch he had shown his friends in the warm bar as I shivered alone.

The log showed pretty effectively our poor progress from Faro to Olhao.

10.45 was the first entry. Our position was noted at timed intervals thereafter. You just had to look at how close Faro is to Olhao on a map to realise that just getting to Gibraltar might take us a whole year. The last entry on that day was 21.15 when he had left me.

We did well from then on.

Olhao to Ayamonte took Saturday. Ayamonte to Cadiz took Sunday and Monday. Cadiz to Tarifa took Tuesday. We were able to bear thirty degrees on Saturday, then, seventy degrees until Monday when we took up our thirty-degree course again. It was the first time I had seen the logbook and I was so impressed that I felt a sense of warmth and pride towards him.

I bowed to the Captain again.

The next page showed another list, more stores, long-nose pliers, batteries, RDF, epoxy wood filler, paint for deck (yellow, three litres), Take lamps (anchor and blue), free halyard blocks, gas cooker and bottles, red Ensign, Perspex (for what purpose I never fathomed), charts, pilot books, (Brandon's), foghorn, 1.5v HP 2 batteries, and spare bulbs for navigation lights.

A meagre showing, he had noted. I hoped one day we would be able to give the deck its final coat of yellow, in Ibiza perhaps.

Some hope.

A shopping list also showed our almost Zen attitude to eating bread, milk (it was the UHT, skimmed stuff), coffee, matches, lots, and biscuits.

It was the simple things in life we cherished. To take cheese on a three-day jaunt is not the best idea and stale bread dipped in coffee is quite palatable once you get used to it. It is advisable to let the brew cool, or a soggy piece of bread can fall off and burn your lip.

Otherwise, the bread was delicious even on its own. Jam was too much of a luxury particularly as it went mouldy after the first day, no matter where you stored it. The truly important navigational information was on the next few pages of the log. We needed the Cadiz to Barcelona Chart No 2717. We had the Ibiza Chart No 3276. We wanted to travel to Alicante at 1372, Aguilas at 774 and Motoril at 773, so my brother had carefully and cunningly decided to navigate by the lighthouses of the Spanish coast.

He had managed to copy part of a chart off a contact of his Gibraltarian friends.

On the following page he had drawn a map in a felt-tip pen. There was Marbella, then what looked like a keyhole, filled in with black ink, beside which was written, 'Calaburras FL 18m'. The next key was just the outline and read, 'Malaga' GP FL 3H 17 m; next, 'Pta de Torrox, GPFL (4) 15m, Motril' and below, 'C Saratif GPFL (2) 25m', 'Adra G Poe (3) 17m', 'Pta del Sabinal (2+1) 16m' past Almeria to 'C de Cata FFL 14 19m'. We were going to follow the south coast of Spain by looking out for lighthouses. It was a stroke of genius. Each one had its own pulse, its own signal, its own recognition symbol, though on paper they were black keyholes.

That was why he had shown me the logbook.

He sat there smoking, obviously pleased with himself, staring at our sketchbook chart in the half-light of one of our lanterns. I flicked ash into the ashtray. Now, on my third Ducados, the black tobacco smoke filled my nostrils.

This giving up smoking idea was not so harsh after all. I knew I would not feel this way the following morning when withdrawal symptoms would gnaw away at my resolve. The giddiness and the constriction of vessels around my brain, the mere thought of such a description made me shudder.

I dismissed such horrible ideas.

Taking another drag, I pretended to study the figures as though I understood them. I had seen enough spaghetti westerns to know how to call someone's bluff. By looking at the figures I was assured that each one had its own significant signal.

It was difficult enough to live down sailing towards the wrong buoy in a channel; aiming for the wrong lighthouse might well delay us even further. Putting my cigarette down in the ashtray, I took a swig from another stubby bottle of San Miguel that my brother had just opened.

There were two shot glasses containing distilled spirit.

After my brother's unfortunate accident with the paraffin bottle, we no longer risked taking spirits directly from the bottle. Rather we poured them out carefully, sniffed and sipped, only then were we permitted to throw the glass back and swallow a whole mouthful. My brother liked to chase his beer with spirit; I liked to chase my spirit with beer.

We could live with that difference between us.

'So, what do you think?' he asked. I could hear the tension in his voice. I had power of veto. I thought that 'C' stood for Cape and 'Pta' stood for Puerta. I had no idea what 'G Pocc' stood for, but it could not have mattered less if I did know. As for 'GPFL', I had not a clue.

I guessed that '18m' was the height above sea level. It was funny in a way because, although the map most definitely showed the south coast of Spain, my brother had drawn a vertical arrow with a capital 'N' at the top. If I had not known this coast from previous holidays, that north symbol would have helped me a lot, but I doubt whether it would have helped me to agree to this part of the journey.

'We have no engine and no chance of getting it going in the foreseeable future, right?'

I let my reply hang in the air, ominously. It was our Achilles' heel, not just his. We would both be giving up the safety aspects of motorised sailing. Sailing into moorings was never easy. The wrong speed on entry and the whole procedure could turn into a shipping disaster, sinking your boat or others, or sometimes both.

It was not a jolly prospect.

'Okay,' I eventually conceded, grudgingly.

'I'll take responsibility for that and for the consequences.'

He sounded like a commander in some Second World War epic.

Perhaps, both of us would have laughed, but this was decision time. My brother could go on alone while I hit the North African coast, by hitchhiking on a boat back to Gib.

We could call it 'Gib' now. All sailors referred to Gibraltar as such. We were sailors.

Crew went there to sail boats across the Caribbean for Europe's winter, the southern hemisphere's summer, I was too early for that, but I could have found work until that time.

The other alternative was to limp on with Waterwitch. I really had no choice. A whole world beckoned out there. The world was my oyster, and more funds were merely a telegraphic transfer away.

However, I had to stay with my brother and do my best to help him sail our stricken and sad vessel to meet his friends. He was relying on my help and his friends were relying on him being there. They had bought their tickets and were entitled to meet Norman as arranged. He needed my help. He needed me.

'We're going to navigate by the beams of the light-houses?' I asked, trying to keep incredulity out of my voice.

I wanted all points clarified. I would move on to more domestic matters later, such as who made the coffee on a Tuesday.

'We sail out during the day, as normal, for three or four days,' my brother said as he shook out another Ducados.

We had to finish the packet or dump it. We were entitled to ten each.

He smoked his leisurely into the night; I would devour mine and go to bed, head spinning from nicotine rush, alcohol-poisoning and terrible constriction in my chest. He lit the cigarette with a match from our lantern supply, within which time I had extracted a cigarette and placed it between my lips.

I was quick on the draw. My brother was impressed both by my swiftness and by my thoughtful economy, saving the use of a second match by sharing his. That all-important last match had been saved by such behaviour.

It could be that match that was used to set the sail on fire as a beacon of distress. We were friends, we were brothers; we understood each other.

'Tell me more,' I urged.

'Then at night we sail towards the coast and pick out one of our beacons. Each one pulses at a different rate,' he explained patiently.

'What if we have fog?'

'We carry on sailing out to sea and avoid the land. We've got to run along the coast. If we overshoot, then we can just head north for Ibiza. We'll hit Algiers if we go too far south and Mallorca or Minorca if we go too far northeast.'

It sounded reasonable and feasible. It was a sensible plan. He had obviously worked everything out. I had to put my faith and trust in him.

'Okay!'

'Otherwise, we hit the east coast of Spain or Ibiza or some yachts heading that way. It's summertime now. There's going to be a lot more pleasure traffic and a lot less commercial shipping to worry about in this area. We've had the tough part.'

'We'll see how we get on.'

Power, even momentarily seized, felt so good. I almost passed out with the weight of my victory.

'Brilliant, we'd better finish these fags and the rest of the beer.'

If I had known what lay ahead, I would have suggested we finish the bottle and a half of spirit as well.

My brother was understandably pleased, jubilant in fact. I've never seen him drink so little; he was that happy.

'To our Periplus,' I toasted; it was a challenge. I was wondering how good his Latin really was.

'To coastal voyages,' he proclaimed.

I was outwitted again. It was there and then that I decided that you can pretend to be twice as clever as someone, but it is in fact just as well to try to be half as clever. You cannot displease them. You cannot disappoint yourself.

The net result is two pleased people, a pleasant outcome in any circumstance.

'Have another smoke,' he urged, I was offered the pack.

'Not for me, I think I have had my ten,' I admitted.

'You've been counting?'

My brother raised his eyebrow, giving me an incredulous look. My bravado was gone. I nodded without looking at him, like a broken man, as if I were admitting some dreadful crime.

'Go on,' he insisted. It was temptation held at arm's length. 'Have one. We've got to get rid of them. I've had my fill, there are still nine left.'

For the first time in my life, I knew how Adam felt when Eve offered him the apple. Cigarettes were my 'Apple of Discord'.

Like the fool I was, I took it, gratefully and gleefully; the last smoke of a condemned man, I thought ruefully. If only I'd known how close to the truth I was.

'Thanks, mate.'

He was my friend. Only friends gave you some of their ration. Only friends gave you their last cigarette.

'It's 'Skipper' to you, number one,' he joked.

There was no room for first mate or ship's mate on this boat.

Both of us were officers. If ever there had been a case of too many chiefs and not enough Indians, too many bosses and not enough workers, then this was it. It was agreed.

We would set sail for Malaga the following morning, a long tack away from Fuengirola and Torremolinos.

Once we sighted Malaga, then we would head towards land again on a north-eastern tack, strictly a bearing east, northeast.

With luck and a favourable wind, we would reach either Nerja in the west, Almunecar slightly further along the coast, or if we were extraordinarily lucky and had made brilliant progress, we might reach Motril, or Castell de Ferro, or Adra.

Our ultimate destination was Almeria, where the Costa del Sol magically changes into the Costa Brava.

Chapter Twenty-One - Pilgrim's Progress

We awoke the next morning feeling jaded. I was feeling delicate; my brother thankfully looked even worse. It would have been murderous if he had been bright and chirpy, I would have hated to sit through his jovial banter while my head throbbed. It was a luxury to make coffee in harbour. Everything stayed in place, and you could actually leave the saucepan on the cooker and do other things.

That morning I needed to do other things.

As the kettle boiled, I rummaged around until I found the small green nylon bag with a white cross in a white circle stamped on the side. Fishing out two sachets of 'Alka Seltzer', I dropped two of the healing discs into the water that I had poured into the ship's glasses. I took one glass through to my brother who was still lying-in bed and drained my own glass in one draught, the bubbles tickling my nose and the effervescence in my throat almost making me choke. I gasped for air, then, recovered, I put the glass on the chart table, looking again at our hand-made map.

If only I had been taught to say no, everything would be fine, but in life we are taught to be so damn agreeable, to say yes to everything, so that we often end up in more stews than they serve at a soup kitchen.

The whistle from the kettle took me away from my ship's cabin philosophy. I was making a kitchen sink drama out of what would be a picnic in the country.

After coffee we had a shower in the harbour facility, changed into clean clothes, ones we had hand-washed, that is, paid our mooring fees and felt much better.

There were no shops to speak of.

We wandered around the harbour one more time, now quiet and still after the vitality of the previous night. Cleaners hosed down the dockside pavements.

As a special treat, I bought my brother a coffee and a roll from one of the restaurants along the quay. The harbour seemed so silent now, along with the boats, their hatches battened down. It was still too, no wind, just the trickle of water dribbling pathetically from a hose and the sound of brush strokes on stone.

We talked of many things, of sealing wax and cabbages and kings. We had experienced most weather. We knew what to expect; like seasoned campaigners in some conflict, we knew that we were up to the challenges. We were naive.

After, breakfast we set sail.

It was 6th June, a Sunday. We were excused church as we were travelling. This was the end of the fourth week of our cruise. We had to make impressive progress in the fifth week in order to catch up with our schedule.

Our journey from Faro to Cadiz involved sightings of the coast, often difficult to see in the heat haze and with a correspondingly blurred horizon.

From Cadiz, life was easier, simply because we had the Sierras as a guide, black shadows visible above most hazes.

Like so much of the Costa del Sol and the Costa Blanca and Brava, where we would later be sailing, it was a flat coast with a shadow of the foothills behind.

Later, when we sailed parallel to the Sierra Nevada after Malaga, the coast was easier to spot and sandier.

As we sailed away from Malaga, there were fewer hotels and tourist developments.

All we could see was a haze.

The beaches seemed more shale in substance and the small villages on the coast seemed more business-like, little modern settlements connected by road.

The village in front of Almunecar, an industrial town, was such a sight.

The land was flat, punctuated by rectangular boxes, some with tall chimneys belching white or grey smoke, others just storage facilities, grey or white, prominent against the blue silhouette of the Sierras.

We sailed along this uninspiring coast until we came to a small port west of Castell de Ferro. It had taken us most of the day to get this far, even though the wind direction had enabled us to take long sweeping tacks at small angles to the shore. Mostly our tacks were forty or forty-five degrees from the coast, that day they were more like fifteen or twenty.

We had covered about fifty or so miles.

The bay was fairly large, big enough for us to tack several times with our forty-two-foot length. At the end was a man-made harbour wall that closed off the sea from the land, except for a gap that would accommodate a large freighter, or, as the designers had perceived, two yachts passing each other port to port with a wide margin between their ruby navigation lights.

The port itself was a beach in such a perfect arc that it had to be man-made. Its depth was dredged to allow yachts to comfortably reverse out of their moorings and chug out to the sound.

As my brother pumped the bilges, I dutifully took soundings with our plumb line. We seemed easily to double our six-foot keel, giving a depth of at least two metres. We had been constantly aware on our voyage that our heavy metal keel could sheer off, either simply capsizing our vessel or taking enough of the wood with it that we would sink like lead.

However, our keel had held through running aground in Faro and outside Olhao. What stress this had put on the infrastructure, it was impossible to tell. It was another of the list of things we could not contemplate.

Like nervous flyers we could not start thinking about wings falling off, otherwise we would have made no progress. An engineer can check stresses on a plane. In a boat you have to go to the expense of putting the boat on the hard and then there is no guarantee that fractures will be discovered.

All the bad had been forgotten.

My brother seemed to drink as much as I did, which was always the case and his worry about the boat and more especially his feeling of responsibility towards me seemed to have ebbed with the tide.

The fact that we had no tide to worry about was obviously a contributory factor.

My handling of myself in a crisis perhaps helped further, but more so than that was the fact that we had survived. Not only did this help us to bury our concerns deep in our sub consciousness but also it bonded us closer together.

We were veterans, veterans of a war against the elements.

From feeling victimised, I now felt that this was a wonderful experience and that I was part of something special. I had been a spoilt brat and my brother had been terribly concerned about both his responsibility to keep his vessel afloat, I still think to this day that he was one of the few skippers who would actually go down with his boat, added to his promise to himself that I would be kept safe and well. It was only within the last few days that his fraternal responsibility extended beyond filial devotion.

I was a sibling that he liked as a friend and whom he truly respected. I, in turn, was the spoilt puppy that wagged its tail and wanted everyone to appreciate me.

If there was one lesson I had learnt, it was that you cannot expect people to constantly reassure you. It is your responsibility to have confidence and to realise that acceptance of yourself with all your faults is worth a thousand times more than acceptance from family or friends. I knew deep down that my brother loved me as much as I loved him.

More importantly, he liked me, which is surely as important. Even today I feel a great sadness for families in which there is love but little friendship. No matter what happened to us from here on in, I knew how lucky I was to have such a fabulous brother and I cursed my churlishness and my capriciousness.

How dare I expect him to change to accommodate me and how dare I expect him to live up to an ideal I had of him! He had always treated me fairly, included me in his social scene and been nice to me, but because I had experienced a few moments of discomfort, I took it out on him.

Worse, I took it out on myself. You can gather from this that we had just had a series of sublime days sailing.

I was in a good mood, but good things never last.

My brother's gift for holding the tiller and, at full stretch, pumping the bilges, often amazed me. Clumsy efforts on my behalf meant either lashing the tiller in a strong wind or waiting until the boat was calm enough to practically steer itself.

As a result, it took extraordinarily good conditions for me to combine the two skills.

Pumping bilges is indeed a skill. The rhythm required to complete the chore quickly and efficiently is something that can only be learnt with practice.

We had to be especially gentle with the perished rubber plunger that sucked up the water. Too much strain and the lever could rupture the rubber; too little strain and the pumping action was so pathetic that a ten-minute job became a full twenty-minute endurance test. Another feature of the bilges, apart from their ability to fill at an alarming rate, was that no matter how full or empty they were, it required the same amount of effort to pump them.

I am not a physicist and therefore will not answer the question, but I suspect that the cause was that if the bilges were filled, then the pump worked efficiently, if they were not, for every drop of water expelled, out came a good lungful of air.

Therefore, we often waited until the boards in the cabin wept water before pumping the bilges. If we had been becalmed this could take hours, but if we had been motoring in choppy seas then it may take only a few minutes for the bilges to fill. As a result, the better sailing we had, the more we had to man the pumps. No matter how we planned it, emptying the bilges took up an enormous amount of time and effort.

Sometimes I felt we were sailing not in a boat, but a sieve. I was relieved that we had this new technology on board. The concept of using a bucket, or worse still a cup, to bale out our boat sent a shiver down my spine.

As it was, every five minutes it was necessary to change arms. Without the pump we should have surely drowned or sunk.

In my experience in Greece, our fibreglass boats did not seep water and even wooden boats had an electrical bilge pump.

How had those sailors of the 1930s managed with so little equipment?

I knew why Venetian and Phoenician sailors had always put into port at night and why they needed slaves to power their boats.

We could have done with someone to make coffee and pump the bilges. As it was, these two equally important tasks were shared between the two of us. It was in fact a totally egalitarian ship, except in a crisis where I failed to panic out of ignorance and my brother panicked enough for both of us out of knowledge.

My face glowed from the warmth of the sun and my heart was lifted by good thoughts towards myself and towards my brother. I was content. The lessons I had learnt were invaluable and I had also developed patience, a gift bestowed on me by both my brother and our clumsy craft. She had taught me that one had to wait for the good things and suffer in silence and with dignity. Like those returning to the land, seafarers become almost insufferably philosophical.

I was feeling exceptionally fit. We had a healthy diet and small, almost meagre portions, just in case we had to eke out what food we had. A hot meal ashore was equivalent to a blowout banquet for others.

We had not used sun block since the first week and, in the dim light of dusk, my arms looked the colour of ebony. My lank, dark hair was the colour of straw now and as dry as wheatears before harvest. There was a cotton softness to it, and it was getting long, which gave me an excuse to run my hands through the strands to keep it from my face.

It reminded me of home and the comfort of my mother or sisters combing my hair by the range at home.

My eyes felt sore from the salt and the sodium chloride in the atmosphere had bleached my eyebrows. They felt wiry like an old man's. Before the trip they were soft, but now they had a coarseness that startled me every time I put my hand to my forehead to wipe away some sweat. It was most disconcerting to have the body of a teenager and the bushy eyebrows of an octogenarian.

Thankfully, we had no mirrors on board so I could not see the depth of this problem. The bars and restaurants we went to had no mirrors, which was fine by us, because there was no compunction therefore to comb our hair.

Brushes, combs, and razors were not part of our standard equipment.

My brother had jettisoned his. Mine was carefully packed in an already moulding sponge bag that I had owned since I was seven years old. The soreness on my face could have been due to the salt or the sun, but it was not too annoying, just an awareness of heat.

My beard, however, drove me crazy.

One night I had taken scissors to it and trimmed the strands that came down too far, but it was still a pathetic mess of tiny hairs, more like a few days' growth on a dark-haired man. My beard refused to sprout like my brother's. He had trimmed his several times in the last two months.

I had scarcely grown mine.

This did not bother me.

The slow growth was a bonus. I did not, therefore, have to hold the hair on my chin and a pair of scissors on a gently rolling boat to make my beard look smart. This is a tricky task with no comb and no mirror, letting your hands work around your face, as your eyes look down, desperate to see what is going on just outside the field of vision.

It was most annoying.

Trimming the beard was a minor worry.

The real bone of contention was the fact that it itched so much.

Like my eyebrows, my beard did not feel soft and downy like my hair but rough and prickly like my now-bushy eyebrows.

I scratched one side and the other side began to itch. When I had itched that side, the other side needed a scratch. Two hands together and suddenly my head felt itchy, just around the scalp. The only way to deal with the situation was to bear the need to scratch for as long as you could, and then to itch gently and leave the face alone. Otherwise, chores on the boat were not possible. You could not pump the bilges with one hand, nor swab the deck with the wet broom, sailing needed two hands- one for the tiller, one for the sail rope or coffee or a cigarette. In fact, sometimes sailing alone needed three hands.

We were not bothered by any of this as long as we had a good sail, which was what we had achieved that day. Hugging the coast, closer than usual (because that was where the wind was) we had zipped along on long tacks between five or ten degrees in angle.

Normally, our tacks were broad and open at forty-five degrees in order to get a coastal breeze, but the wind came off the land now and we could perform tight variations of course, with small deviations of direction. It was superb, like finding a steep slope down a hill when you had previously had to cautiously wind your way down a set mountain road, following the path and maintaining the speed allowed by the small slope.

Our steep slope was the power of the wind. Our bow sent spray splashing on to the deck and a warm breeze tousled our unkempt hair. The waves bowed down before us or were sliced by our keel.

It was brilliant -we were free and cruising. I watched my brother at the tiller, hanging on to one of the backstays to take a bearing from the geography of the coast, which was for the first time clearly visible. We could even make out the contours of buildings on a high hill above the coast.

Normally, the whole Costa was a haze apart from the darkness of a hill if one was there. I moved to the stern from my position at the mainstay and I took the helm as Norman moved forward to look at the map on the chart table. Within minutes he was upstairs again in the aft section, sitting on the cockpit deck as we poured over the waves.

Holding on to the copper windlass to stop him sliding across the almost vertical deck, he smiled warmly at me. This was the type of sailing we enjoyed, the sailing I had signed up to.

Often, I had felt that I had been press-ganged into a life of hardship, a silver King's shilling slipped into my tankard of ale like so many sailors in Nelson's time.

But not today.

It was so exhilarating in ideal conditions: a sea and wind set for sailing, a warm wind set for comfort and sunshine and visibility set for navigating and sunbathing. This was the holiday I wanted. My brother got up and pumped the bilges. He was even doing that for me.

The noise had become synonymous with intrusion and disturbance particularly at night when I was trying to sleep or was woken by the boom-slurp-gurgle, boom-slurp-gurgle of the pump. That day the pump sounded sublime, like the beat of a distant drum or a rhythm of an oarsman. Nothing could spoil that day and it didn't.

It was the evening when things went wrong. It all started with our conversation that afternoon.

'I know exactly where we are,' he announced.

My brother sat on the deck, tantalisingly close to the hatch. Already he was halfway through a sneaky cigarette that he had found stashed down below and had lit contrary to our no-smoking policy, I had made no reply to his statement and wondered how confident he was.

'Great.'

I looked over him at the course my bow should be directed in, at the slope of the cabin and deck as we heeled over, at the full sails that held the wind so tautly and at the compass that for once hovered gently over its mark, rather than veering to left or right as we crossed every wave. I was not ignoring him. The enthusiasm of my reply satisfied him. He knew I had a job to do and for once I was doing it not just passably, but exceptionally well, and no one was going to ruin the magic, least of all him.

'You're doing a great job,' he confided in me, as if to emphasise my own thoughts. He wanted me to do my job exceptionally.

'She's sailing beautifully, today,' I enthused.

I could be cool too.

'Conditions are good. I've looked at our speed, an average of eight to ten knots.'

He paused for me to register amazement. I had been told we were going at these speeds so often, when it felt like we were doing half that speed, that I declined to comment. Perhaps, we were hitting eight knots at best, a very good speed for us, but I knew how hairy and uncomfortable nine or ten knots could be.

The water was kind to us.

We were heeled over so much so that my brother had leant against the gunwales of the boat to pump the bilges and when he sat down again on the starboard side, he had swung his legs around to put his foot on the port deck, so that he could let go of the free windlass that he had earlier held on to for support as he smoked.

We were definitely making very good progress, but I would have been scared if we heeled over anymore.

I had already had to ask for the sails to be reefed down when we had met strong winds several days previously, when I was sure that we would take on water over the side, or simply capsize.

'We'll make more progress than I thought, today.'

His words brought relief. We had suffered so many delays that I felt that it was important we made up for the lost time.

'Brilliant!' I cried.

I could be such a diplomat at times.

'There's a little port I can just see on the map, and we could reach that by nightfall.'

This was the carrot, a hot meal, a bottle of wine and cigarettes.

We had already had our agreed three nights at sea and a fourth one without fresh bread and only powdered milk substitute filled me with foreboding, I had not had a beer for three days and I missed the taste. Even lemonade would have been a change from coffee or water. I told you I was spoilt. The idea of a hot meal, not the one-pot-wonders as my

brother proudly called them, and the chance to smoke filled me with even greater hope.

Cooking on board was my brother's chosen pastime and the brown and orange slop dished out on to tin plates was not only edible, but also delicious. By suppertime we were ravenous and the chill of night at sea made us welcome our nightly feasts; but eating off china plates, with fresh food, not tinned, along with hot doughy rolls smothered in melting butter, not dry biscuits, chipped potatoes, not reconstituted mashed potatoes was a most tempting idea.

I was hooked.

He could have said we were going to have to sail until eleven at night and I would have doggedly headed for port.

We were used to being the only pair dining at close to midnight. We found the waiters quick and efficient, having time to be attentive and determined to see us out before the last diners who had come in perhaps an hour and a half earlier.

Sometimes we lingered over brandy, but only if there was support from the adjoining tables.

When they asked for 'la cuenta', we asked for the bill too. When they left, we left too generous tippers always.

As he outlined our approach, my mind drifted to the meal that awaited us, tapas of different fish, or something grilled. Wine would be nice for a change, perhaps a white from Penedes or Rioja.

Maybe, the local wine would be good- it would at least be worth a taste. We might even be daring and go for a light rose.

Our boat continued to take advantage of the strong winds and it was not until dusk, with our haven in sight, that the wind dropped.

The town behind our berth had not lit up for the night, and I suspected that a little further east in the harbour, the fishing boats were having the afternoon catch taken from their holds and packed in ice for the evening trade.

Under sail still, we made a perfect entrance into the bay. The procedure was the same as always.

Sailing in on a smooth fast tack, we would turn the tiller, let the sails lose wind and bring both jib and main down in a matter of seconds, leaving them unfurled.

The speed that allowed us to turn would dissipate as we drifted gently alongside our moorings, and at a snail's pace with boathooks and fenders we would glide towards our parking space, barely needing to use the boathook or our arms as brakes.

That was the theory and often this practice worked exceptionally well.

At times our speed would be such that we would have to get our oars out and paddle the boat into a berth; or, using our loudhailer, we would try and attract someone's attention so that they would catch our bow line or one or other of our lines, ropes, or painters. It all depended on the current.

Once we were swept backwards and it was only due to a good throw and a long rope that we escaped being swept out into the channel and on to some rocks. Sailing is a tricky affair, like driving, but parking a car can cause immense problems even for competent drivers.

Mooring without an engine can cause as many problems as possible for competent sailors.

That was our disadvantage.

This manoeuvre with variable winds and currents is dangerous in tidal waters, but it is also tricky in non-tidal areas because there is always some undercurrent created by the bay or by the harbour wall.

All was not stillness and light.

As we prepared our turn, we came across a situation we had never encountered. There was no room on the easterly dock and therefore we had to head for the southerly side, not a problem generally, but we were used to going into harbour in another way.

This mooring was not designed by a sailor.

There were two boats, and they were tied up nose first. This meant we would have to enter bow first. Worse still, there was no one about. All the boats had tarpaulin on their cockpits or shrouding their decks; mothballed for the summer or for the weekend. We would get no aid here.

Further complications ensued. We had about a two boats' width gap to bring our vessel into dock.

The turn, perfectly executed, had brought us in too fast. Our fenders were on the wrong side to moor with the easterly boats, and we could not afford to bash our boats or theirs.

We would have to go in bow first because of our speed.

A boat's length might help, so we headed for the gap. I was bracing myself on the bow railing, a habit I had not been able to shake, despite having my shins bruised when we ran aground in the harbour channel at Olhao.

Both of us held a boathook, but it was clear that the current and our momentum were both contriving to smash us against the strong pontoon. Like taxis in the rain, harbour masters are never there when you need them.

With incredible presence of mind, I sat down. Standing in a collision, whether with a sand bank or a dock, is never a safe proposition. I had learnt an awful lot.

As we sped for the pontoon, I held out the boathook and the passage in which Don Quixote charges the windmills in Cervantes's work strangely came to mind.

I knew I would either lose it or it would break.

There was a crack as the boathook hit the metal rim of the wooden pontoon. I was secure, bracing my chest on the bow rail, my legs dangling over the bow.

The force still almost knocked me off my perch and bruised my shoulder. I was leaning heavily on the handle of my boathook, braced against the bow rail, hoping that the tensed muscles in my arms would absorb some of the impact. I was almost knocked flat on my back, but I let my arms bend and the handle rise above my left shoulder.

Still, I could see the water cleaving under me and we had only slightly slowed our progress. As the force-fed the boathook further through my hands, I put my feet out and locked my legs straight.

My plimsoll feet made contact with the dock. I lay flat and slid the useless boathook over my shoulder and on to the deck.

At the same time, I allowed my legs to fold underneath me. It was the most incredible feeling.

Several tons of dock, at my feet, and several tons of boat underneath, separated by my buckling legs.

I resisted as much as I could, pushing against the dock and raising my chest up to hold on to the bow rail which protruded a foot in front of the bow itself. We were slowing considerably but my knees were level with my waist. I held on as long as I could, as the combined forces pushed my knees up to my chin.

I thought that we would break the bow to pieces, I had seen what metal could do to wood, but whether it was a miracle or not we stopped, and the boat bobbed three or four times, stationary. There I was, curled up, white knuckles holding on to the bow rail and my knees touching my chin and a foot between bow and pontoon.

It had all happened so fast that even recalling it now is difficult. One minute we were on a collision course, the next minute, were safe and still. I could not move. My feet still held the metal at bay and my hands still gripped the metal railing.

We swung out a bit at the stern, but my brother fended off the other boats with a languid poke of his boathook on their metal stantions. Fibreglass cracks if it is hit hard and so the metal railing or the halyards, back- stays, mainstays or stantions are legitimate targets for fending off.

My brother leapt on to the boat beside me and tied the two sterns together, making sure there were enough fenders in the right place. We were lower than all the other boats as usual, and in more ways than one. I held on and kept my feet still.

When you tie up at night, you can set up a criss-cross pattern of ropes from one boat to the other known as 'springers'.

It is a complicated but effective method to keep boats from rubbing against each other.

I hoped he would come for me. I still held on, feet locked into place, knees still touching my chin. I could feel my kneecaps being tickled by my beard.

'That was fantastic, I really thought we were going to crash.' The Skipper admitted.

I looked between my aching knees and beyond my feet to my brother's shoes, which were planted firmly on the pontoon.

'Thanks, get me out of here, will you,' I replied.

'Just hang on, that was magic. I wish I had the camera. You did really well, great work. Sorry I came in far too fast. I'll take it easier next time.'

In the silence that followed his praise, I heard nothing but the tying of a bowline knot. I always favoured the reef knot, but he always performed the more complicated knots. He was merely keeping me talking while he tied a few ropes, including the painter I had been holding earlier, around a post and to each other.

I still held on in the same position.

It took an age for him to tie the last ropes. Cramp was beginning to set in, and a cold breeze came from the sea. The wind had changed, and I was starting to get cold. I felt the peeling skin on my shoulders and back contract, and I could see goose pimples and raised blond hair on my arms.

My legs were vibrating with tension, trembling with anticipation of release from this position. I doubted that I could move; yet my legs could not hold this position.

'If you don't tie up the boat soon, there won't be another time like this.'

He left his work, raised my feet off the pontoon and drew them straight for me. I just lay there. It was cold and the wind was getting stronger, but the relief at having my feet in their rightful place overrode all other considerations.

I sat up and asked my brother to fetch my sweater, which he did. I gratefully put it on and as I had lain on the ground in the forest, when I had fallen off his motorcycle, so I did here, savouring the silence that my brother so thoughtfully provided.

I was allowed to get my breath back and to regain control of my limbs.

It was not so much a case of finding my sea legs as being able to stand. I could have quite happily have lain there for half an hour, but that elusive harbour master had beaten a path towards us and was already negotiating a cash settlement for our overnight stay.

As per usual my brother dealt with the situation with consummate ease. There was a lot of sign language, rubbing of beards and chins, admiration of our craft. She was a beauty, despite her present looks; a truly beautiful woman's beauty is not affected by unkempt hair or unwashed teeth, you have the idea. Sign language was followed by a pad and paper being produced. My brother held up a finger.

'Uno notte,' he said firmly.

The harbour master licked his pencil and wrote down the figures for us to see.

'Ah, uno noches,' he replied briefly.

My brother paid him from a wad of notes in his back pocket that seemed dry and crisp. Everything I had, including my traveller's cheques, despite their plastic envelope, was damp. Business concluded and change given, the harbour master sauntered off. When we had paid the mooring fees in Puerto Banus my brother had gone white.

I could tell by his smile and by the wad of notes that he returned to his pocket that firstly, the mooring fees had seemed reasonable to him, and secondly that we would dine well that night.

Hunger forced me from prone position to upright and I unsteadily hobbled to the cabin to change. My brother voiced concern as I went, but I was already of martyr status in my eyes and therefore I could make little of the incident, I told him that I was fine, but hungry.

We had changed in record time and strolled from the boat towards the town.

My brother was tired, I could tell, not mentally drained but physically exhausted. He dragged his damaged leg several times. I noticed, but few strangers would have.

To them he walked confidently with a swagger as I did.

We had attitude, we had purpose; we were going somewhere. It was not the shoulder roll of boys in the hood, but a determined progress accompanied by a sailor's gait.

On land, having spent days at sea, it was difficult to adjust to the stable surface under foot. It is a most unsettling experience. At first you have to adjust to the roll of the ocean on board any vessel, but especially ours, so low in the water and at the mercy of every wave's roll, despite our six-foot keel.

Then, when you are ashore, your whole body is waiting for a roll to wrong-foot you.

Walking on the flat leaves your sense of equilibrium completely confused and I suppose that is why sailors walk the way they do. Your brain is constantly demanding to know why that piece of pavement is not at an angle of forty-five degrees or more. Each step on solid ground is a surprise, the hardness of terra firma a shock to the system.

It must be said that when we walked into the square, we looked the most unlikely sight. Our hair was unkempt; our skin was brown but burnt; our clothes made us look like we were coming back from market, but we walked past a group of girls playing basketball and they stopped. I stopped too.

I was acutely aware that in Franco's day, the ladies of Spain walked one way around the square and the boys in another to prevent them from talking, so I had been informed. To me it seemed a quaint mating ritual.

A girl's glance from behind a fan, a shy smile from the boy and they were halfway to marriage and grandchildren. I was also acutely aware that much had changed since Franco's day, not least the Fascist outlook, but the older generation still carried the remembrance of that extraordinary man.

My brother and I had been oblivious of the girls' sport, but they had stopped their game for us.

We had come up a side street and had decided to cross the road on to the pavement by the square to take a short cut to the docks.

The square was in fact an oblong of dust with two basket- ball nets at each end.

It was open and really, we should have noticed the girls, but we were trying to navigate our way, not a problem at sea, with our Michelin map but a major undertaking with no lamp and no North Star to guide us.

I felt we had transgressed some custom. The girls stopped their game and the ball bounced off to the centre of the square, where it eventually rolled for a time and stopped, having lost all momentum.

We carried on walking, in the hope that we would be across the perimeter of the square and nearer to the harbour before the police could be called. I was conscious of the eyes of almost twenty girls and their spectators, all girls too, staring at us.

Within two minutes, we were bombarded by a chorus of wolf-whistling and clapping.

In any language this is a form of appreciation unless they were trying to frighten us off. For a full five minutes, they whistled and clapped.

My brother and I increased our pace as subtly as we could, but we did not wish to appear scared.

I know of no one that this has happened to, nor had I come across such spontaneous adulation.

Perhaps it is vanity that suggests that this was the case.

They might have been trying to frighten us. It worked, just as a monkey seems to smile when it bares its teeth in anger.

To be realistic, it must have been like seeing a Viking for the first time. No matter our genetic makeup or our actual facial appearance, here were two tall, tanned, bearded blond men who were heading in their direction, to watch their match perhaps.

Teenagers are difficult to understand, but my brother and I felt elated and petrified at the same time.

Perhaps 'petrified' is the wrong word because it suggests being frozen in stone, fixed to the spot and we were far from that; we cleared the square in record time; I'm sure that we looked like two contestants in a walking race. We were of an age, my brother, at twenty-one, and I, at nineteen, that we could not deal with the situation, could not handle the adulation. I am sure that they could not see our faces. They definitely could not see our faces. I am sure they would have jeered and slow-clapped if they had.

It was the overall look, lean, blond, and tall, an unusual sight in Spain. In northern Italy, we would have been treated as the norm, but in southern Spain with the Andalusian colouring and stature we were unusual.

They were kind to us; most people who are different, wherever you go, are just stared at, and perhaps even ridiculed for being different but being different makes you special.

We were special that night and the spontaneous appreciation of our different appearance, our almost alien look, will rest with me forever.

We had those marvellous times sailing and then when we hit land we were welcomed by members of the opposite sex, girls. And what did we do?

Exactly.

We ran away.

On the other side of the square, we took the most likely road and ended up walking into the main harbour. The first priority was buying some cigarettes.

Here our tastes differed.

I liked the Fortuna but preferred the Ducados with its toasted tobacco. My brother liked black tobacco but preferred the blond tobacco if he could get it. Smoking was such a treat that we bought a pack of each from the kiosk.

It was so continental.

In England and America any shop will sell these awful things, but in Spain and Italy and France it is a state monopoly. Only certain outlets can sell them. It reminded me of Canada. There the sale of alcoholic drink is a state monopoly.

In Dubai you are limited to a certain amount of alcohol if you are a Westerner.

All these things some people would look upon as an inconvenience, but with planning any obstacle can be overcome. To my brother and I, the purchase of our cigarettes from a kiosk was a quaint, cultural quirk.

We ate at the Delfin, one of the best restaurants in Adra. Our meal was delicious, but it was marred by my wanting to go off and find our fan club.

I had not played basketball for such a long time, and I felt that I could benefit from a re-introduction to the sport. My brother was quite happy to talk and so we talked, both of us speaking openly about our adventures so far and our feelings about them.

It was much more satisfying than a ball game with seventeen sixteen-year-old Spanish beauties. The food was superb.

Nothing beats fresh fish, even if it is caught in what some people refer to as the greatest lake in the world. I was truly happy. I had squid and anchovy and grilled sardines and all manner of white fish, plus the stress of tidal navigation had been removed. It may have been a struggle to reach this Promised Land, but I was here now.

My brother seemed relieved that we had made it thus far and through the square. He was much more aware of the sailing mythology, sirens tempting sailors from their boats and Greek heroes held up in their progress home by diverting females.

The only problem was lifting our tired bodies off the seats and trying to find our way back to Waterwitch, the only 'she' that we had any interest in. I even found myself saying that we should make a start for home. I considered the boat our home from then on, and when I had to leave her, I had so many memories, not all of them good, that it was a veritable wrench.

From then on, I knew that whatever happened to me, that boat had taught me a valuable lesson. When an adventure ends, there is another one awaiting you around the corner.

I cannot recall our return to the boat.

The square was dark and deserted when we passed by and I think I almost ended up in the drink whilst trying to get aboard, but that is all I can remember.

Chapter Twenty-Two - Plain Sailing

The sun sat in an incredibly clear sky, a pale blue reflection of a heat haze. We untied our boat and sailed smoothly out to sea. The pool was calm, and I pushed us off from the dock, the painter in one hand, the bow rail in the other. I stepped aboard, although it was a stretch step.

Once the boat was drifting backwards, we hauled up the sails, which we had prepared for our departure. The sails were hoisted as we reversed slowly from our berth, employing the usual practice, my brother winching up the mainsail, me pulling up the jib on its rope, the clips already attached to make it smoother and quicker for my inexperienced hands. The tiller was lashed to the bench to ensure a straight path.

Then, the boat stopped in the water, the wind filling its sails as an effective break. My brother bounded back to the tiller. He was incredibly agile despite his injury. He turned the sails into the wind, and we drifted forward towards the harbour walls. I scurried back and we tacked just before the entrance and out to sea.

This manoeuvre sounds easy, but it is no mean feat. Fortunately, we were dab hands at such a performance. I took one last look back at our resting place and saw the Harbour Master standing on the sea wall waving his cap in the air, bidding us farewell.

I felt sure he was also impressed at our superior sailing skills. Although it was my brother's glory, I basked in it too. After all, I had been instrumental in getting us away from the dock and raising our sails, in the last-minute tack and in keeping a look out for jagged rocks as my brother kept the rudder steady with a firm hand on the tiller.

In explaining our voyage, the details of everyday life at sea might have been omitted.

Our cleanliness was important.

We saved our clean clothes for being in harbour, but we washed any dirty articles ourselves out to sea. The main consideration was to get as much sea between us and shore, to pump the bilges and trim the sails.

We were trying to meet friends in Ibiza who had booked tickets in order to arrive when we would be there.

Calculations and chart or map reading, taking into account prevailing winds and fastest routes on each tack, were meticulously entered into by my brother as I sailed the swiftest and most direct course east.

Often, the two elements could not be combined. The quickest route was sometimes the longest, the shortest distance having to be covered by a long triangular journey, all due to the wind. If the wind blew from a certain direction, we would have to sail at an efficient angle to it to get the greatest speed.

This was not always the shortest route.

There was lots to do on board, especially if you were out to sea for three days. On this leg of the journey, my brother had been to the baker's and the cheese seller to get our provisions in the morning while I slept.

The stock of tinned foods was holding out well. We had, after all, spent each day in Vilamoura stocking up when we went to get our daily provisions. Miraculously the freshwater containers were brimming too.

My brother had, obviously, taken care of that as well. He was an excellent quartermaster and sailor, never leaving dock without enough fresh water to drink and for our packet soup at night or our coffee during the day. It was with this very fresh water that we washed our clothes.

A small plastic basin was stowed under the aft deck with everything else.

After we had sailed an hour or so away from land and made sure our bilges were almost dry, it was time to ferret around for this article.

Once found, we took it in turns to either be at the tiller or wash our clothing.

We dare not use a bucket. Once when Patrick was on board, he had put his hand in a bucket to wash his face, thinking it was our shower bucket, and it was full of paint.

He was lucky really, because the other bucket was our toilet, but we meticulously dragged it over the side to rinse it out if we had used it.

Washing clothes was our only extravagance with the valuable commodity. Fresh water was vital for our survival, but we could splash out when doing our laundry.

I had raised my eyebrows when I had seen the packet of hand-washing soap flakes being unpacked by unfriendly customs officials at Faro airport, I felt sure there would be laundering facilities at various marinas, plus I had packed enough clothes for a month, mostly shorts, polo shirts and swimming trunks, but with the mustiness and damp of the sea, the clothes smelt damp before I wore them.

A swirl in soapsuds followed by a good wringing took care of the first part. The dirty water was thrown into the sea, so many disappointed fish following the sound of water on the surface, expecting to find potato peelings or some other edible gash that they were used to feasting on when other vessels passed by. Then, a whole litre or two was used to rinse out the soap. The clothes were wrung again and like suburban householders, we hung the washing on the line to dry with plastic pegs. The line was in fact any piece of the rigging that was not covered in canvas.

Personal hygiene was slightly more involved at sea. We had a back-to-basics existence. Going to the loo involved hanging over the side, either face on or crouched supported by hands that gripped the rigging. So acute was my embarrassment at this procedure that my brother took great delight at trying to photograph this private act.

Each time I squatted over the side with the foaming water only a few feet below me, and the boat ploughing through the waves creating an uncomfortable undulating motion, I would be confronted by the sound of footfalls and the sight of my brother advancing, camera in hand. His camera did not need focusing, being a modest model and so it was a race to stand up and pull up my pants before a photograph could be taken.

This intimidation amused my brother almost to the state of hilarity and annoyed me. I felt it was an invasion of my privacy, but perhaps he was right. There is no privacy when two people share a wooden envelope forty-two feet long, six feet wide with a cabin five feet high.

I just wanted to be left in peace for one crucial moment. It was not as though I was shy.

Equally I could admire a photograph of me at the helm, but I could not enjoy a portrait of me hanging over the side, teeth clenched and knuckles white. Finally personal hygiene took on a new dimension. The sea was everything to us, our highway, our playground, our source of anxiety, our dustbin, our drainage, our loo, and our bath.

In the afternoon, a big black boat called the Solitaire cruised past us coming from the east. She must have been doing almost thirty knots. She was beautiful to behold, jet black, with a white radar dome on top. She left a twenty-foot aquamarine wake in the dark blue water.

She almost ran us over.

We bucked and swayed in her aftershock waves. By this stage the wind had died, but the waves were getting uncomfortable as we luffed in the doldrums. We were low on fresh provisions and bread. We never ate salad; more's the pity and I was surprised we did not have scurvy. Our fruit had gone, as had almost all our fresh water.

The light was fading, and we had spent too many nights at sea. We needed the rest; we needed a salad for supper. Making one on board was too messy, too involved for our galley.

Shore visits alone guaranteed our vitamin intake. Added to this was a diet of Norman's one-pot-wonders while at sea. It consisted of a tin of tomatoes, some form of tinned fish or meat and lots of spices. No wonder we lost weight. Our evening meal cooked to keep out the chill was the only proper meal we had.

Breakfast and lunch consisted of bread and cheese. My brother had eaten the last chunk the night before.

Worst of all we had been at sea for three days without tobacco of any sort. We were pining for any form of nicotine. Smokers will realise our dilemma. We wanted to give up, but there was no real reason to do so.

We had agreed that all cigarettes would be smoked on shore.

That meant ten each from a pack. We stuck to that even if it meant sitting up into the night smoking on board the boat in harbour.

Once we set sail, tobacco was banned.

We could not and would not run a dry ship.

We needed our alcohol too.

Those were the only drugs we allowed our- selves, but they were as necessary as light and water to a plant.

We had finished the last of the crown cork San Miguel and we wanted wine and brandy.

One of our first breakfasts in a Spanish fishing port had been sardines and bread washed down with black coffee and a generous tot of Spanish brandy.

There was no breakfast so sublime particularly after a night of drinking that terrible tasting, but warming, white Portuguese spirit.

Earlier that day, as we sailed towards the early morning sun, we had spied a French registered sailing boat. It was as long as ours, but built for luxury and sunbathing, rather like the boat I had envisaged when I first arrived in Portugal.

Its blue fibreglass hull keeled over, its white sail a bleached triangle straining in the wind. It was travelling fast, maybe ten knots, but we were travelling fast too, dose-reefed, sails hauled in to take advantage of the high glorious wind that blew off from the coast.

The warmth of a lavanta and the strength wrested from the gods, Neptune was on our side. The water was becalmed, almost a mirror in comparison to the high seas we had seen before. It was slightly choppy, and the horsebacks were fairly high, but to us it was almost dull.

Our speed was the only exhilarating factor. Here was a spick and span cruiser, and we with our duck-egg blue and white filter hull and beige-grey dirty sails were gaining.

Not for nothing was Waterwitch queen of the thirty square metres.

She loved the chase and her Sitka spruce sliced unerringly through the foam. Out at sea people get a sixth sense. It develops very much in the same way as a person's hearing in isolated areas is attuned to recognise any sound that is different.

I am not sure whether our French friend could hear us, but one minute he was staring at his full sails with the satisfaction that a lone crewman finds in keeping his sails in trim and his helm steering a true course, then the next minute he turned, perhaps to take a bearing, perhaps just looking for unfriendly tankers that might accidentally run him down.

The expression changed to horror.

There, less than six feet behind was this scruffy ship coming up on his port stern and getting closer. Were we pirates about to ram our old boat against his and take over, did we intend to rob him? These questions must have gone through his mind.

Every sailor has experienced the dread of pirates, theft of their equipment or being lost at sea. Much publicity had been given to incidences of piracy in the Caribbean.

Crews disappeared and boats were re-registered in different continents or in different oceans.

Norman stood at the prow as I held the helm. We bounced as the waves from his wake buffeted Waterwitch, but still we sped on, the gap between vessels shortening all the time. You could almost see his brain computing the various connotations.

Was it the mad boat's right of way?

Were we about to peel off on another tack?

Did we intend to pass behind over his wake?

It was against all maritime law to come in this close and steal his wind. We may not have been burglars, but we were les voleurs if we stole his wind and caused him to luff.

Luffing, that most annoying sensation when wind leaves the sails, perhaps in a becalmed area of the sea and your power is cut off. The wind would drive you around to another tack to get a better breeze, but once you had luffed that was it.

You no longer had the power to tack, and your sails were useless. Above us, he had the advantage of starting the diesel engines, but that was hardly the point. This was glorious sailing weather.

You did not want to motor until you came into harbour. Norman used the loudhailer, a tin cone with a handle, original to the boat with 1930s municipal green paint peeling from the outside.

'Avez vous des cigarettes?' he called.

The French man shrugged. I thought I heard him say or at least mouth, 'Comment?' but my French idiom was as good as my lip reading.

He could have been saying something completely different and much less friendly.

My brother walked back to the stem and took the rudder.

His helmsmanship alone would allow us to shadow the boat without taking the wind out of her sails.

The speed indicator was reading nine knots, a splendid speed. It had to be maintained - too fast and we would indeed be too close and take the Frenchman's 'vent'; too far and we would slip away behind and be unable to negotiate for our needs.

I took up the cry and despite the wind behind me blowing my voice towards him, the Frenchman shrugged, his expression hidden behind his sunglasses. He only glanced back occasionally. He had a big boat to steer and keep moving. I tried again. He realised we were not coming alongside to ask directions.

No skipper of a pukka boat would. Finally, he realised our needs and smiled a knowing smile. These English were mad, shadowing me for a mere packet of cigarettes, skilfully keeping the same distance, just for nicotine.

This would be an interesting story to tell in Sete that summer.

We had been on a marathon watch, four hours on and four hours off. It was with immense relief that we docked in busy Aguillas on Friday, 11th June, three days after the day we left.

We had friends in Mojacar, a small town not far away, so we hitch-hiked there, had a cocktail with them at the Peanut bar in Turre, checked into the Hotel Moresco, had a shower, and went to bed. Mojacar is a beautiful little town, with Puerta del Rio and Cabo Gata to the west, then Garrucha, Aguillas and Puerto de Maxarron to the east.

Already, it was 12th June. The next morning, we had bacon, eggs, and mushrooms for breakfast, our first fried breakfast in over five weeks. Our friends gave us a lift back to Aguillas on Monday evening, after a day on the beach.

On Tuesday morning, we set sail, passing the white conning tower of Almeria airport, which rose up from the sand on the beach.

Chapter Twenty-Three - Cartagena

Cartagena presented its own problems. The equivalent of Portsmouth or Annapolis, the harbour was one part fishing town, one part military base. Cartagena possessed the finest the Spanish navy could muster. Taking an English registered vessel into the port was like sailing into Cadiz in the sixteenth century after the King of Spain's beard had been singed.

We did it, nonetheless.

A warm northwest wind blew us into the harbour at Cartagena. It felt like a lavanta coming off the desert. It was still dry, with just a hint of moisture picked up from the sea, a pinch of salt water.

The main thing was that it was strong and blew hard against our canvas which we pulled in and kept close, but still the wind blew, and we eased off to enjoy its caress and to feel it blow the now-bloated canvas without remorse.

Underneath the bow broke through the calm water, sending spray spluttering left and right as it drove through, slicing through moving waves of fluid, flashing foam and transparent spume.

There was no stopping we now; at seven knots and at the peak of her trim, she ploughed on relentlessly, even though the wind had made the waves grow larger.

She eased through each wave, rocking a little unsteadily, her bow was nudging crest after crest as wave after wave wracked her hull.

Cartagena is a huge harbour at the end of a long thin bay, a natural shelter from the elements. Cape de Palos is a solid rock buffer against weather from the northeast. It is far enough inland for storms from the south to peter out before they reached port.

In fact, that was the problem.

By the time we reached the main harbour our wind was gone. Our lovely strong wind that had rushed us to this point suddenly faded.

A final gasp moved us past the rocks on either side that prevented any penetration by any wind.

Suddenly, we were luffing.

We still had momentum, but the wind had fallen out of the sails. Both jib and main were limp, flapping wildly and uncontrollably and then they stopped and hung off their steel ropes, impotent sheets of canvas.

If you have been there, then you know the sight. We saw the town on the starboard bow, a beautiful old Andalusian village that sprawls up a hill; on the outskirts, more modern houses reflected the growing population. There were two reasons for this port's expansion. The first was trade.

It has to be remembered that many old towns and cities have changed little since the last century, with the exception of Seville, Madrid, and Barcelona. I am of course talking of change in size and shape and not in regard to technology.

Most traditional Spanish towns are nucleated settlements based around a castle, church, or port. No prizes for guessing which category this town fell into. Linear settlement generally signifies a new departure or venture, for example, the towns of Torremolinos in the south and Benidorm in the east.

That way the old towns remain within their boundaries to a great extent and expansion takes place in old villages, which grow into tourist towns.

It was surprising that this town had so few modern buildings that we could see from the sea. I expected Genoa to be traditional, not Cartagena, especially as it was the main port for the southeast coast, supplying Murcia, Lorca and possibly Granada.

This port predated even the Armada.

It was wonderful to behold the busy dock with its rows of freight ships either tied up or at anchor waiting for a berth.

The sun just starting its descent to the west made the bay glimmer and bathed the beige and bright white buildings.

We had no wind, but as the sun beamed down on us, our faces beamed too with satisfaction.

Our smiles were those of tired sailors, grateful to be back in shore, travellers glad to be close to their destination.

We were happy and both of us loved this traditional part of Spain, what we referred to as the real Spain.

As young teenagers we had gone to the Alhambra in Granada and that had taught us that there was another country behind the sea and sand if only one was prepared to look.

Here we had found another nugget, a splendid, bustling, working harbour. We had become bored of the impersonal whitewashed marinas.

We wanted simple cafes, not piano bars; fluent Spanish, not broken English; we wanted tapas, not the savoury crepes on offer in Marbella.

Here we would practise our appalling Spanish, and order chicken as it was the only thing we knew on the menu.

More likely we would order a selection of tapas, ask the waiter what each dish was, repeat the name back to him, be corrected, try again, be corrected and then on our third attempt be reminded that it was 'muy bien' when it was 'calor', but not so good when it was cold.

I licked my lips at the thought of squid in black ink and patatas bravas, Russian salad and fresh anchovy. On our trip we had tried every type of fish dish that we could.

The sea provided both our harvest and our highway. It provided our bathroom too, but we tried not to think about this too much when we ate. The thought of tobacco also stirred longings. I could not wait to taste the black tobacco on my tongue, feel the smoke inside my lungs and smell the aroma through my nose.

My lips longed to touch the white filter, my fingers twitched to strike the match that would light the end that would glow and burn, orange and grey. The satisfaction gained through producing a cylinder of ash was equal to the sense of achievement from a few hours' work.

It was such easily obtained satisfaction, such instant gratification. I had waited long enough for this pleasure; I had suffered my fag-free fast. I had deprived myself long enough.

I had reasons to be cheerful: land was within sight, and it was only three thirty in the afternoon.

We had entered one or two harbours at three thirty at night, Gibraltar for example, which was well-lit by arc lights on long poles up which helped.

On another occasion, in a tiny port, the only light we had was the mirrored reflection of a bar porch light. Our boathook had come in useful then, as had the hurricane lanterns that swung from our bow, our mast and above the cockpit.

The second reason to be gleeful was that this harbour was indeed one of the most beautiful places we had ever been and exploring its winding back streets would be a treat.

The third reason to be cheerful was the food that would be on offer; no one can resist fish fresh from the sea. We had just overtaken three trawlers on our way in.

People who live by the sea catch lots of fish and are therefore far more discerns customers.

That makes the restaurant and cafe owners more demanding and the fishmongers more competitive, wanting to supply only the best to their local customers. Ports are the places for fish.

I mentioned that Cartagena had expanded because of its location. It is practically on the Greenwich Meridian and opposite the Algerian coast. I would say that Cartagena is the closest Spanish port to Morocco, great for trade.

However, the second reason for Cartagena's expansion was military.

Guarding the entrance to the Mediterranean at the southeastern point of Spain, Cartagena had become a military port at about the same time that the Phoenicians started trading here, a while back, in other words.

I mention this military connection not merely out of interest, but because It is important to understand the port's strategic importance. If you were in England, you would consider this town the equivalent of Portsmouth; in Scotland, Lossiemouth; in America, Annapolis.

This was the major league, top-notch, top security naval installation in Spain. It makes Gibraltar with its motor torpedo boats and minesweepers seem small fry in comparison. I hope that I have made it clear that the Falklands conflict, although several thousand miles away, in a different time zone and in a different season in fact, managed to affect holiday makers here.

Protests by the Spanish government had taken up an awful lot of United Nations time and a large section of the Spanish newspapers.

While 'Ola' talked about Princess Diana and other European royals, the government and the press were portraying the British as being bullying imperialists, which Spain as a republic had a duty to stand up to.

With our Royal Ensign fluttering off the back, there were few fewer friendly places we could be, except the Falklands themselves. We were resigned to maltreatment; already our passports had saved us lengthy interrogations at docksides and searches that had left English yachts looking as if they had been vandalised. All this was behind me.

I knew we could blend into the local populace.

We looked vaguely Scandinavian, with our sun-bleached brown hair and beards and once we announced we were Irish we were pretty much home and dry.

I described the bay as thin and long and that we saw the town from our starboard bow. To the port and slightly obscured by our slack sails was a second harbour.

We could only see the entrance as the rest was tucked around behind a rock. At the entrance though we could see a jetty and tied to this jetty was a Spanish cruiser, larger than a frigate, but not as large as a destroyer. It was as if our keel was a magnet that was attracted to the steel hull of the ship.

At first, I was calm, my brother was moving off towards this ship in order to find some wind and complete a neat tack that would bring us into the fishing harbour and a delightful supper, preceded by a few beers at different bars around the town. I would hold that thought.

The wind did not come, a breeze managed to stir our Ensign on the aft stantion, but the Spanish courtesy flag on the main mast remained stubbornly furled.

My brother had told me stories about sailors who had failed to fly the correct courtesy flag at the correct time. It was a sensitive issue. I was worried lest our hosts took umbrage at our lack of respect.

'What's happening?' I asked nonchalantly.

I had stopped admiring the port that I thought we were heading for.

It seemed pointless to dream. It had been seen, but it had slipped past us now and there seemed nothing left to do but ignore its passing.

Both of realised we were heading towards the ship, an aggressive action if ever there was one. We were being pushed by the current.

'There's no wind. I can't turn her,' he replied.

'You do realise that we're heading for that ship,' I subtly mentioned, sounding as casual as I could, assuming that he might have missed all two hundred tons of it, bristling with all manner of armaments.

'That grey thing there?' he responded. I could rely on him to be sarcastic.

'What should I do?'

'I'm not sure. I think it is best to keep still and don't move too quickly. I've just noticed they have started to train their deck guns on us.'

'How many do they have?' I asked.

Being on the other side of the main sheet he could see more.

'There are three anti-aircraft guns trained on us now,' my brother continued helpfully.

'I think I can see the rear gun turrets turning,' I added.

'The two in the bow are turning too. It looks like the crew are armed as well.'

'I hope you realise these are conscripts,' I announced.

'The thought had crossed my mind, trigger-happy and panicky,' he assured me.

'I presume they have live rounds in all their guns,' I replied nervously.

'When we find out, it will be too late,' he noted sagely.

'I think the tide's taking us past them into the next section,' he observed calmly.

'It is not the next section; it's the main military area. There are two submarines there.'

'They won't be too anxious to let us see them, will they?' he explained.

The Riddle of the Sands had left me shaken.

'What's the Spanish for no wind, no power?'

'Wind is venta; I know that much,' he bragged, smiling grimly.

'Can't we just take down the sails and hoist up a white flag?'

'It might do some good to haul down the sails, it will help them see us more clearly.'

'Great, we'll be a better target then. I'll take down the jib.'

'I'll lash the tiller and do the main mast,' he offered/

We were up on deck and across to our stations within seconds.

I released the jib rope and the sail slid down the wire, I unclipped the sheet and furled the canvas.

I turned around and my brother was lashing the already furled main mast. He was much more experienced than me and so much quicker. That is why I always did the jib. It was a smaller and simpler task. I looked to our starboard bow. We had drifted to the port a bit more and we were heading for the submarine pen as my brother had said we were.

I had suggested surrender and I really meant it. The anti-aircraft guns followed our vessel as if they were connected by wire and what was more worrying, the agitated sailors, some of them our age, were even less pleased that we were heading in that direction.

For all they knew we could have been some suicidal death squad, with a boat packed with high explosives.

If that was the case and I was on board the ship, I would be relieved, if I were them, that the floating torpedo was headed elsewhere.

Military regulations always upset civilian rights of progress. By drifting into this part of the harbour we were entering a restricted area, a no-go zone.

By this stage, with our field of vision clear of canvas, I could see the bulbous snouts of two submarines, I could clearly see the marines scurrying about the Spanish boat, their yells of panic, barked orders.

The weaponry was impressive.

I counted seven rifles and twelve sub-machine guns in one glance. Suddenly everything went still. The pandemonium died down. All that could be heard was the lashing of water against our bows and their hull.

Then I heard a click, followed by seventeen others, although I admit I lost count after fourteen.

The loudspeaker on their boat was deafening, although it was most probably turned down to whisper level.

'Halt' or 'halte' or 'halta', in any European language can convey the word halt or stop in English especially if it is delivered loud enough.

The Europeans have learnt much from the English about communicating with people who do not share your language. Speak loudly and firmly. It worked for us, but we could not comply. This was the point where my brother and I, using our miming skills, really started to perform.

Having ourselves learnt much from communicating in foreign lands; we fell back on gesture. The two of us turned our palms heavenward and tilted our heads to the left side. We were both left-handed and shrugged our shoulders, leaving them hanging in mid-shrug. I added a final touch by pouting in a helpless way.

Hopefully, the Captain had binoculars. We hoped to convey our disappointment, as if to say, 'if only we could comply with your request', or 'it is really out of our hands, there is nothing we can do'.

Trying to speak in Spanish to any of their crew could be fatal. It might result in a misheard phrase, perhaps an insult concerning his parentage or the occupation of his mother.

The man with the gun, you keep happy. We could not risk upsetting these people more than they were already. Having several guns trained at you is a worrying prospect. Several thoughts flash through your mind, such as, He is pointing that thing at me, it might go off, or He might be prepared to use it, or He might want to use it to see what happens with a live target.

Everyone has to join the services for a year or two in Spain.

We knew that, as Spanish friends of ours dodged the draft as a matter of course.

Who wanted a seriously short haircut and months of drills when you could be dancing with a girl with a long haircut promising month of thrills, parties, dances, films? The choice was stark, but we understood the sacrifice.

The big question was which service got the brainy people and which one got the troublemakers, the people no one can train, the ones no other service will have? If it was the army, we were fine. The navy in England is the 'senior service', but it did not follow that this would be so for Spain.

Cartagena and a term at sea could well prove to be an ideal ground for the lost causes. If that was so, then we were in trouble. I knew about guns and their safety catches. We were not close enough to see properly, but if I hoped that these sailors did not have their fingers in the trigger guard even, and therefore there was no chance they could shoot me, unless they stumbled and the gun went off, which was highly unlikely.

Maybe one of them hated all the English for their involvement in the Falklands crisis. A few bullets and he would most probably be a hero for killing two English spies. The continental nations are far more lenient on crimes of passion. We should not be there, he realised. We were English and he wanted to strike a blow for his Latin cousins.

End of story and end of our tale.

The big guns worried me. There was no safety catch on those.

The anti-aircraft gun could deliver twelve rounds in as many seconds at a touch of a button. I had seen one in Portsmouth.

The Bophors deck guns I also recognised.

'Those Bophors and that Oerlikon are worrying me,' I complained.

It's amazing how knowledge can diffuse your fear in a situation.

We were going to die, but I was determined to show my brother my knowledge of naval artillery.

Not only could I recognise the manufacturer of the guns by their shape, but I could tell you the calibre and how many magazines of high-explosive shells could be pumped into our boat before anyone could say, 'Cease firing!'

Still, we sailed on, the guns pointed at our bow as we crept towards the cruiser; the guns pointed at our amid- ships as we stripped the deck of sail cloth; now the guns were trained on our aft section.

We could tell they were getting twitchy.

The reflection of sun on the lenses of binoculars on the bridge proved that we were being monitored closely.

The Captain was on the line, as we slipped past, to the Admiral asking for permission to fire. I hoped that he had enjoyed a good lunch and left orders for his siesta to be extended and for him not to be disturbed. Then I wished the Admiral at his desk having had a quick lunch, only because I felt sure that if he had been disturbed during his siesta, he might well give that permission.

'No engine, engine kaput,' Norman shouted as he pointed at our outboard motor. 'No venta.'

It sounds pathetic now, but at the time it sounded pretty good to me, and I was impressed even if the crew was not. The guns trained on us seemed to say, so what?

I saw two of the sailors raise their rifles in the bow of the cruiser.

Suddenly, from inside the submarine pen, there was the sound of a diesel motor, which belonged to a whaler.

The boat reached us in minutes, relieving our tension in seconds. We caught the ropes thrown to us, fore and aft and tied their painters to our stantions.

The boarding party consisted of two young Spaniards, armed with automatic pistols in white holsters and broad smiles. They wore blue trousers and blue shirts; Number Eights as they were called in England, work wear, not dress uniform.

The acquisition of side arms looked rather sudden.

Their holsters were more in keeping with an impressive parade. I guessed that they had just come from the armoury, and I had no doubt that these weapons and all the weapons that had been trained on us that day were carrying live rounds. We were certainly lucky to be alive; not one shot had been fired.

Both of the sailors were slightly older than my brother; one was thin the other was a little bit overweight. The chubbier one spoke. I stole a glimpse of the driver of their boat, one hand rested on the big wheel in the centre of their boat. His raised foot was propped against the wheel housing, his other hand rested on the handle of his gun.

I noticed that the button that kept the holster flap closed was undone.

'Buenos dias,' I tried.

'Good afternoon, you are not very popular, you have almost got yourself blown out of the water here today. What seems to be the problem?' he exclaimed.

He had no accent to speak of and his English was delivered perfectly and fluently. How I wished I could speak Spanish that way, it was faultless.

'Our engine is gone,' my brother explained.

'There is no wind for you to sail. This is a beautiful boat by the way,' our Spanish saviour announced.

'Gracias,' my brother replied, 'thank you, but without wind she is useless.'

My brother liked to impress with his linguistic ability, especially if someone could speak fluently. As if to say, 'I know a word in a different language'.

I kept quiet, watching the thin man who seemed twitchy and the nonchalant driver who I felt was playing it cool, but was in fact nervous.

'Where are you from?' the sailor asked.

'We're Irish,' my brother declared.

'The boat is registered in England?' he noted suspiciously.

'It has to be, it was made in the Isle of Wight.'

I half expected our Spanish sailor to say, 'I've been there', but he was much less interested in knowing the geographical location of the Isle of Wight than in establishing our identity and our nationality.

Once he had checked our passports and read the boat's papers, he was immediately more relaxed. Ireland and Spain had no quarrel. We were fellow republicans and fellow Catholics. They had Basque separatists, we had trouble in the north too; but it was we who got the cold weather.

Our interrogator and translator informed his friends of our status and they seemed instantly more at ease.

The second boarder smiled at us. The driver could not smile, it seemed, but as a token he scowled less.

'We'll tow you into port, the other way. You can dock at the Royal Yacht Club.'

'Thank you.'

'No problem, but next time stay away from this part of the port, or you could be shot"

The thin man stepped back to the bow, untied the painter from the stantion, wrapped it around the bow rail and secured it with a bowline to the anchor chain, then he smiled and leapt into the aft of the boat, standing on the bench seat at the back.

Our friends untied the forward painter from the aft stantion and leapt off the boat. He had barely regained his balance after landing when the driver slipped his gear lever into forward and eased the throttle in the same direction.

The engine had been thudding quietly, in a dull diesel sort of way, but now it came to life. Within half a minute, the motorboat had spun around, and it had taken us with it.

Finally, after an hour of heading west, northwest into danger, we were now travelling east, north- east to safety.

The wake the lead boat produced along with our own wake made me feel as if we were doing five knots. If they had been doing twenty-five knots, they could not have got me away from there quick enough.

As we passed the cruiser, I noticed that the crew's guns were pointed downwards now, trained at the deck, harmless and no longer threatening. The deck guns were trained to the sky. I had noticed the relaxation of weaponry before, just as our boarding party came on board, but my relief at speaking to someone about our situation, even if it was just listening while my brother spoke, was so overwhelming that the passing of danger had not yet registered.

I had observed the situation quickly, but my focus had been on our saviours and nothing else. Thanks to them we were rescued and still alive.

It was an incredible experience, not one I wanted to repeat.

Within the hour we were sitting in the yacht club, a glass and wooden structure built on a pontoon in the 1920s or 1930s. A beeswax smell pervaded the atmosphere.

We lounged in reclining wood and cane chairs and a waiter brought us Spanish gin and tonic on a silver salver, ready-mixed and heady-fixed; there must have been three shots of gin in the tall glass, just a taste of tonic.

Back home it was the other way around; gin passed over the glass, a splash. We asked him what cigarettes he had, and he told us he had Rothmans. We ordered those as a salute to our English existence in London and as a memory of our mundane life there with no guns trained on us. This was living.

Sadly, I let myself down in civilized circumstances. Being a philistine, I ate the lemon in the bottom of the glass.

The sailors had offered us Fortuna cigarettes as they helped us tie up on the jetty. We were the only craft tied on to the five-berth pier.

Waterwitch was made for this berth and the berth was made for Waterwitch, a low-slung dock for her low-slung deck. Those cigarettes tasted sublime. We waited until the boat was secure to light them, tying up knots with our cigarettes behind one ear. The sailors made sure that we were lit, both carrying disposable lighters.

Then, together, as one hand put the lighter back, another reached out to shake hands. It was the warmest of sentiments - saving my life twice, once from the guns and once by providing tobacco at the right moment.

After they shook our hands, they pointed in the direction of the club at the other end of the jetty, gesturing and saying we should go there.

We had followed their advice.

It was built over the water on wooden stilts and was now obviously a curiosity for social venues. We watched and waited for our escort to climb back up into their huge high-sided whaler and we waved them off like old friends.

We sat in the lounge like a couple of lounge lizards. Noel Cowards with blithe spirits. There was no ice in the drinks served here, but the tonic was cold from the fridge and the gin was kept in the pantry, a large bottle of Larios. Two stiff gin and tonics later and we were ready to curl up and go to sleep in our seats. Instead, we watched the sunset send splendid spectrums of the silver-blue sea, first yellow, then orange, red and then blue.

From another window we could see the moon waiting in the wings, ready to take up the dominant role. There was every chance that we might never raise ourselves from our seats, but hunger pangs drove us to look for food.

It was around about suppertime in England when we left the bar. The light was just fading.

We had changed our clothes before going to the club, so we walked gingerly along the bobbing jetty into town.

It seemed incredible to be eating before eight in Spain. Our navigation generally meant we arrived at the tail end of the last sitting. It was amazing to be out when it was not pitch black, but only dusk.

We found the busiest and brightest harbour-front cafe and settled in our seats. Both of us had to have a coffee before we could be capable of choosing our supper.

After a good meal with a lovely white wine, we skipped brandy and sauntered off to bed. We decided we would have an early night that night but managed to slip back into the now-dark club, its faded elegance lit by two standard lamps.

Two couples occupied leather armchairs in another room. Our sailor friends popped back to see that we were fully recovered from our ordeal, and we tried to press them for a drink. Instead, they bought us one and we offered them our fags.

Through sign language, we managed to establish that everyone was happy that the affair had concluded without injury and that it had been a close-run thing.

They bid us goodnight and we thanked them once again for saving us. They had even offered to look at the engine earlier that day, but my brother knew it was hopeless without the right parts.

The Spanish in my experience have always been courteous, kind, generous-spirited, lively, informative, intelligent, and jovial. That day however I saw another side of Spain, Spain at the end of a gun. It was ironic really because just after finishing The Riddle of the Sands, I started to read Homage to Catalonia, Orwell's account of his experiences in the Spanish civil war.

It was not until we tried to untie the boat the next day, at sun-up, that we realised what excellent sailors they were.

It was almost impossible to untie the knots. They didn't want us slipping off in the night. It took both of us and a yawl to get our ropes free.

Chapter Twenty-Four

Mar Menor, San Javier, Torre Vieja, Santa Pola, and Alicante.

The low pressure from the Atlantic brought the storm. How it had got to the coast of Spain I could not tell. Whatever the reason, the bad weather had come. The storm clouds dropped long pellets of rain from the heavens, making our life hell. These pelted on to the roof of the cabin when you tried to sleep, echoing and annoying.

If you were on deck, it soaked you to the skin.

These droplets, the size of a small insect, then released themselves from your hair or clothing in a more lethargic manner.

Equally, raindrops slid past the cockpit windows like fish in a tank.

You could not sleep, and you could not see for the splashes on the windows and the rivers they produced. A mist hung over the coastline, almost like that of a tropical rain forest in the rainy season. There were parts of the coastline that were obscured by the fog, so it was difficult to tell if the sea was land and the land was sea.

The hills were barely visible and in parts they were completely invisible.

We were both on deck, neither able to sleep. Thick beads of water bounced off our clothes, spinning off my brother's oilskins and slipping off my soaked cotton clothes. Alicante lay directly ahead of our rain-lashed vessel. I sat hunched against the chill wind.

The wooden shelf that we sat on to steer was covered in water. My denim jeans, the only warm trousers I had brought, slid across the varnished patina.

At first, I had tried to steady myself, but that was too exhausting. The tiller was lashed to the port stantion and the rope that held it was too awkward to reach.

Holding on to the gunwales took supreme effort and, try as I might; the motion of the boat and my bodyweight overcame the strength of my arm.

Two arms resting on the wood resulted in backache, and like the one-arm method, only resulted in slowing the motion rather than preventing it.

Cold and wet, I resigned myself to sliding from one end of the bench to the other.

I had managed to get two damp towels draped over each end of the bench seat to prevent the jarring pain of my hips hitting wood.

I was miserable.

My soggy sweater, my soaked pants, the darkness, the cold chill of night, the relentless fall of rain and the perpetual sliding made my watch a depressing four hours. We had turned off the navigation lights to conserve electricity.

If I had sighted a boat in the darkness, I would have switched them on, but no boat dared to venture out of harbour. Those wanting to enter Alicante were held up in other ports. Bigger shipping would head for Cartagena or be far out in the shipping lanes.

We were so close to land, five, maybe six miles away, held in a fashion by the canvas bag we called a sea anchor.

It did not seem that we were floating quite still as the waves buffeted us again and again, sending us back and forth, back, and forth, in a boring dance of despair. For six hours we had stayed where we were.

The heavy clouds hung over the horizon, where the land rose above the blue-black sea, constant, motionless. It was too dark to see the waves beyond the end of the boat. Still, we swayed; still I slipped, keeping an eye to stern ahead and gazing left to right, looking for lights.

Even the lights of Aguillas, so bright at dusk, seemed dimmed. All that we could do was sit and wait and hope that the storm would end.

I was relieved when my watch was over.

It was too perilous to brew coffee on our little stove. I wanted something warm; drinking water did not even occur to me. I had enough in my clothes.

My brother smiled and wished me a good night's sleep, assuring me needlessly that he would wake me in four hours. My body ached, especially my bottom and legs. I was so pleased to be out of the rain.

All the bedding was wet, so I grabbed a musty, sodden blanket and took it into the main cabin. I had never felt so tired.

It seemed warmer down below out of the night air. I could hear the waves lapping against the hull and felt almost seasick with the side-to-side motion.

There was nothing else on my mind but sleep.

If the storm had abated when I awoke, all well and good, but I did not care. If it grew into a hurricane, I could not care.

Sleep deprivation had driven me to one simple need - sleep. I collapsed on to the bed, still wearing my damp polo shirt and waterlogged jeans. It was pointless removing any garments as everything down below was wet.

When I hit the mattress, I could feel the water ooze out of the foam. It was not enough to drown me, but enough to make me realise that I was lying on an enormous sponge, which eased water from its fibres every time I rolled over.

The pillowcase and pillow seemed quite dry, but with drenched hair and raindrops still pouring off my face, there was little difference or comfort in a dry pillow.

The comfort was to be relatively still, to be out of the storm, swaying still, but horizontally like a baby in a cradle, not vertically slipping from side to side. I thought how glorious it was to be curled in a foetal ball and so much warmer already.

Soon, I was having the most gorgeous of dreams about a warm beach, a hot lady, and a cool glass of beer. Sleep had finally allowed me to lose my grip on reality and I couldn't have been more pleased.

I had just rolled over in my sleep, or on top of the girl of my dreams, when I was awoken.

It was my brother. Duty called. It was time to raise my head and rise from my waterbed.

Despondent but relieved, we finally approached the harbour wall. My brother was at the helm.

I had been given the erroneous task of being chief lookout and directing us through the channel, past the harbour walls, deciding when to turn and throw the rope to a friendly fisherman.

The likelihood of our being able to navigate such a small harbour under sail without incident was slim. It's all very well to study Royal Yachting Association manuals about ships under sail having priority.

It was quite another matter to convince several hundred tonnes of Spanish boat that you have right of way.

Only someone completely loco would attempt to enter a port under sail. Perhaps we were past masters, but it was not our ability that was in question.

The feeling towards the British in the wake of the Falklands War would convince any red-blooded Spanish skipper to run us down once he had seen the British Ensign.

No matter that a North African colony had been petitioning for independence from the yoke of Spanish imperialism for five years. The bar stewards putting glass in English tourists' drinks did not care about the hypocrisy of their fellow Latins or their government, but about nationalism and jingoistic pride.

Our Irish lineage counted for nothing.

The courtesy flag flying from the main mast was Spanish, but the flag at the stern showed us to be registered in the UK Therefore we were a legitimate target.

Rather than securing our passage, the great Ensign of England was a liability. Latin temperament tends to allow for crimes of passion and shooting first, asking questions afterwards.

The upshot was that we could just about sail through the harbour wall, turn three hundred and sixty degrees and moor where the fishing boats were, but it may not be possible to accomplish this act if a boat ran us down.

I wasn't even sure we had insurance, but in this phoney war we would be at fault.

I focused on my job and hoped that no boat would be leaving harbour until the next day, sure that the storm had past and was not merely abated. I could see nothing in front and nothing behind.

Only we could have been stupid enough to be out at sea when all professional seamen had listened to the forecast and stayed put. Life at sea is uncomfortable enough, without adding to the discomfort by getting yourself caught up in lengthy storms that have no end.

It was with awe and amazement that we made it through the channel and past the harbour walls in one tack. Lesser sailors would have required three tacks at least.

I have seen even well-versed captains coming perilously close to the harbour wall, through not allowing for the strength of the tide and that with the luxury of powerful marine diesels, which should keep anyone who can steer on course.

I was an extremely lucky crewman. In my brother I had an extraordinarily gifted mariner. Within an instant he could judge our course, computing tide, time, and waves, getting us to the exact point we wanted to go.

Admittedly he failed in Olhao, but he had not included the tide in his calculations. How many of us have miscalculated over greater issues? This was a seaman beyond reproach.

I try not to exaggerate, and I would be the first to criticise my family. It is healthy and goes some way to preventing a repeat of the same incidences.

However, I could safety say I trusted him with my life. Here we were, with no engine, under sail, navigating the perilous coast of Spain with a Michelin map and never once with him did I feel in danger, although we often were.

This was one of those times.

I was prepared but not agitated.

I had been in a force eight with an amateur; I could survive with my brother in such calm waters. It was uncanny how still the waters were. I suspected he needed a lot of room to come about.

The turn could not be done tightly for danger of stalling like an aircraft and losing power. Too little wind in our sails and the turn would be incomplete; too much and we would smash ourselves against the harbour wall. With friends waiting in Ibiza, I did not want to wait for a salvage team. Besides, she was a beautiful boat and deserved to stay afloat.

As we entered the pool, Norman aimed for the beach. It was not a time to use the plumb line. I had to judge how late he could make his turn. The later, the better; the closer to shore, the more perfect our entrance would be on the next and vital tack that would bring us slowly enough into the wall and our mooring. We needed that control to avoid any shipping tied up.

Mercifully, there was only one boat that needed avoiding. A tight tack would miss the boat; too wide and we would crash into the metal hulk, sinking us as sure as if we had pulled a plug on board. I looked back at my brother and beyond, just in case we were about to be run over by a fast-running boat.

Only the sun stood behind him and what a sun it was, its glare too much to look upon.

There he sat on the almost-dry bench seat, pumping the bilges, and holding the tiller firm. I turned back to the job in hand. I was ready to lower my arm to signal that we should turn.

I was amazed.

We had spent a rain-soaked night out on the sea, but it was as if we had been in another country.

That fateful day, families crowded on to the shale beach to catch the sun, something I had never associated with the hard-working Andalusians.

I was flabbergasted to see a scene reminiscent of an August bank holiday in Brighton.

There were hordes of people on the beach, young, old, even children, worshipping the sun when I thought worship was reserved for Sunday in church in these Catholic climes. I was admiring a few of the girls of about my age on the beach when I realised there was activity in the water.

They were actually swimming in the harbour. Try that in Dover or Boulogne and see what happens. There were children snorkelling, two older people floating. I could almost see the bottom of the harbour.

It was made up of shale. We would have to turn very soon.

Our keel was six foot and we couldn't afford to run aground yet again or be thrown on to the beach with the others.

Great entrances are one thing, but you can overdo some things.

To my horror, one of the swimmers stood up in two or three feet of water, with us just twelve or fifteen feet away. It was shallower than I had imagined.

Worse still, a lone snorkeler of between the ages of seven and eleven, it is difficult to tell when someone is almost completely submerged but for the sight of flipper and a snorkel, was swimming across our bow. We had to turn now or run him down, it was that close. My arm dropped and the boat swung.

The boom crashed from port to starboard with a bang. The jib was released, and I prayed, as we tacked, that the hull would not crack the skull of the unfortunate swimmer.

How could anyone be swimming while we were in town, or port or harbour? The people on the shore seemed oblivious to the danger, obviously mistaking my blond beard and hair for grey, presuming experience if not wisdom.

The reason why the jib was not being tightened, as all foresails are when a tack is completed, was that my brother was looking at the swimmer, hoping the vessel would miss him.

I heard no crack or thud but felt the rope on the jib being pulled taut, a sign that yet again danger had been averted.

However, the incident had broken both of our concentrations, and, at that very moment, a gust of wind blew from on store, as if to blow us away from the beach, divine intervention, taking the temptation of bikini-clad girls away from my eyes, or perhaps as a very belated revenge for the wind that blew the Armada away from England.

The snorkeler incident had diverted us and there was no reason why this gust should come. Perhaps it was warm currents meeting cold. The result was we were heading for the harbour wall at an alarming four knots. It may not sound fast if you have not studied physics properly.

A five mile per hour impact has a lot of energy to transmit from a steel hull on to one made of sitka spruce and mahogany.

There was nothing we could do.

Norman dropped the sails.

I held the coiled rope.

Spotting a man sauntering along the harbour wall I called out, 'Ola', as if this we would alert him to our danger and galvanise him into action.

I threw the rope anyhow.

Stunned at the sight of old hemp twisting towards him like a striking snake, the man's face registered horror. It was a good long throw.

That rope had to arrest our progress and prevent us hitting the harbour wall and the boat in front.

We were travelling at speed, with only the four fenders, rubber buoys, strapped to our boat to absorb the impact.

I watched as the rope, which had been coiled in my hand, unravelled.

I could do nothing.

Gathering up the wet rope, once it fell back into the harbour, was not on the agenda.

By the time I had recoiled the sopping strand, we would have hit both the harbour wall and the boat in front.

His flaying arms failed to make contact with the heavy end, but once it was on the floor, this man in his fifties bent with the agility of someone much younger.

This was a fisherman. He knew ropes and now, after the initial surprise, he leapt into action. Thank goodness this was no butcher on a stroll along the promenade. Within seconds he had the rope tied!

The boat was in safe hands.

There was no need to take up the slack. The tension brought on by the moving boat tightened the rope immediately. I saw him almost lose his footing, but he regained his stance, pulling on the rope as if he were in a tug of war.

I, then, glanced at my brother, who had a boathook in his hand to fend off the wall, not as hopeless a gesture as one would imagine. The wooden shaft of the boat hook hit the wall and, although Norman allowed it a little give, by feeding it through his hands, in order to stop it from being knocked out of his grasp or from snapping, he managed to slow the momentum by his movement.

Too late, I noticed that the rope had coiled itself around my leg.

As the other two fought to secure the boat or slow its progress, I felt the coil contract around my leg. As the man hauled on the rope, my leg became almost numb with pain.

The jeans I was wearing peeled back as the rope ran over them, burning and ripping at the same time. I could feel the flesh coming off my leg, the nerves registering the heat and the cutting of the old hemp.

I could look down as the blood oozed out of my chafed skin.

I raised my eyes, but all I could see was the black face of the harbour wall and the thin line of sky above its massive bulk. There was no way I could appeal for help.

I dropped to one knee; almost impossible with one damaged leg being pulled vertically upward, bones and muscles resisting, hair and flesh rubbed raw, dots of blood congealing as they met other drops.

I managed to free the rope at the stantion and untangle it from around my leg, but still the tension was fierce. The rope was tied, and the man was receiving the rope thrown by my brother. My hands burned as the rope slid through them, but I was determined not to let the boat swing out or lose the mooring we had so nearly and luckily secured.

My end of the boat was slipping out and we were in danger of spinning around and hitting the tougher larger boat, on our vulnerable side.

All the fenders were placed on the dockside.

The pain was still great, but now it throbbed and burnt. The tourniquet's grasp of the rope had been released and the numbness even this short entanglement had left in my muscles made my leg weak. The rope pulled me vertical, as I felt the last metre singe through my hands.

I pulled hard against the rope and collapsed face down on to the deck, bringing just enough rope with me to loop around the stantion. I looked at my chafed hands as I lay on my elbows and knees.

Then, I rolled over on to my back and managed to raise my knees.

There was a six-inch gash in my jeans, but the skin burnt from hip to knee. The rope burns had covered my whole thigh, but only where the jeans had ripped had real blood been drawn.

Later, when I removed my trousers layers of skin lay shredded over my thigh and the flesh was raw.

It was an extremely painful exfoliation.

I lay on my back and waited until I felt able to move. Norman came up and looked at the leg and was sympathetic. I limped downstairs and washed the leg with some cold fresh water and changed.

We had just had a cup of coffee when the customs arrived.

We had heard horrific stories of the authorities ripping boats apart, but he greeted us in a civil manner, took one look into the dishevelled cabin, felt sorry for us, and bid us a good evening.

Surprisingly, it was twilight when we sauntered into town for supper, dying to buy a packet of cigarettes.

Two police officers stopped us and asked for our passports, inquiring if we were English.

We told them we were Irelandes.

One asked if that was north or south.

My brother cleverly replied, 'Republica, just like Spain.'

The policeman chortled and bid us a good evening. It was a good evening, warm air and hot food, cold beer and strong Ducados. Chicken never tasted so sweet.

Other Books

We hope you have enjoyed the story. You might like to consider the following books by the same author:

The Taint Gallery is the story of two normal people who allow passion to destroy their peace and tranquillity. This is an explicit portrayal of sexual attraction and deteriorating relationships.

Switch is a dark thriller, Chandler meets 'Fifty Shades of Grey'; a nightmare comes true!

Waterwitch, a sailing adventure: two brothers sailing a boat around the Mediterranean during the Falklands War, resulting in disastrous consequences.

Major Bruton's Safari or Uganda Palaver is a witty account of a coronation and safari in Uganda. As a guest of the Ugandan people, a group of disparate people experience Africa with a caustic commentator, not critical of the continent but of his own friends and family.

Innocent Proven Guilty is a thriller on the lines of 39 Steps. A teacher discovers his brother dead in a pool of blood, he wants to find the murderer, but he has left his footprints behind.

Seveny Seven is a 'Punk Portrait' The story of growing up in London during the punk era, a whimsical autobiography that explodes the myth that 'Punk' was an angry working-class movement.

Carom is a thriller about an art theft and drug smuggling. Finn McHugh, and his team pursue Didier Pourchaire, a vicious art thief. The action moves between London, Paris, Helsinki, and St. Petersburg. Everyone wants to catch the villain resulting in a messy bagatelle. Carom is an Indian board game.

One also called *Ad Bec* is a dish best eaten cold; a schoolboy takes revenge on a bully. Stephen is a late arrival at a prep school in the depths of Shropshire. He is challenged to do a 'tunnel dare' by the school bully. When the tunnel collapses on the bully, Stephen has to solve the dilemma, tell no one and be free or rescue the bully.

The story is set in a seventies progressive preparatory school.

Remember the Fifth is the true story of Guy Fawkes; it shows how Robert Cecil tried to destroy all opposition to his power and make himself the hero of the hour.

Karoly's Hungarian Tragedy is Michael's first departure into historical biography. This is the story of Karoly Ellenbacher taken into captivity and used as a human shield by Romanian soldiers during the war, arrested during the communist era and sent down a coal mine, he escaped to England in 1956. His story of survival is barely credible.

2029 is the story of an England where smuggling has returned to the shores and Aubrey goes for a swim with the smuggler's son and the son drowns. Aubrey is accused of murder and has to clear his name. With three strong women to help him, he should succeed but are Adel, Kate and Thomasina on his side or do they have their own agenda?

Michael Fitzalan has written four plays:

Veni, Vidi, Vicky, - a story of a failed love affair.

George and the Dragon, a painter discovers a cache of bonds and sovereigns in a cellar, not knowing that it belongs to a vicious gang. Thankfully his niece's friend is a star lawyer and can help him return the money before it is too late, or can she?

Symposium for Severine is a modern version of Plato's Symposium but with women being the philosophers instead of men.

Superstar is play that sees Thomas Dowting meeting Jesus in the Temple, travelling to Angel to meet his girlfriend, Gabrielle. They convince Thomas to volunteer for work abroad. Three weeks later J C Goodman takes over Thomas's job and moves in with Gabrielle.

Switch and Major Bruton's Safari have been turned into scripts.

Michael is working on a script, which he may turn into a novel.

M.O.D, Mark O'Dwyer, Master of Disguise, a private detective agency, Francis Barber Investigators, is retained to find out why a model was defenestrated from a Bond Street building.

Printed in Great Britain
by Amazon

84062468R00154